Angel Falling Softly

A novel by Eugene Woodbury

ZARAHEMLA BOOKS
Provo, Utah

© 2008 by Eugene Woodbury

ISBN-13 978-0-9787971-6-4
ISBN-10 0-9787971-6-7

Cover design by Jason Robinson

All rights reserved.
Printed in the U.S.A.

Published by Zarahemla Books
869 East 2680 North
Provo, UT 84604
info@zarahemlabooks.com
ZarahemlaBooks.com

What if I told you that one of the best Mormon novels ever written is a vampire story? *Angel Falling Softly* is proof positive that Mormon fiction is not dead. And even if it was, Woodbury has called it from its grave, bestowed it with immortality, and given it a mighty fine set of literary fangs.
— Stephen Carter, *Sunstone* magazine editor

This tale of two women — one a vampire, the other a bishop's wife — is more than a good read. It is a provocative meditation on life and death that will leave readers both satisfied and unnerved. It kept me reading, and it kept me guessing
— Angela Hallstrom, author of the novel *Bound on Earth*

Woodbury captures human relationships with realism and depth of feeling. He also paints a warm and homey portrait of Utah Mormon culture as seen from a sophisticated worldly perspective. All this is woven into a suspense-filled tale of a dangerous friendship as two women — born lifetimes apart — find the desperate courage to bet it all.
— C. L. Hanson, blogger and novelist

In melding the vampire genre with Mormon literary fiction, Eugene Woodbury has created a hybrid that is startling, fresh, insightful, and heartbreaking.

What's remarkable about *Angel Falling Softly* isn't just that Woodbury does something new with vampire themes or that he provides a complex, touching portrait of a Mormon mother desperately trying to save her terminally ill child. It's that he weaves these elements together with well-deployed literary allusions and quotations (often Biblical) that add substance to the questions raised about belief, redemption, desire, sin and death.

The novel is insistently literary while being solidly genre-based. What most amazed me is that he pulls it all off without violating the supernatural and metaphysical boundaries of Mormonism or of the vampire genre. He plays the two worlds against each other in a way that maximizes reading pleasure and says something new about the Mormon experience.
—William Morris, founder of the literary blog
A Motley Vision: Mormon Arts and Culture

This isn't just a vampire story. It's a character study of the things Latter-day Saints might do when pushed into a corner with no apparent way out. The theme of the entire book can be summed up in one line: "Christians claim to believe in eternal life. So why are you so afraid of death?" Woodbury does nothing the easy or expected way in this story. There are a lot of questions and almost no answers—and I liked that. More, please.
—Moriah Jovan, novelist

    Full of doubt I stand,
Whether I should repent me now of sin
By me done and occasioned, or rejoice
Much more, that much more good thereof shall spring,
To God more glory, more good will to Men
From God, and over wrath grace shall abound.

—John Milton
Paradise Lost

Chapter 1
The devil lives next door

Bedlam beat against the boards. The oaken beams shuddered. The reverberations echoed through the great hall of the manor house. The sound of thunder, perhaps. Or the Master slamming through the empty rooms in another one of his senseless rages. The child they'd brought him had not satisfied. He would beckon her soon enough, glower and remonstrate, pace lines on the drawing-room carpet, smacking the leather of his riding crop into the palm of his hand.

Always the same accusation: "You have wrung her dry! Do you hand a hard sponge to a thirsting man?"

Always her plea: "But there are three of us and only one of you!"

Always his dismissive answer: "You are children. You need hardly a drop!"

She closed her mouth and clenched her teeth and repeated to herself: *I am not a child, and one day you shall know this.*

Another harsh report. Milada's eyes flew open. The darkness hung around her like funerary curtains. Her heart raced. She listened closer. No, these were not the echoes of the Master's temper. It was not lightning, nor was it thunder. It was the sound of angry men and their fists pounding on the door.

Kamilla turned to her, eyes glowing in the dark. "What is going on?" she demanded. *"What have you done?"*

The heavy iron hinges were beginning to give.

Chapter 2
Fortune favors the bold

THE SONIC BOOM ECHOED ACROSS THE CITY from the West Desert bombing range, rattling the window frame. White light struck Milada hard in the face. She jerked her head away from the growing patch of sunlight. A draft of air from the vents had caught the curtains away from the glass. She covered her eyes with her hands and groaned. So early, and the day had defeated her already.

Milada climbed out of bed and pulled on her nightgown. After retrieving her cell phone from the dresser, she approached the window and cracked open the curtains. Then leaned back as a veritable blast of light sprang into the room.

From her safe vantage she contemplated the Salt Lake City metropolis. What a strange city it was, housing no more people than Yonkers yet filling a county half the size of Long Island. The urban landscape flowed down from Federal Heights and out from Temple Square like the gush from a fire hydrant flooding onto Brooklyn asphalt. Zoning was left to nature, and nature was an undisciplined commissar.

Her cell phone chirped. Jane's wake-up call. "Morning, Milly," Jane said in her always-cheerful voice. "How are you finding Utah?"

"It is very bright," Milada replied.

An understatement, to say the least. There was nothing subterranean here, no shade that was not filled with light. Late yesterday afternoon, while she waited for the Hilton limo to pick her up at the airport, the air had been as hot as an oven and as dry as sandpaper.

On the phone Jane was saying something about Garrick. Milada shifted her attention back to her executive assistant as Jane said, "He left a note. 'Ask Milly about the last time she's had anything to eat,' it says."

Milada had to laugh, though she was really laughing at herself. A biting truth underpinned the kidding reprimand. She did not live by bread alone.

"Oh, and I have Kammy's local phone and pager numbers," Jane said.

"I should be seeing her later today, but let me have them anyway."

Jane ran through the day's itinerary. Milada half-listened as she talked, and mostly to the comforting familiarity of her voice. Two thousand miles, and it sounded like she was next door. Milada already felt a touch of homesickness. She not only understood her stepfather's solitary ways, but she was starting to take after them. That's what worried Garrick.

Jane said, "Your contact at Loveridge & Associates is Merrill Loveridge. Odds are they'll push some flunky on you."

"Just as well," Milada replied. Most corporate officers equal to her in status were wont to treat her like a precocious teenager.

The hotel room phone rang. Jane heard it as well. "I'll let you get that, Milly. That's all I've got on my end."

Milada said good-bye. The call was the concierge saying that her driver had arrived. Before returning to the bedroom, she paused again before the window. As she gazed down from her aerie on this unrolling sod of civilization, it appeared to her as Mars might have through Percival Lowell's telescope: an exotic, unexplored country. No, it was definitely not New York. But she was intrigued by what its people had to offer her.

The game would soon be afoot.

Chapter 3
Only the good die young

RACHEL FOLDED HER ARMS ACROSS HER CHEST. The doctor stopped talking. He'd used a lot of acronyms: Jennifer's ANC (absolute neutrophil count), her FDP (fibrin degradation products), and the wicked joker in the deck, GVHD (graft-versus-host disease). Nothing had changed: her daughter's levels were all flat. In this business, no news was bad news.

But her husband nodded. He was the bishop, after all. Being understanding was his job. Not two years ago, over a span of six months he had blessed a newborn child, married the parents, and then conducted the funeral for all three. He understood that suffering came with the territory, that death was part of the job description.

The bishop's wife did not. She hadn't understood then, she did not now, and the good doctor hadn't said a thing that meant anything to her. His empathy did not inspire in her any confidence. She didn't care if he could feel her pain. She didn't want him to *feel*, she wanted him to *do*.

"Tell me her chances."

The bishop said, "Rachel—"

"Give me a number," she insisted. Something she could hang her faith on. Otherwise, the substance of things hoped for was no better than a child's wish for a pony on her birthday. *We can't afford a pony, dear.* That's what they were telling her.

The doctor pushed his hands into the pockets of his white lab coat. He shook his head somberly—he had somber down. She pressed. "Sixty-forty? Eighty-twenty? One out of ten? One out of a thousand?"

She was beginning to sound hysterical. But she knew they understood. Hysterical mother was her job description, and they were very understanding men. The bishop put his hand on her shoulder. It took all of her self-control to resist jerking free of him. She stood there, Lot's wife turned to a pillar of bitter salt.

The doctor's eyes briefly met hers. "There's no way to say in cases like this."

There are no other cases like this! she wanted to scream at him. *This is my daughter—she didn't come with a spare in the trunk!* Instead, she calmly said, "So it's all or nothing."

The doctor sighed. Rachel took the sigh as a yes. Like boys shooting free throws: *How about double or nothing, God?*

In the waiting room outside the bone marrow transplant unit, a big picture window framed the Salt Lake Valley. The smoky city skyline shimmered in the midmorning sun. The Great Salt Lake sparkled in the distance, the brown-blue brine dissolving into a tan horizon etched by the rocky outlines of Stansbury and Antelope Islands and the hazy sky above.

The bishop said, "I've got to get back to work."

Rachel searched out the golden spires of the Salt Lake Temple, dwarfed by the stressed-concrete-and-glass façade of the Church Office Building. She looked for Moroni and his trumpet, the angel perched on his golden ball like a little toy soldier, bugle raised toward deaf heaven. But it was too far away, the smog too thick on the ground.

The bishop said, "You're squishing the dragon."

She looked at the golden wyvern clenched in her fist. She relaxed her hand. The stuffed animal uncurled its wings in her palm. The bishop put his hands on her waist and kissed her on the cheek. For a moment, she melted at his touch.

And then he had to leave. Rachel remained at the window. *I'm okay.* What a lie that was. Her daughter was dying. She didn't care if faith no greater than the grain of a mustard seed could move mountains. The mountains could stay put. All she was asking for was the life of one small child. So where had her faith been weak? What prayer, what blessing, what sacrifice hadn't been good enough? She'd offered the marrow of her bones.

Children died all the time. She knew that. The Bromley child hadn't been six months old. But if that was the way God was parceling out justice these days, he could stop being so ironic about it. They'd beaten the cancer. Now it was *Rachel's marrow* that was killing Jennifer. She had a vicious immune system. Not content with her ovaries, now it was bearing down on her offspring. She drew air deeply into her lungs. Her heartbeat slowed. Time stopped. Nothing bad could happen.

She exhaled. Her shoulders slumped. One breath always followed the next. She returned to the sterile pale-blue room and sat by her daughter's bed. Again, she found herself counting the breaths. She closed her eyes and shook her head to clear her ringing skull of the siren's song. She reminded herself, reprimanded herself: there was still Laura, the daughter who would live, the daughter who needed her attention as much as the daughter who didn't even know she was there.

Chapter 4
Butter wouldn't melt in her mouth

MILADA'S DRIVER FROM EXECUTIVE GROUND TRANSPORT was young, well groomed, and extraordinarily polite. His name was Steven Day. A premed student at the University of Utah, he was married and had two children, a fact she found stunning in this day and age. Steven met her at the front desk and accompanied her to the limo.

"Eagle Gate Plaza," she said. She placed her parasol on the seat next to her. It was a short ride, so she kept on her gloves and hat. The Lincoln merged into traffic. Milada said, "Steven, I gather that you're working your way through college."

"Yes, ma'am."

"Is this not difficult, with a family to support at the same time?"

He glanced at her reflection in the rearview mirror. "It's a lot of work, ma'am, but we're getting by."

"You must have married young to already have two children."

"We met at Brigham Young University my freshman year. We got married right after my mission."

"Your mission?" She recalled her *Frommer's Utah* guidebook. "Ah, you mean a proselytizing mission."

"Yes, ma'am."

Steven turned onto South Temple and stopped beneath the pink granite facing of Eagle Gate Plaza. He walked around the car and opened the door. Milada said, "I shouldn't be needing you for the rest of the afternoon." She added, "From now on, we shall use the parking garage entrance."

Milada rode the elevator to the seventeenth floor, where Loveridge & Associates occupied all but two suites. She presented her card to the secretary at the front desk. "I'm here to see Mr. Loveridge."

"Just a minute, ma'am." She digested the information on the card. "Your sister's in the south conference room."

Kammy could be counted on to be punctual.

A minute later, a man walked up to her. "I'm Edward Christensen. Mr. Loveridge has asked me to take care of any concerns you might have."

As Jane had predicted, they'd assigned her a handler. Milada supposed that her embossed business card reading CHIEF INVESTMENT OFFICER, DARANYI CAPITAL MANAGEMENT was not by itself persuasive, especially when the woman presenting it looked barely twenty.

They shook hands. "Milada," he said, motioning for her to accompany him, "we've arranged for one of our conference rooms to be at your disposal whenever you're in town. Here we are."

Milada strode ahead of him into the conference room. Kammy was leaning back in a chair reading a medical journal. Her stocking feet rested against the edge of the heavy oak table. Her platinum-blond hair was tied back in a ponytail. Her fedora and slicker sat on the table. She was wearing green hospital scrubs.

Kammy looked up at Milada, her eyes shielded by her wrap-around sunglasses. "It's about time. The seminar starts in thirty minutes."

"The seminar?" Milada echoed.

"The Biomedical Informatics Seminar at the University of Utah. You insisted, remember?"

Milada remembered.

The room faced south. She closed the curtains, removed her hat, and took out her small Sony laptop. Edward stood in the doorway like a bellhop waiting for a tip.

"Is there anything else, Milada?"

From the corner of her eye, Milada was sure she saw Kammy smirk. She said, "Edward—"

"You can call me Ed."

"Edward," she said again. "You may begin by addressing me as Miss Daranyi." Still wearing her sunglasses, she looked directly at him. "Before I left New York, I asked Mr. Loveridge to prepare the SEC filings on Wylde Medical Informatics. I'd like to see them now."

"Yes, *Miss* Daranyi." Edward wheeled around and marched out of the room.

She said to her sister, "You *have* read the prospectus I sent you?"

"You couldn't have bought a company in Seattle or San Francisco? The UV index got up to *nine* yesterday."

"You tolerate sunlight better than I do. Be thankful this isn't Phoenix."

"I'm just saying."

"The prospectus?"

Kammy shrugged. "Did you know the company started out as a chain of funeral homes? Love the irony." She grinned, showing her sharp lateral incisors. "The informatics stuff looks solid. The long-term demand for genome-sequencing data is all upside as far as I can tell. Tie it into the genealogical data and you can do deCODE Genetics one better. I figure that's the market you're aiming at."

"*You* can do deCODE Genetics one better. You're going to be running it."

"Yeah, right."

Milada sighed. "But it looks solid, you said."

"The people in charge of the science seem to know what they're doing. I think it's the same Wylde guy who funded a wing at the hospital." She glanced at her watch. "I'm going to be late." She leaned over and pulled on her shoes.

Milada said, "I'm going to try and get you onsite. It's what they're *really* doing that matters. Not what they *say* they're doing in press releases."

Kammy's head popped up. "What? Oh, sure. That's cool." She rose to her feet at the same time Edward returned with the folders.

"Is there anything else?" he asked stiffly.

"No. This should keep me busy for the time being."

Kammy grabbed her slicker and hat and followed Edward out the door. She said in a loud-enough voice for Milada to hear, "Hey, don't take it personally. When she travels, my big sister's a bitch to *everybody*."

Milada shut her eyes. Hearing the door close, she opened her eyes and scanned through the folders. The filings for the current year-to-date were missing. But she'd had her fill of Edward. Instead she spent the rest of the morning answering correspondence, devoting her attention to anything from Jane, her broker Garrick Burke—the family was his only client—or her stepfather, Michael.

The conference room door opened. A young secretary said, "Ms. Daranyi? You've got a call from Ken Garff Mercedes." Noticing the absence of a phone, she darted out of the room and rushed back in with a telephone, which she plugged in next to the network cable. "Line two," she said.

Milada hit line two. "Milada Daranyi."

"Ma'am?" said a male voice on the other end. "Oh, yes, Ms. Daranyi. The S500. We don't have the tinting you ordered in stock. It should be here by Thursday, Friday at the latest."

"That's fine. Please call me when the car is ready."

She gave them her cell phone number and hung up. The secretary again poked her head into the room. "Ms. Daranyi? Um, want to get some lunch? The Seagull Room." She bobbed her head toward the ceiling. "It's pretty good." She spoke with a complete lack of conviction.

Milada said, "That sounds nice—" The sentence trailed off with an obvious question mark at the end.

"I'm Karen, Karen Talbot."

"Well, Karen, shall we plan for twelve-thirty then?"

The secretary took a deep breath, showing more relief than she'd probably intended. She nodded and smiled and ducked out of the room.

Chapter 5
A good example is the best sermon

Rachel opened her eyes. The book she'd brought with her lay open in her lap. The clock said one o'clock. She always tried to be home when Laura returned from school, so she'd better get going. There was no telling what might come up between here and there.

She bade the nursing staff good-bye with a smile and a nod to Veralee, Jennifer's critical-care nurse, who returned her pleasantries. "See you tomorrow, Sister Forsythe."

Yes, tomorrow, Rachel thought darkly. *Tomorrow and tomorrow and tomorrow.* When Jennifer started on the chemo, Rachel had stayed overnight at the hospital for a week. She was better acquainted with the night shift at Deseret Children's Hospital than with most of her neighbors.

She walked down the open staircase from the third floor. Freed from the calm cocoon surrounding her daughter's bedside, she found that the vague feelings of anger, the glimmering sense of upset, returned. It was something more than the cosmic injustice of it all. It was David. He'd powered Jennifer through the chemo with prayer and raw emotional muscle. But then came the GVHD and the coma, and he was out to sea. He *did* things with the kids or did things *for* them. Faced with a child who did *nothing,* he had nothing to give. It was easier to work and tend to his flock. Easier to deal with other people's problems.

But hadn't she wanted to be a bishop's wife? Come to believe she'd earned it? Deserved it? No, not growing up. Not when they were first married. And not even when David was briefly elevated to the stake high council. Nevertheless, there was little subtlety in the politics of picking a Mormon bishop. When David was called as first counselor four years into Bishop Ackerlind's term, everybody knew David was going to be the ward's next bishop.

She found herself looking forward to that which she'd once scoffed at. It would be like being first lady, enjoying no *de jure* authority but having all she said taken with extra seriousness.

Though by now it was beginning to wear. All things being equal, it was the hours of David *not being home* that truly gnawed at her. Not being out in the garage, or at the computer, or mowing the lawn. Just not being around.

Worse was the pedestal. How did her brother Carl put it? "Sooner or later they stop admiring you and start looking up your skirt." She dreaded the day that Laura hit puberty full on. David would be done as bishop in two years, and then the pressure would be off. With luck they could escape all those idiotic arguments between parents and their teenagers that David was always being called on to mediate.

Such as another piercing, two in each ear like Kathy Reid. Laura had brought up the subject twice already. But she couldn't. Not while David was bishop. Not while any other kid in the ward could turn to the bishop's child, *her* child, and make *her* the example.

Once he was released as bishop, Laura could turn her lobes into sieves—that'd be fine with Rachel.

She pulled out of the parking garage and drove down from the University of Utah campus. The mountains rose up behind the hills in the east. To the west, the bright city slowly hid itself behind a green curtain of trees.

Chapter 6

Look before you leap

THE SECRETARY RETURNED TO THE CONFERENCE ROOM promptly at twelve-thirty. As they rode the elevator to the penthouse suite, Milada said, "I take it the invitation was Edward's idea?" While Karen stammered for an answer, Milada continued, "No matter. I appreciate the thought."

The city looked deceptively cool through the tinted windows, but Milada asked the waiter to seat them away from the wall of plate glass.

Milada said, "What do you recommend, Karen?"

"I usually get—" She didn't seem too sure about what she usually got. "I usually get the chef's salad."

Milada said to the waiter, "Two chef's salads."

The waiter retrieved the menus and left. Karen said under her breath, "To be honest, I don't eat here *that* often." She quickly added, "But the chef's salad really is good."

Milada smiled. She appreciated that the girl was not good at lying and knew it. "Tell me, Karen, are you married?"

Karen shook her head. "Engaged. Well, almost."

Milada took a sip of water. "An employee at the firm?"

"Tom Wilkins." She brightened saying his name. "He's an accountant with Smith Barney. We met at the Salt Lake AICPA conference last fall."

"Where do you live?"

"I share an apartment with Cindy—at the front desk. Tom's building a house in Draper up on the bench. It's got a great view of the valley, but it's a little far from things, you know? At least it's not as bad as commuting from Lehi or American Fork. Draper's the only place on the east side that's affordable these days."

"Where would you prefer to live?"

"Sandy would be nice, or Granite. But you've got to be totally rich to live there." Karen reflected for a moment. "It's going to be a real nice house, Tom's."

Milada put on her sunglasses and turned toward the windows. "Where is Draper from here?"

"You can't really see it because of the haze. It's due south, right before Point of the Mountain."

"And Sandy?"

Karen pointed off to the left. "Right there, where you can see the entrance to Little Cottonwood Canyon. That's actually Granite. Sandy is west a bit."

The waiter came with their salads. Milada straightened her chair and unfolded the napkin in her lap. She selected a fork and inspected it briefly. "Karen, is there a real estate firm that Loveridge employs on a regular basis?"

Karen thought for a minute. "Mr. Christensen uses Valley Real Estate Management."

"When we have finished lunch, would you get them on the phone for me?"

Karen cheerfully said that she would.

After lunch Milada found the missing SEC filings on the table next to her laptop. *Better late than never.* She got out her cell phone and called Kammy. Some conversations she preferred not to make over company lines.

"What's up, Milly?"

From the background noise, Milada guessed her sister was at the student union. "Where are you staying?"

"The Crocker Science House. It's a dorm for post-docs. Why?"

Milada frowned. She lowered her voice to a few decibels above a whisper. "Where in the world do you keep blood in a dorm room?"

"Gee, Milly, a medical college. Where could I get my hands on whole blood? Hmm, let me think that one over and get back to you."

"I was only asking. How was the seminar?"

"Not bad. I've got rounds, so don't go penciling me in for dinner or anything."

"You know, you could apply for a residency or open a practice—"

"Not going there, Milly," Kammy replied in the singsong voice she used whenever her sister started waxing maternal. "Bye. Gotta go."

Milada knew she shouldn't be surprised. For the last two decades, a significant portion of the charitable donations made by the Daranyi Foundation had ended up buying internships and fellowships for Kammy. Or maybe Kammy being so *content* playing the eternal student was what annoyed her. She, on the other hand, did everything she could to come across older than she appeared.

Why couldn't her sisters settle down and *work* for a living? She could only dream of Zoë disciplining herself sufficiently to even attend school.

The intercom buzzed. Karen's voice announced, "LaDawn Gunderson from Valley Real Estate."

Milada thanked her and picked up the phone. "This is Milada Daranyi. I'm an associate of Mr. Christensen's. I'm going to be in Salt Lake City on and off for the next six months or so. I was thinking of renting a house in the area."

There was a block of upscale apartments a hundred yards north of Eagle Gate Plaza. But the thought of sharing walls and floors and ceilings with strangers—not to mention the halls and lobby—made her skin crawl. At least in a hotel the people next door had no pretensions of being her neighbors.

"Mr. Christensen's a wonderful man, isn't he!" The voice of an older woman, bubbly and overly enthusiastic. "What part of Salt Lake?"

Sandy would be nice, Karen had said. "Sandy," Milada casually suggested. "A small ranch or rambler with a finished basement. A covered porch facing north."

The line fell silent. It was a clear connection. Milada could hear a pencil scratching against paper. LaDawn said, "I'll see what I can find. I'll phone Karen, okay?"

"That would be fine."

LaDawn called back half an hour later. "Miss Daranyi, I have just the thing for you! Came on the market two weeks ago, a split-level rambler, three rooms up, bedroom and full bath in the basement. It's in Cottonwood Estates. A *really* nice neighborhood. Right on Dimple Dell Park in Sandy. Would you like to see it?"

Milada tried to remember what time the sun set. "Would eight o'clock be acceptable?"

"Eight o'clock? Um, tonight?" The woman's hesitation was obvious.

"Would seven be better?"

LaDawn collected herself. "Oh, sure!" she burst out, revealing a Midwestern accent tinged with Scandinavian roots. "The address is 1204 Larkspur Lane. Do you need directions?"

"I'm sure my driver can find it."

"That's just great. I'll see you tonight, Miss Daranyi."

"Seven o'clock," Milada confirmed. After hanging up the phone, she opened the folder and thumbed through the SEC filings. *LaDawn,* she repeated to herself. In her long life, she'd never met a woman named LaDawn before.

It briefly occurred to her that she had no good idea about what she was getting herself into. She kept too many secrets not to know what she was getting herself into every minute of her life.

Chapter 7
Don't judge a book by its cover

IN PURELY UTILITARIAN TERMS, being the mother of a dying daughter was not that difficult.

Every morning Rachel had someplace to go and something to do. It was almost like having a job again. She hustled the husband and the daughter out of the house, showered and dressed. And then hung around children for several hours in a teaching institution staffed by busy, competent professionals. Yes, many of the children were dying, but other than that . . . And it was only part-time employment. She was done every day by noon, one o'clock at the latest.

And so the days came and went.

In Sandy she stopped at Smith's to get a few things, a few things that quickly filled her shopping cart. How many people had they invited to family home evening, again? Charlene was bringing a tossed salad. She'd talk to Doris at church on Sunday and get everything else on Monday.

She moved to the checkout queues. "Rachel!" A woman hurried up to her, a woman in her late forties stuffed into a Liz Claiborne pantsuit that would look much better if the person inside it lost twenty pounds and didn't use quite so much makeup.

"Guess what!"

Rachel didn't guess. A tree falling in a forest wouldn't make a sound until LaDawn Gunderson told somebody about it.

"I've rented out the Lindstrom place!"

"The Lindstrom place? Oh, yes, the Lindstroms."

"You're going to have *quite* an interesting neighbor." LaDawn spoke with an almost rapturous intensity. "Though I don't think she's a *member*. Didn't seem at all like the kind of person you'd expect at Relief Society, if you know what I mean."

"Not a family?"

"Oh, no. Single, early twenties. *Very* professional. *Immaculately* dressed. *Quite* attractive. The whitest skin you've ever seen. Rather a strange girl. No, *eccentric,* that's the word. She wanted to see the place at night! Probably one of those supermodels you're always reading about—doesn't want to be seen in public. I didn't recognize her. She drove up in this fancy car with her own chauffeur and everything!"

LaDawn lowered her voice. "I shouldn't be telling you this," she said, patting her friend's arm for emphasis, "but she paid six months all in advance. Wrote out a twelve-thousand-dollar check, just like that—like she was buying groceries! Can you imagine?"

"Ma'am?" said the checkout clerk, leaning over the scanner to get her attention.

"Sorry," said Rachel.

LaDawn said, "Well, I'd better get going, myself." She stopped and asked, "And how is Jennifer doing?"

"She's doing fine."

Such transparent lies no longer bothered Rachel when it came to greasing the wheels of social conviviality.

She pulled out of the parking lot and turned onto Sego Lily Drive.

Cottonwood Estates was the quintessential Salt Lake subdivision. Pluck this plot of earth out of the ground and deposit it outside the beltway of any Midwestern American city, and nobody would notice.

It was so unremittingly normal that the developers felt compelled to mess up Brigham Young's commonsensical east-west, north-south street-numbering system with meandering mazes of ways, lanes, places, trails, circles, and avenues. She had to wonder when a neighborhood got too good for plain old streets.

Still, it was safe, quiet, and clean. The neighbors' kids behaved. The neighbors' pets did their business on their own lawns. Yes, she had in her youth sworn that she would never end up in a place like this, just as she had sworn she would never end up a bishop's wife. But right now she was perfectly willing to sacrifice a small part of her principles for nothing jumping out and surprising her.

She drove up Larkspur Lane. There was the Lindstroms' house. Mary had been second counselor in the Relief Society. Rachel missed her. But the Lindstroms were a young, upwardly mobile couple, and their future lay in Sacramento, not Salt Lake City.

An R.C. Willey furniture delivery truck was parked in the driveway and a pair of rusty pickups out by the curb. A small crew was busily trimming the lawn, washing the windows, sweeping the porch, flushing out the sprinkler system. This was a tenant LaDawn wanted to impress.

A supermodel, LaDawn had suggested. How did one welcome a supermodel to the neighborhood? Would a supermodel appreciate a loaf of homemade whole-wheat bread? Or would that be like giving a chicken bone to a cocker spaniel? She had no idea.

Rachel made the dogleg from Larkspur Lane onto Willow Way and drove up the driveway of their three-bedroom rambler. The garage door opened at a touch of the remote. She popped open the back door of the Honda Odyssey and hauled the groceries into the kitchen.

After dumping the groceries haphazardly on the table, she ran a glass of water at the sink and paused at the kitchen window. The lots bordering Dimple Dell Park were a cluttered no-man's-land of yellow backhoes and concrete foundations. Men with sunburned shoulders and tool belts slung low around their waists marched around like a small army on maneuvers, making war with circular saws and air hammers.

One good earthquake would topple the whole street into the Dry Creek arroyo, to be carried away with the alluvial flow.

The front door opened and slammed shut. Laura tromped into the kitchen. Rachel asked, "How was school, Laura?" and began putting away the groceries.

"Okay."

Rachel had read an article the other day about how to get a child to reply to such questions with more than one-word answers. She'd have to read it again.

Laura asked, "What's with the Lindstroms' place?"

"Oh, yes. I ran into Sister Gunderson at Smith's. She said she rented it out."

"Who to?"

"A woman, she said."

"Any kids?" Laura got the orange juice out of the refrigerator and poured herself a glass.

"I gathered she was single."

"So why's she moving *here*?"

"I don't know. LaDawn did say she was quite attractive. Like a model."

"She's a model? Really?"

"She said she *looked* like a model."

"Oh," said Laura, disappointed. She put the glass on the counter. "I'm going to Heidi's."

"Be home by five."

"Yeah, Mom."

Rachel returned the orange juice to the fridge. It was time to start thinking about dinner. She looked in the refrigerator and found the pork chops left over from Sunday dinner. A bell pepper, an onion, a can of stewed tomatoes, tomato paste—she could whip together a cacciatore in thirty minutes.

That was enough thinking about dinner. She went down to the family room and turned on the computer. "Move it, cat," she said, nudging the animal with the toe of her shoe. The cat had a habit of camping out next to the warm power brick. It jumped up and headed to the living room to find a patch of afternoon sun under the bay window.

Three e-mail messages were waiting for her. Two from her brother Carl and one from her brother Phillip. The first was a programming question from Carl directed to Phillip. Unless it was of an expressly personal nature, Carl mailed his messages to everybody on his list, regardless of relevance.

They want me to add all this interactive garbage to the website, Carl wrote, *and I can't remember the JavaScript routines and I'm too lazy to look them up and I figured you'd know it off the top of your head anyway.*

"They" were Carl's investors, or the government, or the church, the forces of nature, the Godhead. Whatever. His was a binary view of life: thumbs up or thumbs down. Things were okay or they were stupid, and most things in life were stupid.

The message from Phillip was a solution for Carl.

Carl's second e-mail was addressed to her alone. *Debby hates our guts and wants new parents. You have a spare bedroom available these days. What do you say?*

Rachel had stopped being offended by Carl soon after he was born. She hit the reply button and typed, *No thanks. We already have one pubescent teenager. Maybe Mom & Dad will take her.*

Carl would get the joke. They grew up in Maine until their dad took a job in the physics department at Utah State University. No surprise, then, that their parents had retired to Great Diamond Island in Casco Bay. It was, if not in the middle of nowhere, then within shouting distance. The week they'd spent there last summer for the family reunion, Debby and Laura had died multiple deaths from boredom.

Rachel pushed the chair back from the computer and stared out the sliding glass doors. New neighbors were always interesting. *A model,* she thought again. Michelle Montgomery still did some modeling for Macy's. Maybe Michelle knew the new woman.

She shook her head in self-reproach. No, that was as absurd as the habit Utahns had of assuming that any two Mormons living east of the Mississippi must necessarily know each other. Still, a model for a new neighbor would be interesting. Not as interesting as having a daughter dying in the hospital. But even tragedy got boring when it dragged on long enough.

Chapter 8
Money and a room of her own

MILADA HAD NOT SLEPT WELL since arriving in Utah. The sun came up no earlier than in New York, but the fine weave of the curtains made it impossible for her to escape the light. Better to have drapes of rough canvas. Had she planned on staying longer, she would have had them replaced forthwith.

No need for that now.

The house in Sandy turned out to be a champion idea. Both the house and the neighborhood were utterly prosaic. But the view was not.

The Wasatch Front, the ragged range of mountains running north to south along the eastern rim of the valley, was not the subdued Catskills. It strained meaning to use the word *mountains* to refer to those rolling hills. Here at the mouth of Little Cottonwood Canyon, the Wasatch Front was a skyscraping battlement of stone, as if giant slabs of granite had been punched upward through the earth by some aggrieved Plutonian god.

The financial transactions proved simpler than she had expected. A dollar certainly went farther here than it did in Manhattan. The lady with the funny name recommended an interior decorator named Brittney. Milada gave Brittney a budget of four thousand dollars and told her to keep it simple.

"The bedroom set goes down in the basement," she told her.

"You don't want the upstairs rooms furnished?"

"I suppose you could put a couch and an armchair in the living room, in case I am forced to entertain." Milada did not think it likely. "And a kitchen table, a few chairs. Put the telly in the family room — is that what you call it? And a sofa and a coffee table."

"Some plants perhaps? I know where you can get the most wonderful hanging macramé holders. Maybe some wall coverings?"

"Macramé? I am not enthusiastic about plants. Nothing that requires extra effort to keep alive."

What Milada ended up with was subdued Western chic, sandy tans, light blues, and off-whites. A Remington knockoff in the foyer—she supposed she could hang her hat on it—and a couple of not-bad Monet prints on the walls. Considering the milieu, Milada would have recommended O'Keeffe, but Brittney must have been working under the assumption that people of East Coast extraction went for French impressionists over American abstract modernists. Though that didn't explain the bucking bronco in the foyer.

Saturday evening she picked up the S500 at Ken Garff Mercedes. Steven was confused. "Will you need a limo on Monday?"

"As always. Driving for me is strictly an after-hours pleasure. Fetch me Monday morning at seven-thirty. You know the address."

She settled into the Mercedes. Feeling in a very déclassé mood, she hit the search button on the radio until she landed on a country station at the high end of the FM dial. She turned up the volume and drove home to the suburbs with Tim McGraw booming out the windows.

Chapter 9

Every rose has its thorn

RACHEL COULD STILL REMEMBER when they slept in on Sunday mornings.

Once upon a time, even with church running on the early schedule, they didn't have to get up until seven or eight o'clock. There were so many things a person could do with an extra hour or two of sleep—other than sleep. She was sure she'd conceived Jennifer on a Sunday morning. Maybe if she convinced President Forbush that she became fertile only on Sunday mornings, he'd give her husband an early release, put him in charge of the nursery or something.

She lay in bed waiting for the alarm to go off. Other than daylight saving time, they hadn't reset the alarm clock in two years. But even this was a big improvement. When David was first counselor in the bishopric, Bishop Ackerlind insisted on holding bishopric meeting at six A.M. in the bloody morning. Good man, Bishop Ackerlind, but he liked meetings too much.

When David became bishop, she'd laid down the law. Short of the Second Coming, he wasn't leaving the house before six-forty-five. So he moved bishopric meeting to seven, cut it in half, and hacked Priesthood Executive Committee meeting down to thirty minutes as well.

The ward had survived.

The clock radio clicked on. The radio was tuned to KUER, the University of Utah station. Sunday morning they played gospel music from six till nine. Not music she'd ever hear in a Mormon sacrament meeting, but she liked it. It got the blood moving in her veins.

"*Yolanda Adams and the Union Temple Concert Choir,*" the disk jockey intoned in his low, rumbling voice, "*singing the Lewis E. Jones hymn, 'There is Power in the Blood.'*"

The music started in a slow blues rhythm, the piano leading off, Hammond organ filling in between the chords. Rachel found the tune more familiar than the lyrics. Yolanda Adams began in solo:

Would you be free from the burden of sin?
There's power in the blood, power in the blood;
Would you o'er evil a victory win?
There's wonderful power in the blood.

The choir came in on the second stanza, repeating the last three lines in counterpoint:

There's power in the blood, power in the blood;
Would you o'er evil a victory win?
There's wonderful power in the blood.

Yolanda sang in recitative shout and response, "*You've got to make yourself free from your passion and pride. There's power in the blood, power in the blood!*" The chorus belted out in the background:

There is power, power, wonder-working power
In the blood of the Lamb;
There is power, power, wonder-working power
In the precious blood of the Lamb.

David climbed out of bed, stretched and yawned, and shuffled into the bathroom. Rachel put on her bathrobe and headed down to the kitchen. She got bacon and eggs out of the refrigerator, the frying pan out from under the stove. Except that today was Fast Sunday. She sighed, put the food back in the fridge, and stowed away the frying pan. She found a mug in the cupboard, ran the water hot at the sink, and added a teabag, herbal orange. There were limits to how far she could take this fasting business, and dehydration was right out.

To be honest, she'd never found much spiritual value in fasting, at least not in the warm-fuzzies department. It wasn't that she didn't believe it worked for other people—she was willing to give any faith-promoting rumor the benefit of the doubt. And it wasn't like she hadn't given it her best shot. The first time the doctor had used the words *cancer* and *Jennifer* in the same sentence, she'd fasted every week until the bishop told her to cut it out.

"I'm doing it for Jennifer," she'd insisted.

"You're not exactly being spiritual about it." He meant she was getting to be a real pain to be around. He was right. Low blood sugar made her grouchy and gave her migraines. Besides, she knew perfectly well what she was doing. If she couldn't control the world, she'd settle for controlling herself. But God certainly knew the difference between faith and an obsessive-compulsive disorder.

Herbal tea, she rationalized, didn't have any calories.

The bishop walked into the kitchen wearing a white shirt and tie, black pinstriped suit coat, and matching slacks. He hardly ever wore a suit to work, and once a week he really looked fine in one, the junior exec with the power marriage. Well, they could pretend.

"Hi, handsome," she said.

He kissed her. "You taste nice."

"It's the orange." She put the mug down on the counter and straightened his tie. "By the way, Norma and DeMar are up in Pocatello today. Grandchild number three. So I'll see you at PEC."

Since there was no breakfast to prepare, she held onto him a while longer. But they had their morning ritual to attend to. David fetched the scriptures from the hutch. They sat down at the kitchen table. Alternately, one read aloud from the New International Version while the other followed along in the official King James.

It was a practice her husband had first observed when they visited her parents after getting engaged. He confessed to her later, "When I saw your mom reading out of that NIV Scofield Study Bible, making lengthy references to Dummelow, I thought I was marrying into one of those families of Mormon radicals. Next thing, you'd be trying to convince me that women ought to get the priesthood."

"That's sweet," Rachel replied. "Wait till you meet my brother Carl."

After meeting Carl once, David had done his level best to avoid ever meeting him again.

They were presently working their way through Isaiah, dense going no matter what the translation. David glanced at the clock. "I'd better get going." He got up from the table, leaned over, and kissed her forehead. "See you at church."

He picked up his briefcase and left. Rachel replaced the bookmarks and then flipped back through the pages to Job. She had developed an affinity for the last ten chapters of Job, even more so in the King James Version. Perhaps that was because the poetry of the language pretty much disguised the fact that for all the grief they give Job, Elihu and God don't come up with much of a philosophy of suffering. She always imagined Robert De Niro as God, saying to Job at the beginning of chapter 38, "You talking to me, Job? Huh? Are *you* talking to me?"

Basically, God's philosophy was: "I'm God. You're not. Trust me on this."

Nevertheless Job was somehow reassuring. No reasons, no answers, no profound philosophies of life. But Job gets his reward anyway. As if Job had his lawyers sue God and they settled out of court, big time. New house, new family, a whole bunch of sheep and camels to boot. *Hey, sorry for the trouble.* The moral of the story: complain hard and long enough and maybe the check won't bounce.

She closed the book and put the bibles back on the shelf.

The bishop glanced at his itinerary, tugged at his necktie. With nine people stuffed into his office—his two counselors, the elders quorum president, high priest group leader, Young Men president, the ward clerk and executive secretary, and his wife representing the Relief Society—it was getting stuffy. Stuffy meant it was time to get it over and done with.

"Brent, you still need the Scout fundraiser totals, right?" Brent Millington was the Young Men president. "Catch Glen after church before we start tithing so he can print it out for you. And make sure he deposited the fundraiser checks against the Young Men account. He's still learning the ropes." He paused, shuffled his papers, and said, "All right, anything else?"

"Fast offerings," said Bill Garner, the second counselor.

"Right." Back to Brent: "Can you cover half the routes before church?"

"I'll round 'em up."

Brother Ellis, the elders quorum president, said, "I heard someone moved into the Lindstroms' place."

Brother Garner said, "Sister Gunderson's been trying to rent it out for a couple of weeks now."

The bishop's wife said, "LaDawn told me she has a new tenant."

Everybody turned. Other than to explain Norma's absence, Rachel hadn't spoken up till now. A good Relief Society president knew more about what was going on in the ward than anybody else, including the bishop. But Norma was out of town, and so was Mary. And so here she was filling in.

"It's a single woman. LaDawn didn't think she was a member. That's just her impression, though."

"We'll have to make sure someone stops by and says hello."

Brother Clark said to Brother Ellis, "Hey, Troy, hear that? She's *single*."

The bishop said to his wife, "Did Sister Gunderson say how old she was?"

"Mid-twenties." No need to add *attractive*.

Troy said, "Okay, okay, you talked me into it."

Rachel didn't think Troy Ellis was the best person to head the welcoming committee. The bishop didn't either. "Hold your horses, Troy. We'll let the Relief Society handle this one."

After the prayer everyone but the bishop's wife filed out. The bishop kicked a jam under the door to let in some fresh air. Rachel said, "You're going to be through at three, right?"

The bishop barked, "Todd!"

The executive secretary stepped back into the room. He opened his three-ring binder and shook his head. "Nothing three to six. Interviews at six-thirty, seven, seven-thirty."

"There you go."

The same routine every Sunday. Odds were fifty-fifty he'd be home on time.

The shower was running when she got home. Laura was up. Good. What else? Make a few calls, make sure Amy Lewis had the Relief Society lesson ready—

The doorbell rang.

She opened the door. Gary Reed and Kyle Matheson stood there in their Sunday best. Kyle was Laura's age, Gary a year older. Kyle said, "Hi, Sister Forsythe." Gary handed her a donation envelope.

She looked at the envelope. Across the flap she'd written the month before, *Pay with tithing*. Glen, the ward finance clerk, was supposed to pull all the pay-with-tithing envelopes, but he was still learning the ropes. She said, "How about I keep this, okay? I'll give it to the bishop."

"Okay," said Kyle.

Rachel closed the door and tossed the envelope on the coffee table and went back to the kitchen. She put on an apron and got the roast out of the fridge.

Chapter 10
An open door may tempt a saint

MILADA WAS PRETTY SURE somebody was at the front door. She rolled over and tucked the covers around her shoulders. The clock radio on the nightstand flashed 9:05. In the bloody morning.

The doorbell rang again.

She groaned. *It's Sunday morning!* Her visitors were impertinent *and* impatient. She could ignore them. Probably. Maybe it was some neighborly thing they did here, some city statute about welcoming new residents on Sunday morning. Hell, she didn't know. This was new territory for her.

She pulled on her *yukata*, tying the sash as she marched up the stairs. She turned the deadbolt and flung open the door. Sunlight reflecting off the roof of the house across the street nearly blinded her. She squinted and took a step back, raising her hand to shade her eyes.

"*What?*" she said.

It was more a command than a question. The two boys heading down the steps stopped in their tracks and returned to the porch. The taller one said, "Um, Sister Lindstrom?"

Do I look like a nun? Instead she said, "You must have the wrong address."

The boy held up a pale blue envelope. "This is 1204, isn't it?"

She had to think about it for a moment. "Yes."

"Oh," the boy said, stymied.

"May I see that?" She plucked the envelope out of the boy's hand. The label on the envelope read: *Ryan & Maryanne Lindstrom, 1204 Larkspur Lane*. She said, "I suspect the Lindstroms were the previous occupants."

The boys shrugged in noncommittal agreement.

The cardstock envelope was sealed at the top with a Velcro flap.

Below the address label it said in black block letters, FAST OFFER-INGS.

"What, pray tell, is a fast offering?"

The sunlight was beginning to irritate her skin. She hadn't had time to put on any sunblock. "Why don't you boys come inside and explain it to me?"

The two exchanged nervous glances. But she had the envelope, and that was the only way they were getting it back.

The foyer opened onto the living room. Milada settled into the overstuffed armchair. She indicated the couch against the opposite wall. The two boys sat side by side with nervous civility. Milada pried open the Velcro flap. Inside was a three-by-five form with a yellow carbonless copy attached. Along the top of the form was printed in bold type: TITHING AND OTHER OFFERINGS. She read down the columns: TITHING, FAST OFFERING, MISSIONARY, HUMANITARIAN.

"The two of you are collecting religious contributions?"

The taller boy gulped and reddened. Milada realized without looking that the collar of her *yukata* had relaxed when she sat down, revealing most of her left breast. She suppressed a smile, tightened the sash, crossed her legs, and smoothed the *yukata* over her thighs.

"Yes, ma'am," the boy squeaked.

"Explain to me what a fast offering is again?"

The shorter one piped up. "You're supposed to skip two meals and donate the money you would have spent."

"I am?" Milada was beginning to enjoy herself. "Two complete meals? Not just meat? Or fish instead? So this is a Mormon practice? And what are these contributions used for?"

"For poor people."

Milada smiled again. These kids wouldn't know a poor person if one smacked them up the sides of their blond little heads. But good intentions did count for something in the breach of actual experience. "A noble thought," she acknowledged. She went into the kitchen and retrieved her checkbook. "I gather I keep the yellow copy?"

"Yes, ma'am," they chorused from the living room.

"And to whom do I make out the check?"

There was a flurry of deliberations. The shorter one spoke up: "Cottonwood Estates Second Ward."

Milada slipped the check into the envelope. When she returned to the living room, the boys bounced to their feet. She handed the taller one the envelope and said good-bye.

They escaped as might a pair of mice freed from the clutches of a hungry cat. Milada returned to the kitchen and pinned the yellow copy to the message board next to the telephone. A trophy of sorts. She shook her head in wonderment and almost giggled. Some things were worth getting up early for.

Chapter 11

Little pitchers have great ears

A SENTENCE THE BISHOP'S WIFE hadn't heard in church before: "She didn't have a *thing* on under it!"

She slowed her stride. She didn't stop and turn, having learned long ago that paying close attention to what a teenager was saying was the worst way to find out what he *was* saying.

"Get out!" That was Brian Shore.

"I'm telling you, I was sitting five feet away from her!" That was Gary Reed.

"What were you doing five feet away from her?"

Yes, Gary, what were you doing?

"Hey, she invited us in. And she gave us a contribution. She's gotta be a movie star or something. Like that *Touched by an Angel* chick. She had a funny accent and this unbelievable hair. I mean, it was so white it was almost *silver*."

Were platinum blondes so rare these days? In the church foyer, the boys walked past her and pushed through the doors into the bright sunlight. *Ah!* Rachel said to herself. LaDawn's new tenant. Glen hadn't sorted *any* of the fast offering envelopes. So they must have stopped at the Lindstroms' place too.

Rachel walked home with Laura. At times like this, without Jennifer by her side, she ached to hold her daughter's hand, but Laura was long past the hand-holding stage. Instead Rachel whispered to her, "You look very pretty in that dress."

"Mom!" Laura protested. But her mother saw how her daughter beamed when she turned away.

The house smelled of roast beef. Rachel turned the swamp cooler on low. She changed into a blue paisley housedress and set to work on dinner. Her husband walked in the door at a quarter to three. Small miracles did happen. She called out, "We'll be ready to eat in ten minutes. Laura, come down and set the table!"

David hung his suit coat on the banister post. He got the plates out of the cupboard and handed them to his daughter. "So, Laura, what did you learn in Sunday school today?"

"Some *babe* moved into the Lindstroms' place." She said it in such a way to indicate that the source of the information was a jerk. "Gary said they were collecting fast offerings and this half-naked lady answered the door." She added quickly, "That's what *Gary* said."

"That's right." The bishop went to the banister and extracted his cell phone from the inside suit coat pocket. "Glen mentioned a contribution from a new member. Ah, yes. A fast offering contribution from Milada Daranyi, 1204 Larkspur Lane. Must be LaDawn's new tenant."

"Milada Daranyi," Rachel echoed. "What an interesting name."

Laura said, "Like I'm sure she's a member."

"Still, we should say hello," Rachel said. "No one's been assigned to the welcoming committee yet."

"I assigned you, as I recall." David glanced at his watch. "We're going to the hospital after dinner to see Jennifer. Do you want to come with, Laura?"

Laura gave him a pained look. "She's always the same, Dad. She just lies there."

"Okay, Laura. You don't have to."

Laura sat down at the table and announced, "I'm hungry. Let's eat."

Her mother returned to the stove. She said over her shoulder, "Why don't we stop and see Sister—Miss—Daranyi on the way back from the hospital?"

David thought that was a good idea.

Chapter 12
Behind every good man is a woman

AS HAPPY AS MILADA WAS with her Ozzie and Harriet accommodations, it occurred to her that the Mormons might take some getting used to. Early on in the project, Jane had prepared a fact sheet on the state's demographics and overall fiscal health. It alone convinced Milada that they should consider acquisitions of several high-tech firms she'd been following on the NASDAQ small cap index.

What Jane hadn't mentioned was that Salt Lake City proper was approximately fifty percent Mormon. Cottonwood Estates, Milada was beginning to suspect, boasted a higher-than-average concentration.

Two more were now arriving. Late thirties or early forties, she guessed. The man still preserved some of the athletic slenderness of his youth. His wife was attractively dressed in peach, a bright blue sash tied around her waist, tight enough to show her figure.

Milada observed them from her comfortable perch in the wicker chair, standing only when they climbed the steps to the porch. "Milada Daranyi?" said the man. He extended his hand. "I'm Bishop Forsythe. This is my wife, Rachel."

Milada shook the woman's hand as well. She said to the bishop, "You don't wear a collar?"

It took him a second to parse the statement. He said pleasantly, "The Mormon church is run by a lay priesthood at the local level." He thumbed the lapels of his jacket. "Everyday business attire."

"Not every day." His wife smiled.

"And when you are not being a bishop?"

He handed her a business card. Milada motioned to them, "Please." They sat on the bench against the porch railing. She returned to the chair and examined the business card. "Zions Bank?" she said, a touch of surprise in her voice. *So you have a real job then?*

the question meant. "You must be kept busy, running a church congregation at the same time."

His wife laughed, "You can say that again. I'm counting the days."

Milada decided at once that she liked her. She seemed determined not to be just another desperate housewife. If that was why he married her, then that made him a smart man as well. "Then it is a temporary position?"

"Five years on average."

The bishop's wife asked, "And what brings you to Salt Lake, Milada?"

"I run a capital management fund. We're exploring investments in the area."

They both nodded.

After a little more small talk, the bishop and his wife got to their feet. "Well, we'd better get going."

"Oh," the bishop's wife said, remembering something at the last minute. "Milada, we're having a few friends over tomorrow night. It'd be nice if you could join us. It'll be an informal affair. How do you feel about barbecued chicken?"

"I feel fine about it."

"If you're not busy, why don't you come by around seven? We're up the street a block and around the corner, 445 Willow Way."

Milada said, "I assume this will be a backyard affair. May I ask what direction your backyard faces?"

Rachel did not understand the relevance of the question. Then her husband said, "East. The backyard faces east."

"Very well," Milada said pleasantly. "I'll look forward to it."

Chapter 13

A lonely person is at home everywhere

RACHEL DRAINED THE MARINADE from the chicken breasts. The doorbell rang. "Laura!" she called out. "See who it is!"

A minute later her daughter walked into the kitchen with a curious look on her face. "There's this *lady* at the door."

"What? Oh, that must be Milada. Invite her in." She shooed her daughter out of the kitchen with dripping hands.

She heard the front door close, footsteps in the hall, Milada saying, "So this is your family then?"

Milada must have noticed the genealogy of photographs on the wall.

"Yeah," said Laura, with no great enthusiasm. "That's Grandpa and Grandma, my mom's parents. When we were in Maine last year. Mom and Dad. Me and Jennifer. She's seven years younger than me."

"And the dragon?"

Rachel smiled to herself. Nobody could miss the bright purple reptile crouched over the picture frame. "Barney Junior," they called him.

"Oh, yeah. Jen's in the hospital. It's one of her guardian angels."

"Her guardian angel? I hope she gets better. And what is your name?"

"I'm Laura."

"I'm pleased to meet you, Laura. My name is Milada."

Laura said, "That's a weird name."

Her mother winced. Milada answered pleasantly, "It's Czech."

"Is that where you're from?"

"I'm from Romania, but a long time ago."

They entered the kitchen. Rachel said, "Hello, Milada. I see you've met Laura. Sorry I couldn't come to the door, but my hands are full."

Milada was holding a broad-brimmed fedora reminiscent of Ingrid Bergman in *Casablanca*. She was wearing a gray jacket over a blouse and matching slacks. Sensible shoes, gloves, sunglasses. A parasol was tucked under her right arm.

She needed some place to put them.

"You can leave your things on the piano in the living room. Laura—"

Laura showed Milada to the living room. When they returned, Milada had removed her sunglasses and tucked them into the pocket of her jacket. Her high cheekbones gave her face a catlike appearance. Her eyes were the clear color of rain. Her shimmering white hair, cut short and brushed even with her ears, was white down to the roots, as were her eyebrows. The conclusion struck Rachel forcibly: *she's practically albino*. Hence her concern about the light, the direction of the yard. The previous evening on the shaded porch of her house, it hadn't been that obvious.

"Anything I can do to help?" Milada asked.

Rachel was afraid she'd been caught staring. "Why don't you get that other plate of chicken." She pointed with her elbow at a glass pan next to the stove. As Milada picked up the pan, Rachel was seized with a vision of marinated chicken spilling down her suit, which she didn't think came off the rack at Dillard's.

"Laura, get the back door." She said to Milada, "Careful, it's a step down."

The bishop was holding court with Brent Millington and Tom Forbush at the GrillMaster 550. His apron was illustrated with a silkscreen of a DEER CROSSING road sign bent across the hood of a pickup, with the words *The buck stops here* stenciled underneath. A Christmas present from Carl.

"Ah, the main course," said David. He was cooking hot dogs for the Millington kids, who were already running low on blood sugar. He picked up the tongs and announced, "All right, who wants one?" A boy and a girl ran over. David plopped a hot dog into a bun for each of them.

Brent Millington said to the boy, "Go ask your brother if he wants a hot dog."

The kid ran off, chewing the end of the bun. A few seconds later, a pudgy, round-headed kid came shambling over. The whole

Millington family was large. Big boned, with big appetites to match. Rachel could not begin to contemplate the Millingtons' grocery budget.

"Here you go, Andy," said David, serving up another hot dog.

Rachel and Milada placed the chicken on the table next to the barbecue. David began laying the meat on the grill. "David," said his wife, "why don't you introduce our guest?"

"Yes, of course." He rapped the tongs on the edge of the grill so as not to fling marinade at his audience. "Tom, Brent, this is Milada Daranyi. Milada, this is President Forbush." He indicated the man on his right, a graying executive type in his late fifties. "And this," he said, putting his hand on the shoulder of the ox-sized man to his left, "is Brent Millington. And his four kids." He gestured at the yard.

"President," she said to President Forbush. She shook his hand.

"Call me Tom."

David said, "Tom's the president of our stake." He explained, "A Mormon stake is akin to a Catholic diocese."

"Also a lay position?"

President Forbush nodded. "I work for FranklinCovey."

"And Brent here's a produce manager at Smith's."

Milada shook his hand as well. It enveloped her own.

"What brings you to Utah, Milada?"

"I represent Daranyi Capital Management. We are considering some investments in the area."

"Daranyi . . ." President Forbush thought about it for a moment. "That wouldn't be a division of Daranyi Enterprises, would it? Covey did some work for DEI a few years back. Training and orientation for the Blackhaven buyout."

Milada remembered as well. "Small world."

Rachel broke in. "Enough shop talk. I'd like to introduce Milada to your better halves."

That was when Troy Ellis arrived. Rachel had to stop and remind herself that she *had* invited the elders quorum president the week before. Reluctantly.

"He's going to think we don't like him," the bishop pointed out.

I don't, his wife thought. She wasn't sure why. He struck all the wrong chords with her. He was too—something. *Too Mormon.* Like Hugh Nibley's quip about people who thought it was better to get up at six A.M. to write a bad book than at nine to write a good one. That's how Troy struck her: the first one up in the morning with nothing to say.

"Because people like Troy *need* a calling," David had explained. "Busy hands, and all that. Besides, he's good at it. Zeal is preferred to knowledge in some cases. There's a lot to be said for just getting a thing done on time. He turns in the best home teaching stats we've ever had."

Rachel was glad she wasn't a home teacher.

She managed to make it to the picnic table with Milada and say hello to Doris Forbush and Charlene Millington before Troy strode up and introduced himself. He couldn't have helped but notice Milada. Even in the shadowed backyard, she looked like she was standing center stage under a spotlight.

"Hi. I'm Troy Ellis."

"Milada Daranyi."

"You new in the ward?"

Milada gave him a bemused look. Rachel said, "She's renting the Lindstroms' place."

"That's right! Are you moved in okay? That's great. What brings you to Salt Lake, Milada?"

She didn't have to answer. The bishop called out, "Troy! Priesthood powwow."

Troy's shoulders slumped. "Sorry, I'm being paged. Hey, don't you go anywhere." He ambled over to the barbecue pit.

Briefly, across the patio, David caught his wife's eye and winked. Rachel was sure Milada saw it too. She found herself blushing with chagrin at the obviousness of the maneuver. The four women resumed setting the table. Plastic knife, spoon, and fork, paper plate, paper napkin, paper cup.

Doris said, in as offhand a manner as she could muster, "Forgive me for asking, Milada, but I'm intrigued by your name. It certainly isn't common around these parts."

Rachel winced again. She didn't think uncommon things in New York City provoked such a constant need to be commented on. She said by way of apology, "Doris is the ward genealogy specialist."

Unperturbed, Milada replied, "I was named after the daughter of a gentleman by the name of Boleslaw the Cruel, a pagan who murdered his Christian brother on the steps of the cathedral." She went on setting places as she talked. "No little irony that Boleslaw's son went on to establish the Bishopric of Prague. His daughter became abbess of the Benedictine order of Saint George." Milada paused. Then she said impassively, as if reciting a lesson learned long ago at her mother's knee, "And thus do the children atone for the sins of the father."

Doris obviously hadn't expected this level of detail. "Well," she said, "that's certainly an interesting story! Your parents must have been quite the historians."

Milada smiled a small, knowing smile. "No, but in their time it was like it had happened only yesterday."

There certainly wasn't much more they could add to the subject. Charlene asked Rachel, "So — are you going to teach school this year?"

Milada said, "You teach school?"

"Substitute teach. But not this year." Not while her daughter was in the hospital, she meant. She called out, "How are things looking over there, guys?"

"Almost done." David waved.

She said to Milada, "Why don't you help me get the rest of the food?"

In the house, Laura was sitting on the couch in the family room reading a paperback. Her mother said, "Laura, put down your book. We're ready to eat. You can take out the punch."

Laura responded with a groan, but she set aside the book and slouched up the steps to the kitchen. Her mother opened the refrigerator and took out two pitchers of pink lemonade and set them on the counter. She handed one to Laura. "Here you go. Don't spill it."

Laura sighed. "I won't spill it, Mom."

Rachel glanced at Milada and was relieved to see that she was amused by her daughter's angst-ridden attitude. After Laura left the kitchen, Milada said, "I have the feeling you wish to keep some distance between Troy and myself."

"I'm just afraid he'll try to convert you before the night is through. He can be awfully persistent."

Milada smiled. "That's about the least of my worries when it comes to men. Usually all they're interested in is my number."

"He might want that too." Rachel handed Milada a green Tupperware bowl, Charlene's tossed salad. She got the potato salad, tucked it against her hip, and grabbed a bag of potato chips off the top of the fridge.

David rationed out the first round of chicken and threw on a few more hot dogs for the kids. Sister Millington herded her flock to the picnic table. Laura was curled up in one of the deck chairs, reading her book. Her father said, "I guess we're ready to begin. Laura, put down your book. President," he said to President Forbush, "could you offer a blessing on the food?"

"Certainly," said President Forbush. He folded his arms and bowed his head and blessed the food to their health and strength. Rachel silently added: *We ask thee to keep the cholesterol from clogging our veins. We ask thee to keep the cellulite from collecting on our thighs.* Lastly, he asked a blessing on Jennifer.

These days, if David asked somebody else to pray Rachel could count on the person throwing in a heavenly petition on Jennifer's behalf. Spiritual pandering, perhaps, but Rachel had long ago determined not to be above it.

They chorused an *Amen* and sat down and commenced to eat.

Troy positioned himself across from Milada. As he casually deboned a chicken breast, he asked, "So, Milada, what do you know about the Mormon church?"

"Very little, I'm afraid."

"Well," he said, "if you want to find out more, this is the place."

Milada clearly didn't get the pun.

"You know, Darin Pelton—he lives right around the corner—he's the ward mission leader. We could round up a couple of the full-time missionaries. You got a free night this week, say Wednesday or Thursday?"

Milada surely had no idea what he was talking about.

"A new sister missionary got transferred into the ward last week. She's from Finland. Amazing, don't you think?"

Milada didn't reply. Instead she did something that Rachel hadn't expected at all. Troy's left hand was resting on the table next to his plate. Milada reached over and lightly touched his hand with the tips of her fingers. "We shall talk about something else now. Sports, perhaps?"

Her voice was so low and direct that Rachel wouldn't have caught it if she hadn't been paying close attention. It wasn't a suggestion. Troy didn't mull it over. He stopped mid sentence—mid thought, even. He said to Brent Millington, "Hey, Brent, what do you think about the Y's chances this year?"

Rachel said to Milada, hoping to help push the conversation onto that track, "Brent was an offensive lineman at BYU."

"Second string," responded Brent. "Warmed a lot of bench."

Milada politely acknowledged the honesty in the qualification and turned to Laura, perched on the end of the picnic table bench. Laura was eating a hot dog with one hand, holding the book with the other. Rachel was about to tell Laura to put the book down, but a passion for reading was something a parent shouldn't mess with. After all, Laura dutifully read her Bible and Book of Mormon. That her taste in literature had grown more gothic over the past year should have surprised no one.

Milada asked, "What are you reading, Laura?"

"It's this book by Annette Curtis Klause." Laura showed her the cover. "It's about a guy who's a vampire. But he's a *good* vampire, like Angel on *Buffy*. Except he has a little brother who got turned into a vampire when he was little and never grew up. So he's evil."

"It is nice to know that there are good vampires around," Milada said. "Bram Stoker gave us Carpathians such a bad reputation. And they do grow up. It only takes forever and a day."

When Laura was sure she wasn't being made fun of, she grinned.

Rachel felt the tension oozing out of her neck and back. The chicken was edible—David was demonstrating some real skill at the barbecue. With Troy distracted and her daughter's attitude on hold, things couldn't have turned out much better than this. She excused herself and went into the house to get boxes of Popsicles and ice cream bars out of the freezer. Outside she distributed them to the Millingtons, making sure Andy didn't get anything with milk or soy in it. She sat down and listened as her daughter and Milada talked.

"I was born in Romania," Milada was saying, "but I grew up in a little town in Hungary called Szeged, on the Tisza River. It's grown to the size of Salt Lake City by now, or so I am told. I haven't been back in centuries."

"You sound like you have a British accent," Laura said.

"We resided in London for many years. I live in New York now. I'm what New Yorkers sound like when they're trying to rise above their immigrant roots."

"New York City, you mean? Wow, what's New York like?"

"*It's a helluva town,*" she said, half-singing the Leonard Bernstein melody from the Gene Kelly and Frank Sinatra musical.

Laura asked, "Is there really a Transylvania? Isn't it in Hungary?"

"Hungary and Romania have been fighting over it for the past five hundred years. Since World War II it's been a province of Romania." She quipped, "Our loss. Or theirs."

Rachel asked, "Do you have family in New York, Milada?"

"My father—stepfather—and my two sisters, Kamilla and Zoë. Kammy's a doctor." The pride was evident in her voice. "She's a fellow at Saint Jude Children's Research Hospital. She's currently a visiting professor at the University of Utah." Milada paused, and a distant, fleeting look came to her eyes. Rachel knew that look. Milada hadn't mentioned her mother or her natural father. She hadn't said what Zoë did. *They do grow up. It only takes forever and a day.*

And Rachel said to herself: *I could understand this woman.*

Everybody was pretty much done eating. They munched on potato chips, sipped lemonade, digested. The men argued sports. BYU versus the University of Utah. Jazz basketball. The long-term viability of the major league soccer franchise. Charlene, her littlest one on her shoulder, chatted with Doris, casting an occasional glance at the three older Millingtons gallivanting across the yard.

"Do you wish the plates left in a certain place?" asked Milada, picking up hers.

Rachel said, "Oh, no, we'll get that later."

Laura said, "Meaning she'll make me do it."

"We'll do it together, okay, Laura? Why don't we sit over here?" Rachel indicated the pair of faux-redwood deck chairs. Rachel took the one on the left, the one with the right arm missing. Laura sat down on her chair sideways, her legs swung over the side, her back against her mother's shoulder.

Milada settled into the deck chair, her countenance white and ghostly in the falling light. "Forgive my ignorance, but do you deify dragons as guardian angels?"

It took Rachel a moment to realize what she was referring to. She laughed. "It's got nothing to do with Mormon theology. When Jennifer was diagnosed with cancer, she took to the idea of having a guardian angel, like on that one television show. But she felt that *her* guardian angel should be as strong and terrible as the thing she was fighting. She's got quite a collection of them."

Laura said to Milada, "What do you do in New York?"

"I buy things. Companies, mostly."

"You buy companies? Wow. Like Wal-Mart?"

"Not Wal-Mart. Small-cap, high-tech companies."

"Is it fun?"

Milada smiled. "For the most part, yes, I do enjoy my work."

Almost absentmindedly, Rachel drew back her daughter's hair and began to braid it. Laura didn't duck or shake her head the way she was wont to do. Perhaps, her mother thought, they should have Milada over more often.

Laura said, "Is your hair like that naturally?"

"It does run in the family." Another small smile. She was not a woman easily offended by personal questions. Or perhaps not easily offended by children. She had taken to Laura—or was it the other way around?

Just then, Brother Millington bellowed—and the man could bellow like a water buffalo—"Andy!" He stood at the edge of the patio and stared out at the yard and field beyond.

Laura jumped up, the braids falling out of her hair. Her mother stood behind her. Charlene hurried up to them, her eyes full of fear. Rachel said, "Charlene, what's going on?"

She gasped, "We can't find Andy."

Chapter 14

Every cloud has a silver lining

THE MEN COALESCED IN A PHALANX around them. President Forbush asked, "Where did you last see him?"

"Maybe he wandered down to the creek bed," the bishop suggested.

Brother Millington shook his head, but not in disagreement. "I'll just bet that's what he did. If I've told him once, I've told him a thousand times—"

Troy said, "He probably followed the trail the Cub Scouts use."

Milada joined Rachel. Laura said under her breath, "The Pillsbury Dough Boy bounced away." Her mother didn't bother admonishing her. Laura had much experience babysitting the Millington children.

Rachel agreed with her husband about the creek bed of the arroyo. "It's like a magnet for kids around here. A boy drowned there last summer in a flash flood." She grimaced to herself as she spoke. *Why in the world did I say that?* Perhaps it was to state the worst-case scenario so anything else would be an improvement.

The men fanned out across the field and snaked down the crumbling, sandy slopes, Brent Millington's voice blaring like a foghorn.

With a dispassionate expression on her face, Milada watched the men move off. Then she kicked off her shoes and stepped up on the picnic table bench, her gaze moving slowly like a predator scanning the Serengeti for fresh prey. She stepped down, put on her shoes, and walked to the edge of the property line.

Laura took off after her. Rachel said to Charlene, "It'll be okay."

Charlene sighed wearily, then snapped at her two older children, "Mary, Brent Junior, get over here and sit down. Don't want you getting lost as well, for Pete's sake."

High along the ridgeline of the Wasatch Mountains, the setting sun gleamed off the granite walls of Twin and Lone Peaks. The contrast threw the shadowed valley floor below into an exaggerated darkness. Milada waded through the tall, dry grass with unhurried strides. Not toward the arroyo but toward a John Deere backhoe parked next to a gnarled apple tree at the edge of the new housing lots. Rachel jogged to catch up with her, and then fell back a step behind with Laura. The field hummed with the buzz of cicadas. Mormon crickets sprang out of their path. The grass, charred from the harsh September sun, shattered at the touch.

A nervous droning sound grew louder as they approached the backhoe. It wasn't the droning of cicadas. It reminded Rachel of the sound the vacuum cleaner made when it grabbed a penny off the carpet and jammed it against the belt. Laura ran ahead, stopped, let out a shriek, and retreated to her mother's side.

The evidence of the crime lay scattered on the ground. The spent can of Raid left behind by the work crew. The survey stake Andy had managed to heft and swing with unfortunate accuracy, knocking the nest from the overhanging limb. The crumpled hive buzzing with angry yellow jackets—

And Andy's still, flaccid body a few feet off, his puffy skin dotted with red welts. "Milada—" Rachel started to say, but Milada hardly hesitated. She picked up the nest and flung it a dozen yards into an open house foundation. Not a yellow jacket lit upon her. She knelt next to Andy. Rachel said to her daughter, "Laura, go get your father."

She didn't move. "Laura!" her mother said again. Laura took off across the field.

Rachel kneeled next to Milada, who said in her calm voice, "The boy has stopped breathing." She pressed on his sternum with the palm of her hand. Air rushed hollowly out of his mouth. She compressed his chest twice more.

Andy's head lolled to the side. She picked up his right arm, the ball of her thumb pressing tightly at the bend of his elbow, lowered her mouth to his wrist—

And then—

Rachel's mind went blank. Literally blank. Static on an empty television channel. She blinked and shook her head. Her brain fired up, jerked her back to reality. Milada looked at her, her crystal-clear eyes filled with concern. She touched Rachel's cheek with her fingertips. "Are you all right, Rachel?"

She nodded. She hadn't fainted, had she? She didn't faint over something like this—after all, she'd handled bloody catastrophes at girls' camp. She was still kneeling at Milada's side. Only a moment had passed, but whatever had happened in that moment had evaporated into nothingness.

Milada said, "The boy is breathing."

"He's breathing?"

Milada scooped the boy into her arms and stood up. Rachel remained on her knees, still dazed. Milada said, "In the right pocket of my jacket—"

Rachel leapt to her feet. Andy was a big boy for his age, but Milada's voice was not even strained. The thought struck her: *Good heavens, she's strong.*

"My cell phone—"

Rachel reached into her jacket pocket and found the little Nokia. She popped it open and dialed 9-1-1. "An eight-year-old boy just got stung by yellow jackets. I think he's in anaphylactic shock. We did CPR. He's breathing now. We're at 445 Willow Way in Sandy."

People ran toward them. Laura arrived first, her eyes wide. "Andy!" Brent Millington shouted. Milada carried Andy to the lawn and set him down on the grass next to the patio. Andy stirred, twitched, and kicked like a sleeping dog. He coughed, his stomach heaved, and he threw up pink lemonade, half-digested hot dog, and melted orange Popsicle onto Milada's jacket.

Brother Millington sat Andy up and patted him on the back, making sure he didn't choke. "You all right, Sport?"

Andy weakly bobbed his head.

A police cruiser drove up, siren screaming in the quiet twilight, strobe lights painting the street with ribbons of red and white and blue. The ambulance arrived soon after. The paramedics hefted the boy onto the gurney and started an IV drip.

A small crowd gathered in the street in front of the house. Bill Garner—the Garners lived three houses down—approached the bishop. "It's Andy Millington," David explained. "He got himself tangled up in a yellow jacket nest. But it looks like he's going to be okay. Brent's riding with him to Alta View Hospital. I'll take Charlene and the kids and meet them there."

Troy Ellis asked, "You need any help giving Andy a blessing, Bishop?"

The bishop gave Troy a pat on the shoulder. "Tom's going to

follow us down. He can assist us there." Between Troy and Bill Garner, the news would get out, a mostly correct version. "He's going to be okay," the bishop said again.

The ambulance roared off. The police officer waited while David loaded the Millingtons into Rachel's Odyssey, and then he escorted them to the Alta View ER.

The small crowd dispersed.

Rachel took a breath, exhaled. "Well," she said without any irony, "that was interesting." Her nose caught the sour smell of bile. "Oh, Milada, your clothing—"

Milada glanced down. "Most of it's on my jacket," she said, as if that was a good thing. She scraped a spot of vomit from her thigh with the side of her hand and flicked it off.

"For heaven's sakes. Come inside. Let's get you cleaned up."

In the kitchen they daubed off the puke with paper towels. The foul odor remained. "I'll have to soak that," Rachel said. "You know, we're about the same size, Milada. Why don't I give you an old sweat suit to change into? I'll take care of the cleaning."

"I think I can make it home in one piece."

"No, no. I insist."

She steered Milada up the stairs to the master bedroom. Milada disrobed. Rachel carefully set aside her jacket, blouse, and slacks. "The bathroom's right through there."

Rachel dug out her old BYU top and drawstring bottoms. The water stopped running, and Milada came out. She wore a sheer white chemise and panties cut high on the thigh. Rachel felt the bite of envy. The chemise hung short over a flat stomach that showed only the hint of a belly. She looked like she'd modeled for the sculptor of those ancient Roman statues, the women with the perfect round breasts, skin polished smooth as glass—women who, after two thousand years, still looked great.

Oh, to have the body I had at twenty. The body she married David with. She wondered if her husband missed that body too.

Rachel held out the BYU top for Milada to see, the one with the cougar hunched over the big block letters. Milada's eyes lit up. "It's darling!" she said. She drew it down over her breasts and pulled on the bottoms. Her figure showed well even through the loose fabric. "You're right, it does fit." She peered down at the blue silk-screened logo. "You graduated from BYU?"

"Yes, that's where David and I met."

"It's precious," said Milada. "Zoë will be jealous. Why don't we call it a trade?"

"A trade?"

"I certainly couldn't get one of these back in New York."

"But—" Rachel meant to say that she could buy several dozen sweat suits for what an outfit like Milada's must cost. "I'm sure you could get one at any mall or sports shop around here. And Provo's not that far away—"

"I detest shopping for clothes."

She was serious. Running out of reasons, Rachel gave in. "Okay," she said. Now that the possibility was real, she found herself looking forward to trying on Milada's outfit. After she got it cleaned.

Milada said, "One thing, though. The dry cleaning will prove dear."

Expensive, she meant. It couldn't be that much, Rachel assured herself.

Rachel walked with Milada back to her house on Larkspur Lane. "I'm sorry about tonight," said Rachel. "Our dinner parties are rarely so eventful."

"Think nothing of it."

"Still, it sure was a good thing you were there. I think you're the only one who kept her head on straight."

"You would have done fine without me."

"I'm not so sure. You probably saved Andy's life."

"To be honest, Rachel, I am not the Good Samaritan type. It is the kind of thing Kammy would have done."

"Then thank her for being such a good influence."

Milada flashed a weary smile and wished Rachel a good night.

The bishop got home shortly before ten. Rachel heard the younger Millingtons piling out of the Odyssey, climbing into their big Chevy Suburban. She walked outside. "Oh, Rachel," gasped Charlene, running up to her. They hugged. "The doctor said Andy's going to be fine."

"That's wonderful!"

"I forgot to thank you before. It was just so—"

"That's okay. But it's really Milada you should thank."

Brent Millington and David finished talking. They shook hands, and Brother Millington gave him a heartfelt whack on the shoulder. Big guy emotion. "See you Wednesday, Bishop." Brother Millington and Charlene climbed into the Suburban, and they drove off.

Laura was waiting for them in the kitchen. "So how's the doughboy?"

Her father gave her a scolding look. "Surprisingly well. They're keeping him overnight at Alta View for observation. But it looks like he'll be no worse for wear. Remarkable, considering the severity of his reaction." He paused. "There was one odd thing, though. A pair of marks on his wrist—" David touched his right arm.

"Bee stings?"

"No, they're pretty sure it wasn't that. More like needle marks. Maybe one of the EMTs—" He shook his head. "Who knows in cases like this—all the excitement and everything. At least he's all right." David paused for a moment. "How did you know where to find him?"

"Mom didn't find him. It was Milada. It's like she has radar or something. Like she can see in the dark."

Her mother agreed. "She does have very good eyesight." Then she hesitated. "When we found Andy, I think she started doing CPR."

"You think?"

Rachel opened her mouth to go on, but she didn't know what to say. She tilted her head to one side, her brow furrowing. "I—I can't remember."

"Can't remember?" Laura was incredulous. "How can you not remember? Mom, you were right there!"

"I know." A gnawing frustration welled up inside her. "She started doing CPR and then—and then Andy started breathing and she picked him up and carried him back to the yard."

End of story. Good enough for them, but not good enough for her. Something was missing. Something she couldn't remember. Something she'd *lost*.

David gave her a reassuring hug. "It's been a most interesting family home evening."

"Yeah," said Laura. "We should have Milada over again."

Have Milada over again. Rachel smiled. Laura was rarely enthusiastic about their adult guests. But at that same moment, something jolted inside her like an electric shock. She ran herself a glass of warm water and drank it slowly.

It was only later that night, her mind hovering at the edge of sleep, that she understood what she had felt. Not fear—not the fear of imminent harm or suffering—but surprise, astonishment, even awe.

Just then, out of the corner of her eye, she saw a shadow creeping across the room. She felt a quick stab in the gut. Her eyes opened wide. But it was only the curtains fluttering against an open window, the bright street light beyond.

It's nothing.

So in her dreams, she went back to cranking the handle of the music box with a quiet if impatient amusement. Listening to the playful melody. Yet feeling the uneasy expectation that when the trap door flipped open, the little clown would pop out bearing tooth and claw.

Chapter 15
Don't take no for an answer

MILADA ASKED JANE, HER ASSISTANT, "Is Garrick on the line yet?"

She heard a click in her headset. Garrick Burke said, in the lower Middlesex accent he'd never bothered to shed, "Morning to you, girls. At least to you, Milly. Still morning there, isn't it?" He was on speakerphone, sounding like he was in the middle of the Holland Tunnel.

"Talk to me about Wylde Medical," she said. "I don't like what I'm seeing."

"Neither do I. I'm looking at thirty-seven and change on the big board right now."

Milada sucked air through her teeth. Garrick said, "I'm telling you, Milly, the float is a bloody mess. Every time I buy into a position, the day traders are all over me. It's like throwing a stuck pig in the Amazon."

"What are we holding?"

"I figure we've got over a third of outstanding. With the churn we're kicking up, we could sell off right now and make a killing. All that irrational exuberance, don't you know."

"Get it up to half first."

"How high are you willing to go?"

"Forty."

She knew Garrick was shaking his head when he said, "It'll go there, Milly, on a rocket. But I wouldn't pay ten for the whole shebang. They've sunk fifty million into that new biotech venture of theirs—fifty million in new debt on marginal earnings, and not a dime of profit so far."

"Those are real assets, Garrick. Fungible R&D resources. Push come to shove, everything else depends on the unregistered shares. That's what's flogging the float. Have your elves start digging."

"Hi-ho, hi-ho."

"That was elves," Jane interrupted. "Not dwarves."

Milada laughed. "Jane, have we heard anything from corporate? Let them know I've come all the way out here just to look at DEI's investment. Considering their stock buybacks, we're putting a lot of money into their coffers. In the meantime, have research do another patent search. I don't want this to be easy for the wrong reasons."

Jane agreed. Then she asked, "How're you doing, Milada? The Hilton treating you all right?"

"I moved out of the Hilton. Rented a house in the honest-to-God suburbs."

"You did what?"

"It's a great improvement. I'll fax you the papers. You can pull off the contact information in case my cell goes out."

Garrick chuckled. "The suburbs? No kidding? You mean the quarter-acre plot, the two-car garage, the neighbor kid who comes over every week to trim the lawn—"

"That describes the situation."

"You know what the old song says about mad dogs and Englishmen, Milly."

"Yes, I know, Garrick. I will stay out of the midday sun."

"And watch your diet. You must be a mile high. The blood thins out at those altitudes."

She ignored him. "Jane, ride their little backsides and FedEx me by Thursday latest. I want hard copies."

Jane cheerfully said she would. Milada hung up the phone and called Karen back into the room. "I have a job for you." She handed Karen the annual report for Wylde Medical Informatics. "That Post-It note marks a listing of the board of directors. I want you to find out who they are, where they live, who they're related to, how many kids they have, what charities they contribute to, other boards they sit on, and what they eat for breakfast. Especially Darren Wylde. Does Loveridge have an Edgar or Morningstar account?"

"I don't know. Probably."

"Find out. If not, you can use mine. I'll show you how it works."

"Okay!" said Karen. She sounded excited to find out, to get involved in The Big Project. Better than pushing the mail cart and making coffee.

• • •

The first batch of SEC reports arrived the next morning with the FedEx courier, a thick wad of Xeroxed forms crammed with tiny, practically indecipherable print, the dirt hauled out of an economic archeological dig. The valuable artifacts wouldn't show themselves without a good deal of sifting.

Milada called in Karen, and they started going through the forms. "How is your research going?" Milada asked.

"It looks like the biggest stockholder in WMI got into the business as a funeral home operator."

"Yes, that's Darren Wylde, the CEO. A well-run funeral home is a veritable cash machine, so that's no surprise."

"Up to 1979 the only hits in LexisNexis had to do with Wylde Funeral Homes and his work on the board of the National Funeral Directors Association," Karen said. "Wylde remains the largest locally owned chain of funeral homes in the Intermountain West. Listings related to Wylde Medical Informatics start in the late 1980s, and then there's a bunch more in the last five years."

"So he stays out of the spotlight. How much of the company does he own?"

"About twenty percent." Karen looked at the papers they were stacking in small piles around the conference room table. "What exactly are we doing?"

"We are trying to determine the size of the float. When a company goes public, the stock they sell to you and me is called the float. The rest gets divided up among the company's officers. Since the volume of held stock determines who controls the company, the principals will try not to sell off their holdings—their unregistered shares—even after the lockup has expired and their options vest."

"So we're trying to find out how much of the company Mr. Wylde controls?"

"Precisely," said Milada, rewarding her pupil with a smile. "The stock he *owns* and the stock he *controls*. Love, money, and in-laws."

The phone rang. It was Jane. "Yes," Milada confirmed, "we've received the first batch."

"I just had a pleasant conversation with Dr. Richard Brickey, CTO at Wylde. He's *dying* to show you the place. Sorry, I couldn't resist. The meeting's set for tomorrow at two."

Milada rolled her eyes. "Yes. That works for me."

"They're off the Van Winkle Expressway in Murray. I assume that means something to you. You have the address?"

"I'm sure Steven will be able to find it."

"Garrick promised the rest of the WMI statements will reach you by tomorrow."

"Good work, Jane. I'll ring you tomorrow after the meeting."

Jane hung up. The phone intercom buzzed. Cindy at the front desk said, "I've got a call for Ms. Daranyi."

"Who is it from?"

"A Mr. Troy Ellis."

"Ellis?" Milada glanced at Karen. Karen shook her head. "Ah," said Milada, remembering. "*That* Troy Ellis. Well—" She thought it over for a minute. The pious had always proved adept at her game. It was the historical perspective that religion provided, the willingness to believe in devils and angels. The greater the challenge, the greater the reward. "I'll take the call."

"Line four."

Milada hit line four. "Good morning, Troy."

"Milada! How are you?"

"I'm doing fine, Troy. And yourself?"

"Better that ever." Milada could hear the sound of printing presses running in the background. He said, "I was wondering if you might be free Friday night?"

"I might well be."

"The Utah Symphony Orchestra is playing at Abravanel Hall. They're performing Scheherazade."

"I have always enjoyed Rimsky-Korsakov. When does the concert begin?"

"Eight o'clock. I was thinking dinner first. How does Japanese sound? There's a little place in Sugarhouse that has great sushi. The Bamboo Grove."

"Japanese sounds fine. Why don't we meet there around—"

"—around six-thirty?"

"My driver will drop me off at the restaurant, and we shall take it from there."

"Great. I'll see you Friday."

"Good-bye, Troy." Milada took off the headset.

Karen said, "You've got a date! Who is it? Who asked you out?" She made it sound like an accomplishment more profound than taking over a publicly traded company.

"Some of my neighbors invited me to a barbecue yesterday. Mr. Ellis was one of their guests."

"That's nice."

"Curious thing is, he's a bishop. Or maybe that's not so odd."

"Mr. Ellis?"

"No, my neighbor. I wonder how he got my number."

"Your bishop?"

My bishop? Did one have a Mormon bishop whether one wanted one or not? Milada shook her head. "Mr. Ellis."

"Oh. Well, a good bishop can find out just about anything."

Thursday afternoon, following a pleasant if unproductive meeting with Richard Brickey at WMI headquarters—he steadfastly refused to promise her a face-to-face with Mr. Wylde—Steven picked up Milada at the Wylde headquarters in Murray. Milada had Jane on the phone by the time the car door closed. It was six o'clock in New York, but Jane had hung around for the call.

"How'd it go?" Jane asked.

"Give Bob a holler. He's got himself a new client. They don't know about it yet, but lay the groundwork."

"Are you sure you want Prince Machiavelli consorting with those nice Mormons?"

"Bob knows when to put on his family values cap. The man has that Dobson fellow on speed-dial. Or is it the other way around? He'll know what to do."

"He's a son of a bitch—" Jane began.

"Yes, but he's *our* son of a bitch."

"About the tender offer, how soon do you want to start getting proffers from Garrick?"

"Not until I can talk to Mr. Wylde himself and hopefully prevent a hostile takeover and the predictable poison pills. But tell Garrick to get his team together and start chipping away."

Steven exited Highland Drive and drove into the north Sandy suburbs.

A girl was walking by herself along the sidewalk, carrying a clarinet case and a backpack slung over her right shoulder. "Steven," said Milada, "pull over. The girl we passed, her name is Laura Forsythe. Ask her if she would like a ride home."

As Steven pulled over and stepped out, Milada watched through the tinted side window. For a brief, unbearable moment, her mind flashed back to the wet, reeking alleys winding off the Borough High Street. She remembered wending her way through the stews of Southwark, through the theater crowds at Bankside, past the brothels and bear-baiting arenas—trolling the dens and warrens for that impressionable, lost girl to bring home to Rakoczi and her sisters.

Laura walked over to the limo. *God, she was trusting.* It jarred Milada. Some things, like the inherent trust of children, never changed. Steven opened the door. Laura peered in, her hair haloed in sunlight. Her face brightened with recognition. Milada said, "Good afternoon, Laura."

"Hey, hi!" She climbed into the car. Steven shut the door behind her. Laura confided, "I've never had a chauffeur before."

"Steven is a very good one."

Laura said, "What are you doing here?"

"We are returning from a trip to Murray. Do you go to school nearby?"

"Alta High. Over there." She pointed over her shoulder.

"I see you play the clarinet."

"Yeah. I'm in marching band."

"I saw Benny Goodman in his Carnegie Hall concert. That was when Harry James and Teddy Wilson were still with the orchestra. Do you have any of his CDs?"

Laura shook her head, and Milada suspected she had no idea who Benny Goodman was. Just some dead jazz guy. Still, it was fun to match wits with children, even more so than with priests. The church ladies at the Forsythes' backyard barbecue politely had refused to take a thing she said literally, but children always believed her. She would pick out a child and stroll beside her and smile and say, *Come with me, and I will show you things, things you have never seen before and never will see again.*

The child would hear her strange accent and hesitate—

Come, she would insist, *and you shall see. My Master lives in a fine merchant's house. He shall treat you as he has always treated me.*

She did not lie. That was *exactly* how he would treat them. And so she won them over with her lilting voice and with her poisonous, compelling touch. With the promise of money or food. She would promise them the whole world, if that was what was required. *It's a game, don't you see?*

They sang and giggled as they skipped along: *Ring around the rosy, a pocket full of posies—*

Milada shook the melody out of her head. Her mouth tasted dry as ash. She'd left that life behind her so long ago. But the memories could still gain a powerful momentum, screaming at her out of the past. The oldest habits were the hardest to break.

The limo wove slowly through the sculpted suburban streets. Milada said, "It's not easy being the big sister in the family, is it?"

"You have a sister? Oh, yeah, two."

"And when one of them gets into trouble, who does your father pay his attention to?"

"Yeah," said Laura with wry empathy.

Steven announced, "Cottonwood Estates." He glanced over his shoulder at the back seat. "Where do you need to go, Miss?"

Laura giggled at the formalities. "It's 445 Willow Way."

Steven stopped in front of the Forsythes' driveway, got out, and opened the car door for Laura. Laura said, "Thank you, Steven."

Steven answered with a polite bow and a tip of his hat.

Chapter 16
Opportunity knocks only once

RACHEL WAS IN THE KITCHEN when Laura arrived home. "You're later than I expected."

Laura answered with a teenager's shrug. "I was going to ride home with Heidi, but she had an orthodontist appointment. So I walked."

"I could have picked you up."

"That's okay. Milada gave me a ride."

"Milada? *Milada* gave you a ride?"

"Yeah. She was driving by — I mean, she has this chauffeur who drives for her. He has this cute little hat and everything."

"A cute little hat—"

"Yeah. You know, Milada, she's not quite human."

Rachel froze. "What did you say?"

"I said she's a nice woman."

"Yes. Yes, she is." Rachel shook her head, listening for the clunk and rattle of loose parts.

Laura said, "What are we having for dinner?"

"What? Oh, dinner. Spaghetti."

"That's okay, I guess." Having signed off on the menu, Laura headed upstairs. "I've got homework to do," she announced.

Her mother stood there, wondering why she had heard what she thought she had heard. *She's not quite human.* She was sure that's what her daughter had said.

The next morning, the phone rang. It was her brother Carl.

"Hello, Carl," said Rachel. She checked the time and began making a series of mental calculations, scheduling the rest of the morning — what had to be done, what could be put off. Because once Carl got on the phone, it was hard getting him off, especially when he called during the day. That meant he was bored at work and had run out of more constructive ways to waste time.

Not that she minded talking to Carl. The world was chock full of people who could fill the spaces between any two points of time with words. Churn them out nonstop. LaDawn, for example. Every other church high councilman. She didn't quite know how they did it. That's why she didn't carry a cell phone. Why invite the bother?

But Carl always had something to say that was worth listening to. Offensive, but interesting.

"What's up, Rache?"

"Same old, same old, Carl." She paused. Carl wasn't in his office. Instead of a low electronic hum in the background, the telephone transmitted the echoing hustle and bustle of crowds moving through large, open spaces. "Where are you?"

"I'm at the Salt Palace."

"You're in Salt Lake? What are you doing in Salt Lake? Why didn't you tell me?"

"Hey, so I'm telling you. I flew in this morning." Carl said it like it was something he'd done at the last minute and just for the heck of it, which he probably had. For Rachel, even flying to San Jose was a chore not to be undertaken without thorough planning and preparation.

Carl said, "How about lunch? I'll buy. Mullboon's on Sixth South, is it still there? How about twelve-thirty? Just a second." He turned away from the phone. "Just start without me," she heard him say. "Five minutes." Then to her, "Gotta go."

"Bye, Carl."

Rachel hung up the phone and smiled to herself. A one-and-a-half-minute phone call from Carl and the promise of compelling company for lunch. There were worse ways to begin the day.

She left early and checked in at the hospital. Her daughter was no better, no worse. The glass was half empty or half full. But leave a half-full glass sitting around in Utah and it would evaporate soon enough. The expanse of the Bonneville Salt Flats stretching out beyond the lake proved that fact well enough.

Rachel didn't intend to stay long, but she hated leaving so soon. So she rearranged the dragons. The nurses didn't always put them back in the right places after rounds. The blue dragon guarded the heart monitor, the red dragon stood watch on the head rails of the bed, a pair of golden wyverns hung by their tails from the IV stand—things that went into her veins, Jennifer well knew, needed particular looking after.

On the wall opposite the bed—the first thing Jennifer would see when she woke up—was a full-color poster of the magical world of James Christensen's *Voyage of the Basset*. A land of dragons and elves and mermaids and endless possibilities.

She touched Jennifer's quiet, composed face, kissed her cheek, and prayed a silent prayer for her to wake up and be well.

At the restaurant, the maitre d' escorted her to the table. Carl was tapping away at his laptop. He stood to greet her, grinning broadly as he always did. He was wearing a tweed blazer over a faded T-shirt with a metallic-blue Digital Moviola logo emblazoned across the chest. He'd been wearing that T-shirt for years, filling out more of it every time she saw him. A Popsicle stick all through high school, Carl was Laurel slowly turning into Hardy.

They hugged. Rachel said, "Nice jacket."

"Mom gave it to me for Christmas. She still acts like I can't afford clothes."

"You dress like you can't afford clothes."

The maitre d' seated her and handed her a menu. She scanned the lunch entrees. Salmon, she'd have the salmon. Spending Carl's money bothered her not at all. "What brings you to Salt Lake, Carl?"

"ViFEE-West." Carl closed the laptop cover. "Video and Film Editors Exposition. I was going to give it a pass. But the sales guys picked up some big new account, and Bruce wanted me to come out and brownnose the clients. Make them feel so good about not going with AVID or EDIUS."

Rachel thumbed through her mental Rolodex: Bruce, the CEO of Carl's company.

"And how is work these days?"

Carl shook his head. "I'm surrounded by idiots, Rache. You wouldn't believe what a pain in the ass it is to hire competent coders these days. I'm telling you, we get this next rev out the door and I'm gone."

Rachel smirked good-naturedly. Carl had been threatening to quit every time the subject came up over the past five years.

"So why don't you, already?"

"Every time I try, Bruce has the board throw more options at me." He made it sound like an injustice of World Court proportions. "And then it's another eighteen months to get vested again."

"Yes, wealth can be such a heavy burden."

"It's these damned Scottish Calvinist genes we've inherited. Can't resist the urge to sock away more acorns for the long winter months to come. You remember how much Grandma had on her when she died—and she couldn't bring herself to put in air conditioning. Air conditioning! In Saint George! Anyway, do you have any idea what a house and yard like yours would go for in San Jose? A million, easy."

"So move here."

"Hey, don't think I haven't thought about it."

The waiter brought water and a bread basket and took their orders.

"The thing is," Carl explained, though she had heard it all before, "I wrote the thing in the first place because none of the video-editing tools out there are worth shit, not because I had some burning desire to design software for a living. But here I am, designing software for a living. I gotta get back to what I was doing in the first place."

"I thought you hated film editing. I thought that's why you got into programming."

"Yeah, yeah, you're right. I wanted to *be* an editor. Turned out I didn't want to *do* editing for a living. Producing, then. I'll be the one telling people what to do for a change."

"You could go back to rattlesnake wrangling."

"Now, there's a thought."

They both laughed, remembering the summer Carl had talked her and Phillip into helping him catch snakes for a study their Uncle Warren was doing at Utah State University. "What, you'd rather flip burgers at McDonalds?" Carl had argued.

"Burgers won't kill you."

"Give 'em fifty years and they will."

But she had done it anyway, because Carl was right: she didn't want to spend the summer flipping burgers at McDonald's. Her brother's driving need to avoid boredom at all costs had its side benefits.

She said, "I'm still amazed you didn't get us killed."

"Hey, we got lucky. Some other kids, it'd be sobbing parents on the six o'clock news wondering why God let it happen." He tore off a piece of bread and chewed it contemplatively. "The thing is, Rache, one of these days I'm going to have to wake up and face the fact that in my entire life I had one good idea in me. That's it."

"One good idea is good enough for most people. Especially an idea like yours."

"Yeah, good enough." He sat back in his chair. "It's like David O. Selznick. Produced *Gone with the Wind* and then spent the rest of his life trying to top himself. Never did."

The waiter brought their salads, refilled their glasses.

"The real depressing part," Carl continued, "is that I know I couldn't do it again. The field is too crowded. Like I said, no one wants to write real software anymore. It's all XML and Perl and ActiveX controls. What a joke! And then you have the dot-com punks eating up all the venture capital. That bubble is still burst, as far as I'm concerned. I happened to be in the right place at the right time. That's what it comes down to. I got lucky. I rolled sevens."

"Pretty depressing attitude when you put it that way, Carl. Success depends on a lot more than getting lucky."

"What else do you call it? God's will? God wanted Carl Cameron to be rich and bored? Okay, I'd like to believe that too. Though if God were so okay with the rich part, you'd think he could do something about the bored part. But I really don't think nonlinear video editing is something God takes a profound interest in. For that matter, neither do I. That's what Bruce is for."

He shook his head. "You know what our problem is? We *way* exaggerate what we think God cares about. It's like—like that time we went down to Saint George to see Grams and Kris had that stupid doll she was always dragging around whenever she went anywhere—"

"—and she left it behind."

"Yeah, and she didn't remember until Dad got to, like, Parowan—"

"—and Dad turned around and we went back and got it. I'm amazed you still remember that. That was twenty years ago."

"Hey, I was pissed royal. We had a monster D&D session set up for that evening—Dan, Pete, the whole gang. I ended up missing half of it. But the thing of it is, there was nothing intrinsically valuable about that doll. It was only valuable because Kris valued it. And because she was pitching a fit. That's what our lives are to God: kids pitching a fit. Maybe if we pitch a big-enough fit God gives in. But odds are, it's just some piece-o'-junk doll. Do you think she even remembers that dumb doll anymore?"

"Not like you'd ever let her forget it."

"Yeah, well—"

"Lucky you're not God."

"Nah, I'm an old-fashioned deist these days. Whatever happens happens. Man makes plans, God laughs. Getting born is ninety-nine percent of the game right there. The rest is frosting. Hey, and I don't blame God one way or the other. You want a universe with free will and all that, this is the universe you're gonna get. At any rate, if I ever run my car into a tree, it's because I'm a bad driver, okay? Believe me, God's not going to be calling me anywhere."

"I don't doubt that for a second," Rachel said.

"Speaking of dolls—" Carl reached down and took a box from his carry-on bag. "Here. Something for Jennifer."

Rachel opened the cover. Inside was a stuffed Dilbert doll astride a bright green dragon, like a wrangler riding a bucking bronco. She burst out laughing. "How clever! Was this your idea?"

"More of a family project. But that *is* what my job is like. Riding the dragon."

"We'll forgo the business metaphors. I'm sure she'll love it."

"So, how is Jennifer?"

Rachel started to say, *Okay, she's okay,* but with Carl there wasn't much of a point. She said lightly, wanting to get past the subject, "You and Liz thinking of having any more kids?"

Carl gave her a shocked look. "Hell, no. I'm getting a vasectomy. I thought I told you."

"Told me?" Rachel echoed. She gaped at her brother. *It's a joke,* she told herself, *one of Carl's gross jokes.* "You're *what?*"

"Yeah, as soon as I can take a couple days off without Bruce freaking on me." He caught her expression and said, "We *never* planned on having five kids. Mom and Dad only had four. It was *always* going to be two. Okay, okay, by Utah standards we're pikers in the procreation department. But in our neighborhood, with five kids we're the population explosion on the corner. Besides, Liz is getting up there. Hell, we're all getting up there. The odds for things going wrong in a major way are starting to get scary. The last thing I need in my life right now is a kid with a screwed-up chromosome or two."

"*I'm* getting up there, Carl. I'm only two years older than you. I'm not over the hill. Yet."

"I mean, come on. It's not something *you* have to worry about, Rache."

She leaned toward her brother and said in an insistent stage whisper, "There are other ways, less *permanent* ways."

"How do you think we ended up with five kids? Our gametes laugh at latex. Anyway, I thought they figured out what was wrong with you, some autoimmune thing."

"*Alloimmune*," Rachel corrected him. Yet another medical subject she knew too much about.

"Whatever. Look at it this way—your body zaps the little bastards before they get planted. You've got yourself a built-in IUD. Think of what I've got to do to get myself similarly equipped." He squirmed in his seat.

Rachel sighed. Carl's way of looking on the bright side of things was not always the brightest way of looking at things. Her immune system was like a gang of sacking and pillaging Goths. Her husband's sperm, her daughter's marrow, it showed no mercy. Had they left things to God and nature, the family would have stopped with Laura. The prednisone worked—once. Jennifer was the result. An IUI was next on the list and then in vitro, but Rachel had her doubts. For all her faith in the miracles of modern medicine, she found herself unsettled when it came to messing with the powers of procreation. So she'd convinced herself that two children were enough. Two children were all she really wanted. Two was God's will.

It was drawing too late in the day to take back that lie now. Easier to go on believing it.

Their entrees arrived. Rachel commenced eating with studious intent. They'd started out talking about software and ended up talking about their gonads. Par for the course when it came to Carl.

Rachel drove south on State. She'd invited Carl to dinner, but he had clients to schmooze and a nine o'clock flight to catch back to San Jose. David would be grateful—not grateful that she'd invited Carl, but grateful that Carl couldn't make it. David didn't get along with Carl. Most people outside their immediate family didn't get along with Carl. Even Laura thought her Uncle Carl was an odd duck, but a child could hold worse prejudices.

And Carl getting a vasectomy—that *was* weird. Only in Carl's *que sera sera* view of the world was the whole thing not a huge, cruel joke—Carl getting his plumbing cauterized to keep the little bastards from doing what God and nature intended them to do, while she was stuck with a womb armed like the Maginot Line.

The traffic light turned red. Rachel stepped on the brake and numbly watched the cars flashing by. Come to think about it, what was she doing driving a minivan anyway? What, with her one-point-five children? Talk about wishful thinking. Sure, she hauled girls to church camp once a summer, but that was all rationalization.

She hit the steering wheel, hard, with both hands. A shock of pain shot up her wrists. *Buy it and they will be born,* was that it? Was that what they were thinking? She hit the steering wheel again. *Bam!* And again. *Bam! Bam! Bam!* Until she had to stop, holding onto the wheel like she was going down with the Titanic and grasping at a life preserver. A car horn blared behind her. Her head jerked up. Through her blurred vision, the traffic light was a smear of green. She coasted through the intersection, turned into the Chevron station, and put the transmission into park.

She sat there with her head pressed back against the headrest, eyes squeezed closed. *Inhale, exhale. That's right. Inhale, exhale —*

"Mom," said a small voice.

She answered automatically. "Yes, Jenny."

"Mom," her daughter said again, looking at her with quizzical eyes. "What's the matter?" She was sitting in the passenger's seat, wearing her Oshkosh denim overalls and a Tigger T-shirt, the clothes she'd worn the day they had taken her to see the doctor, the last good day before everything went so terribly wrong. She hugged Carl's Dilbert dragon to her chest.

"Jennifer —"

"You have to remember, Mom."

Rachel told herself to breathe. "Remember what, darling?"

Jennifer's expression grew taut with concern. "About Milada. All you have to do is remember, and then you'll know what to do."

Somebody tapped on the driver's side window. "Oh!" Rachel exclaimed. A kid was standing there, a Chevron cap pressed down over a mat of curly brown hair, the name DALE stitched across the pocket of his stained white overalls. She lowered the window. The kid said, "Can I, um, help you, Ma'am?"

She had pulled into the full-service lane, which she never did. But she didn't want to think about it right now. "Sure," she said, "fill it up, regular." She reached down and pulled the gas cap cover release.

When she looked again, her daughter was gone. The box containing the Dilbert dragon sat alone on the seat.

This wasn't dinner table conversation. Not that Mormons didn't believe in miracles. But nobody spoke in tongues and cast out devils by smacking people on the forehead and hollering, "Be healed!" Carl was right. Too many pragmatic Scots in the family tree to tolerate that sort of nonsense. Nobody saw visions that didn't go through the chain of command. There had to be a reason, and the Mormon God was big on "working it out in your own mind."

"You have to remember, Mom," wasn't much of a reason. A ghost in the front seat wasn't subtle at all.

Instead Rachel said, "I saw Carl today."

Her husband stiffened noticeably, a purely Pavlovian response.

"Don't worry, dear. He came for some expo at the Salt Palace. He's flying back tonight."

"I wasn't worried."

"You were worried."

Laura said, "Uncle Carl is weird."

"Laura," said her mother.

"He is! He's always swearing at stuff. Uncle Phillip doesn't swear. *Dad* doesn't swear."

Her father beamed at her.

Rachel sighed. Her brother, the bad influence. Laura had spent two weeks over summer vacation in California with her cousins. She had since derived a certain syllogism to explain the experience: her uncle was rich, her uncle was weird, so rich people were weird.

The Dilbert dragon. That would rescue Carl's reputation for the time being. She retrieved the box and handed it to Laura to open. "Something Carl and Liz and the kids made for Jennifer."

Laura opened the box and lifted out the dragon. "It's so cute!" she exclaimed, swooping it through the air like a kid playing with a model airplane.

Even her father was impressed. "So," he said, still trying to prove that the mere mention of his brother-in-law's name didn't bother him, "Carl still threatening to quit Digital Moviola?"

"He never stops."

"So why doesn't he?"

"Because then he wouldn't have anything to complain about." Except the cost of living, the cost of raising five kids, the general state of the universe. For a silly, insane moment she considered alluding to Carl's vasectomy. But that *definitely* wasn't dinnertime conversation.

Not bedroom conversation either. Not a subject you casually brought up with the man you still dreamed might father another child someday. And lying on her side of the bed, she saw Jennifer clearly in her mind's eye, sitting there in the car. She was so real, her voice exactly what Jennifer would sound like. But what did she mean about remembering? Why would she imagine Jenny saying something like that?

Her husband emerged from the bathroom, brushing his teeth. She said, "David, have I forgotten something?"

"Forget something?" he mumbled, trying not to drool toothpaste. He ducked back into the bathroom and rinsed. He called out, "You think you forgot something?"

"If I knew, I wouldn't have forgotten it."

"Um, the dry cleaning?"

"I didn't forget that. They had to do a special order on Milada's outfit. I'll pick it up next week." She looked at him. "You can wear the navy blue on Sunday."

"Oh."

Yes, he preferred his black pinstriped suit. Even though he was forty, the navy blue tended to give him something of that freshly scrubbed missionary look.

David crossed the room and turned off the light. He knelt down at the side of the bed. She joined him, clasping his left hand in her right. They prayed every night like this, side by side. And while David prayed aloud, Rachel silently asked God to help her remember what she could not remember forgetting.

For once, it felt good to ask for something other than her daughter's life. Even if it was only for herself.

Chapter 17
And one more for the road

BRIGHAM'S BEER HOUND WAS THE NAME of the bar. Kammy's idea. Her non-Mormon students had recommended it. The bar was located at the east end of South Temple, where the avenues climbed the east bench to the University of Utah campus. They had to buy a four-dollar membership to get in the door—the product of some strange nexus between state liquor laws and the teetotaling Mormon population, Kammy explained.

Down-tempo lounge tunes played in the background. When they sat at the bar, the bartender paused in front of them. "What can I get you?" he asked, stepping to the side so they could see the sign boldly displayed on the wall: WE CARD EVERYBODY. IT'S THE LAW! Even serving the watered-down brew that passed for beer in the state, he obviously didn't want to risk them not being over twenty-one.

They handed over their New York driver licenses. He made a show of comparing their license photos to their actual selves. Kammy was wearing her Indiana Jones outfit, as she called it. She tipped back the fedora and pushed down her sunglasses and smiled coquettishly at him over the rims.

"Huh," he said, handing back the licenses. He added under his breath, "Nice fake IDs."

"They are," agreed Kammy, playing along. "The weird thing is that we're a lot *older* than it says."

Based on the name alone, Kammy ordered a microbrew called Polygamy Porter. "Not half bad," was her opinion. Milada played it safe with a midrange white wine.

Kammy said, "I hear you moved to the suburbs. Living a life of quiet desperation, eh?"

"Garrick telling tales out of school again?" Milada twiddled the stem of the glass, slippery and cool with condensation. "It is tolerable, actually. The welcome wagon all but rolled out the red carpet. I was invited to a *barbecue* on Monday. It turned out rather—interesting."

"And when they found out you aren't Mormon?"

"Only seemed to pique their curiosity. One eager young man, had he been a dog, would have been humping my leg by the time dessert was served. I have a date with him later this evening."

"No kidding?"

"He asked. I was intrigued. I don't see that much of a downside."

"As Garrick likes to say, don't go hunting in your own back yard."

"The same Garrick who otherwise treats me like a neurotic anorexic. Anyway, it hardly counts as hunting. More like catch and release."

"The action around here picks up in a few hours. If your young Mormon proves as well behaved as reputation suggests, you might find something here more to your liking."

"You should take your own advice."

"Nah, it's too complicated."

"Complications can be dealt with." Milada lowered her voice. "Besides, you know blood tastes so much better fresh. And that's not the *only* thing that tastes better."

"I mean, complicated for *me*. I prefer to keep my dietary demands and my social life separate. Like I said, not a problem in a hospital. It goes good with V8. Protein rich. And nobody can tell if our thermoses get mixed up."

The combination sounded truly revolting. "Get thee to a nunnery, sister."

"I'm no ascetic. Abstinence is just easier in the short term. I save up my emotional nickels and dimes, settle on a nice guy, and then blow it all on some grand, tragic relationship."

"Tragic?"

"You know, like, 'We'll always have Paris.'" Kammy continued in a husky growl, "Stick by me, kid, and you'll regret it. Maybe not today, and maybe not tomorrow. But soon and for the rest of your life."

She did a pretty good Bogart, Milada thought. The fedora didn't hurt. "How romantic."

"How pragmatic. Zoë's the romantic, waiting for her Cinderella to come dancing into her life and sweep her off her feet."

"You mean Prince Charm—" Milada shook her head. "No, you're right."

A group of students bustled in the front door. One of them waved in their direction. Another called out, "Hey, Dr. Daranyi."

Kammy waved back. "My students," she explained. "I'm subbing for Dr. Dennett. He's off to Lake Powell somewhere. That's near the Grand Canyon, isn't it?"

"What rotation are you doing?"

"Geriatrics."

"You did your residency in pediatrics. Why not—"

"You know why," Kammy said in a quiet voice that told Milada to drop the subject. "Besides, as you can see, I'm teaching."

"So get yourself on a tenure track, then."

"Like I have any desire to dive into a time suck like *that*."

"Ah," said Milada, a bit too smugly. "Then you should have *plenty* of time to serve on the Wylde board."

Kammy collapsed with a melodramatic groan. Resting her forehead against the dark, varnished hardwood of the bar, she asked, "Why are you so obsessed with me living your idea of a productive life?"

Milada had to smile to herself. The eternal teenager was still hiding inside her sister, just beneath the skin. "Because you *are* perfectly capable of living a more productive life."

"Why aren't you giving this lecture to Zoë?"

"If she'd sit still for five minutes, I would."

"You're just compensating," Kammy grumbled.

"You're just sublimating," Milada snapped back.

Always the same routine. The same questions and the same answers. But she had to ask, she had to nag. "Well, I'll let you get to your friends." Milada cringed as soon as the words came out of her mouth. She sounded like somebody's mother.

"Have fun with your Mormon boy."

"It should be an adventure."

Milada paid the tab. She glanced over her shoulder as Kammy joined her friends—or colleagues, or classmates—at a table near the back. Kammy had friends. Friends that came and went without the world ending or beginning, something Milada had never been able to manage. She rationed her friends the same way Kammy rationed lovers.

Returning her billfold to her inside breast pocket, Milada felt the envelope and sighed. She was getting forgetful in her old age—the envelope was the reason she'd arranged this meeting with Kammy in the first place. She wrote a few lines on the back and strode over to the table, ignoring the intrigued looks that turned in her direction. "Here," she said, handing the envelope to Kammy.

Kammy opened the envelope and took out a Wylde corporate ID card.

"No rush," Milada said. "But try to get some hands-on experience in the next couple of weeks. Kick the tires, take the databases for a spin. Whatever one does with whatever they do."

"I'll think about it."

Milada patted her on the shoulder. "I wrote my address on the back. Stop by some time and enliven my life of quiet desperation."

Kammy turned the envelope over and nodded. "Sure. If you say so."

"I'll see you, then."

"Yeah, later, Milly."

She wasn't out of earshot when somebody at the table said, "Wow, so it really *does* run in the family."

"What, you guys didn't believe me?"

"Pretty rare, though, isn't it? A trait like that?"

"Rare doesn't mean zero."

They were referring to her hair and skin. Kammy described their observable condition as hypomelanism. In simpler terms, they were albino. It was genetic, and it did run in the family. Except that they got it from the first of their stepfathers, long after their parents had died.

Chapter 18
A man's known by the company he keeps

THE STRESSED-CONCRETE ENTRANCEWAY to the Japanese restaurant was tucked in between the parking garage and a movie theater. Steven pulled into the parking garage and said, "Are you sure this is the right place?"

Milada looked again and replied that it was.

"When do you need to be picked up?"

"I should be fine for the evening. If not, I will call a taxi."

Once she got inside, Milada felt more reassured. The sharp scent of *shoyu* and boiled rice at once brought back a decades-old memory of strolling through Shibuya a quarter-century ago, before Japan's real-estate bubble burst.

The sushi chef called out a greeting from the bar. The floor area, crowded with tables, wrapped around the varnished pine sushi bar. A waitress, a small Japanese girl, bowed to her.

"I'm here to meet a Mr. Troy Ellis—"

"Milada!" Troy stood and waved. Seeing the eager young Mormon again, all square jaw and broad shoulders, she knew he was the boy who as a child sat through all the elementary school self-esteem courses and believed every word he heard.

The waitress led her over to the table. Troy came around the table to hold the chair for her. The waitress gave her a menu.

"Did you find the place all right?"

"My driver has a talent with addresses and directions."

"The sushi's quite good. Take your pick. I usually go with the tuna roll or California roll."

Milada nodded. She put down the menu and took a sip of water.

"So," said Troy, "how's your knowledge of Mormons coming along?"

"It's still pretty much confined to what you don't do. I'm up to tobacco, alcohol, and caffeine.

"Technically it depends what the caffeine comes in. Coffee — that's a given. Diet Coke — that's how you separate out the true believers."

Milada smiled. She wasn't certain whether the boy was trying to be funny on purpose. The waitress returned and took their orders, picked up the menus, and left.

Troy toyed with his water glass, spinning it around on its coaster. "Not to get too personal, but do you consider yourself a religious person?"

"No," Milada replied bluntly.

"You mean, you haven't ever thought about, say, whether you existed before you were born, whether the soul continues after death—"

"Those are as much philosophical questions as religious questions."

"Then do you consider yourself a philosophical person?"

Milada said again, "No."

Troy gave her a guarded look. "Not even the purpose of life? Your place in God's creation?"

"A long time ago, I spent a century thinking about it. Not any more."

"And what conclusion did you come to?"

"The purpose of life is business."

Troy raised his eyebrows.

"I am serious. Religion preaches values, ethics, love of your fellow man. But where do those virtues touch everyday life? Other than in our own homes? In commerce. Yes, we aspire to loftier pursuits — to art, music, literature. To the priesthood. To lives of charity and self-sacrifice. And how do we pay for them? What must we sacrifice at the end of the day? Not only our lives and honor, said Thomas Jefferson, but our fortunes. The Good Samaritan, when he asked the innkeeper to watch over the man he rescued along the road to Jericho, he left the man with an expense account."

Troy objected. "But business by itself is hardly virtuous. Without a foundation of belief, isn't life reduced to little more than a series of economic transactions?"

Milada nodded. "Yes, business is hardly virtuous. Neither am I. It is not the place to expect sainthood. Or even fair play. But it is the place to practice. Immediate gratification tempts. But patience rewards in the long term. That and the miracle of compound interest." She smiled to herself. "Now, if you are looking for a more Manichean philosophy of life, I would have you ask Zoë."

The waitress and busboy arrived with the dinners. The two set out the sushi and tempura, miso and rice. Troy thanked them in Japanese. The waitress grinned and bowed in return.

Milada cradled her miso bowl and sipped the hot, salty tea. She hadn't tasted miso in a while. She had forgotten how much it reminded her of blood.

Troy dipped a slice of the sushi roll into the soy sauce. He used chopsticks with a practiced dexterity. "Zoë?" he said, picking up the thread of the conversation.

"The younger of my two sisters."

"What does she think the purpose of life is?"

"Killing people she doesn't like."

The surprised look on his face was followed by a suspicious expression that his leg was being pulled. Milada shrugged. "She battles evil, if you like. Rather haphazardly. I agree, I can think of better occupations."

"Is she a police officer or soldier or something like that?"

"Something like that."

The sushi wasn't bad, Milada thought.

"So you believe in evil then."

"I believe people can be bad, can be cruel. Perhaps can be clever enough to be evil. But even the clever ones eventually end up against the wall like the Ceausescus. Or erased from history like the Gang of Four. Evil accumulates. It eats away at the core. It destroys its host. For evil to survive, it must find some good that justifies its existence. Some higher purpose—if nothing else, making the trains run on time—or else it collapses almost as soon as it begins. So kingdoms rise and fall. In the meanwhile, a well-run corporation outlasts any government. And most nations."

"Which means you do or don't believe in the devil?"

"I believe there is evil enough in ourselves. I've never met the creature myself. I have met a few of his foot soldiers. And in their time most were thought to be—and thought themselves to be—good and decent men."

Troy nodded.

Milada said, "I knew someone once, a person who did evil with purpose and intent." Briefly, she looked past Troy, through the window at the shadowed sidewalk, at a man and woman pushing a stroller, a boy coasting by on a skateboard. "She thought she was doing the right thing. Or perhaps was doing the only thing she could do. Or perhaps was merely frightened. Fear and ignorance are so easily confused in the moral imagination."

They ate in silence until Troy asked, "What about God?"

"Were I to believe in God, a personal God, as Christians would have it, I must believe in a God who values life much differently than we do."

"But in the end, good triumphs over evil."

"No, my experience is that mediocrity triumphs over all. Hence the need for grace, would you not say?"

He conceded the point.

Milada finished off the last of the tempura. "This is quite good."

"As good as what you can get in New York?"

"Hardly Nobu Matsuhisa. But not bad."

Troy checked his watch. "We'd better get going."

He paid the check at the front desk with a Platinum Visa card. They arrived at Troy's car, a red Jeep Wrangler. Milada's initial reaction was dismay, and she didn't stop it from showing.

"Don't worry," Troy said, "I keep it clean."

The Jeep was indeed tidily kept. Milada's concern had not so much to do with cleanliness. She had a phobia of convertibles, regardless of the time of day. It was light, though the sun had settled safely behind the Oquirrh Mountains. *Get a grip,* she told herself and buckled herself in.

Steven had pointed out Abravanel Hall on their informal tours of downtown Salt Lake. It stood kitty-corner from Temple Square, southeast from Energy Solutions Arena. If she were still around later in the year, she should take in a Jazz game.

Salt Lake's Brahmins mingled together on the polished tile below the glass façade of the concert hall. A line of gushing fountains along the edge of the plaza cooled and moistened the air. Milada spotted a few tuxedos and evening gowns, here and there a black-felt Stetson on top of starched cotton and pressed jeans. It looked like a collision between prom night and Sunday school.

And Milada found that comforting. She had worn her black Mondi to work that day — she'd given her gray to Rachel Forsythe — and though it was a ridiculously expensive outfit, it was cut for utility, not show. Had she appeared at the Met thus attired, the immediate question would have been whether she was dressing down on purpose or by accident. No one cared here, and what a relief that was.

They collected their programs and found their seats. First tier, stage left. A brief inspection told Milada they were just behind the best seats in the house, the corporate patrons. She opened her program and said, honestly surprised, "Keith Lockhart?"

"He splits his time between here and Boston."

A couple came down the aisle along the railing. The man saw Troy. "Hey, Troy," said the man, "didn't expect to see you here tonight."

"Brother Newhall." They shook hands. The man said, "So who's this fine young woman you're with?"

"This is Milada Daranyi."

"Sister Daranyi, I'm Greg Newhall. My wife Cynthia."

Milada shook Cynthia's hand and then Greg's.

Greg said, "By the way, Troy, how's the press run on the new Monson book coming along?"

"We begin shipping to the bindery tomorrow."

"Good, good."

The Newhalls continued up the aisle to the corporate seats. A few minutes later, a man came walking back down the aisle, a man who knew how to wear a tuxedo. He made a beeline for them, for her. He said, "Milada Daranyi, I presume?"

She didn't contradict him. He introduced himself. "I'm Russell Stander with Piper Jaffray."

"Mr. Stander."

"I hear you're making a play for WMI. We all know that Daranyi doesn't buy into positions just to run up the price. Besides, you gotta know by now that the only way in is through the old man." Russell chuckled. "Good luck cracking that nut. Say, you still with Garrick Burke? We can give you better margins at Piper Jaffray." He flicked out a business card.

Milada took it and gave it a cursory glance. "We're very happy with Mr. Burke."

"Can't blame me for trying."

Milada smiled politely.

Russell Stander moseyed back to his group. Troy said, "What was that all about?"

If she had meant to impress the boy with her importance, she had succeeded all too well. "Blood in the water, as Garrick says.

Sooner or later the sharks start to circle." She handed him the business card. "Here. I do hate throwing away these things myself. Bad luck or something."

The house lights dimmed. Keith Lockhart strode onto stage. The concert began with Ravel. They didn't play *Bolero,* thank God. Instead, *Valses Nobles et Sentimentales* and the *Piano Concerto in G.* The soloist who performed the latter was proficient and the conducting competent, and passions were kept in check. The orchestra was saving its best for last.

The pianist bowed, the musicians were acknowledged. Mr. Lockhart left the stage. The lights came up for the intermission. Milada excused herself.

The plaza outside the hall was almost devoid of cross traffic, vacant compared to New York. She took out her cell phone and dialed Garrick's number. The tall granite spires rising above the high walls of Temple Square were lit up in the blue-green glow of the mercury vapor lamps. The Angel Moroni shone like Gabriel at the Second Coming.

She got Garrick's answering machine. "Garrick, it's Milada. I'm at the Utah Symphony. Did you know they have Keith Lockhart out here? Anyway, a Piper Jaffray rainmaker picked me out of the crowd and started chatting about Wylde Medical. Told me we'll have to deal with the old man. Meaning Darren Wylde controls fifty percent. Worst-case that scenario, please. I do not want to be blindsided by a proxy war. I'll check back with you on Monday."

When Milada returned to the balcony, Troy was talking with the man she had been introduced to before, Mr. Newhall. He saw her and said, "Ah, Miss Daranyi."

So her religious status had been amended.

The house lights dimmed. The audience found its seats. Mr. Lockhart appeared again, turned to the orchestra, and raised his baton.

Milada closed her eyes, steeled herself for that great explosion of brass that begins the prelude to *Scheherazade,* a fanfare that bursts out, recedes, dies, fades to near silence before the solo violin echoes the theme, the small, soft, seductive voice of the storyteller herself. The prelude always struck Milada as Rimsky-Korsakov's ironic reply to the excruciating foreplay in Wagner's *Tristan and Isolde,* the waiting, waiting, *waiting* for the climax. All classical music was about sex. Or death. Or death and sex, if it was Wagner.

None of that for Rimsky-Korsakov's sultan, who hops in the

sack and gets it over with first thing. Then it's up to Miss Scheherazade to entertain *him* for the next, oh, thousand and one nights. Talk about having to be resourceful in bed.

The music burrowed into the recesses of Milada's mind, into the places where memories moldered like rotting corpses in forgotten graves. It turned over soil and brought up bones on the blade. She could remember so much if she wanted to, and she did not want to. *Sufficient unto the day is the evil thereof.* Or the year, the decade—or, frankly, the whole bloody century. The past was the past, and she didn't live there anymore.

She opened her eyes. The one thing even the best of recordings on the best of sound systems lacked—*all that movement.* The weave of the baton, the stroke of the bow, fingers blurring on glittering brass. A symphony was a life lived in exaltation and killed with triumph. Eternity made the best of music monotonous, the best of lives meaningless. The performance was made wondrous by the fact that it would end. Dramatically. She lived in that moment and died with the last, fading notes, in the vanishing echoes before the applause.

She preferred experiencing death in music. She'd experienced too much of it in real life.

Chapter 19

Desire is nourished by delay

MILADA ENJOYED THE DRIVE HOME, enough to put aside her phobia of open-top automobiles. The city, at street level, was quiet and orderly. Composed like a postcard. The headquarters of the Mormon church occupied several blocks in the heart of downtown, a Vatican City in miniature. Gray granite buildings with heavy stone foundations. A kind of architectural temperance movement.

Back in the suburbs, they'd long since rolled up the sidewalks. Porch lights were on. Bedroom windows glowed behind drawn curtains. Troy drove up Larkspur Lane. He pulled into her driveway and switched off the engine.

"I've had a great time this evening."

Milada smiled at him. "So have I."

The boy returned the smile sheepishly. He hesitated, making an internal calculation. Milada added up the numbers for him. "Why don't you come in for a nightcap?"

They got out of the car. Out of the corner of her eye, Milada saw him take a package out from under the front seat. "What is that?"

Troy held up a box slightly bigger than a video case. He seemed pleased she had noticed. "I'll show you inside."

The night only gets more interesting.

Contrasted to the desert night, the house felt musty and warm. Milada took off her blazer and went around opening windows. Troy said, "You've got a swamp cooler, don't you? You can air out a house pretty fast at night just turning on the swamp cooler fan."

As she slept in the basement, Milada rarely bothered with it. The switch was located on the wall at the top of the stairs. She stepped up and turned it on. A gush of cold, damp air poured down from the louvered vent in the ceiling.

"An interesting contraption," she observed.

"The air in New York is too humid for swamp coolers?"

"Very much so." In the kitchen, Milada took a bottle of Martinelli's Sparkling Catawba out of the fridge.

"Umm—" Troy said.

"Don't worry. It's just expensive grape juice. I purchased it the other day on a whim."

She twisted off the foil-wrapped top. The bottle opened with a pop. She retrieved two glasses from the cupboard and filled each half full. She raised her glass. "*Kanpai,*" she said.

"*Kanpai.*" They clinked their glasses together.

"Hmm," said Milada, "like very good Sprite." She set down the glass and leaned toward him, her elbows on the counter top. "So what do you have in that box?"

"Oh, yes." Troy set the box on the countertop and lifted off the cover. It was a book. The book had a black leather cover of middling quality. Her name was embossed in the bottom right-hand corner: MILADA DARANYI. Spelled right, even. Milada wasn't sure whether to be taken aback or amused. She removed the book from the box. Gold-trimmed pages, scriptures of some sort.

"It's a triple combination," said Troy, quite proud of himself. "That's what we call it. The Book of Mormon, Doctrine and Covenants, and Pearl of Great Price. Three books—"

"Hence, a triple combination. The Mormon canon, I take it."

She was familiar with the title of the first. "I don't know what to say," she said, which was the truth. She idly flipped through the pages as she walked from the kitchen and down the half-flight of stairs to the family room. She flopped onto the couch, kicked off her shoes, and rested her feet on the coffee table.

Troy said, "I think you could read better if you turned on the light."

She hadn't noticed the darkness.

He sat on the couch and looked at her like she was a young charge he'd been asked to babysit. He said, "I marked a place. Verse four."

Milada tugged on the black ribbon. The book opened near the middle. She found the verse and began. "*When ye shall receive these things, I would exhort you that ye would ask God,* and et cetera, and et cetera—" She scanned to the end of the selection. "Well," she said, "that's nice. To paraphrase André Maurois, in religion as in love, we are readily astonished at what is chosen by others."

"The things people believe in are often true."

"Perhaps *valid* is a more accurate term than *true*. And perhaps not *often*. But, yes, they are." Milada closed the book and ran her fingers across the textured leather. "I am not unsympathetic to the religious impulse, Troy. I was born into what is called the Eastern Orthodox Church. My parents had belief to spare. But belief did not spare them from cholera. I don't blame God. I don't even feel that my faith is less now than then. I have only as much as I was born with. No more, no less."

Troy took the book from her. "I believe this book is true."

"I respect that. You could say I have faith in other people's faith. A disciplined passion is an admirable thing. It is good to have believers in the world to keep alive the possibilities of transcendence. My passions, however, tend toward a more earthly nature."

Milada took the book from Troy and placed it on the coffee table. Her little discourse had left the boy stymied. She gave him a delectable smile. "You Mormons are full of surprises." She plumped the cushions and snuggled up next to him. She smelled his aftershave and then his apprehension and took it as a challenge. She kissed his cheek, nipped at his earlobe. "But to tell the truth," she breathed, "I really do not have an overwhelming passion for theology at the moment."

She draped her arms around Troy's neck and kissed his mouth. Her weight pushed him back on the couch. His hands played across her blouse, slipping across the silk from her waist to her breasts. He was probably just trying to push her off, but she permitted herself a small, encouraging moan.

His whole body recoiled.

Men simply did *not* recoil from her. But this man leapt—in a single movement—from the couch and backed away hunched over, hastily buttoning his jacket. Milada could feel the heat beating off his face, the strong scent of testosterone mingled in his sweat. She stared at him, stunned. She came dangerously close to grabbing him and throwing him against the wall and screaming, *Where do you think you are going?*

Troy turned and fled up the stairs, as Joseph fled from Potiphar's wife. The front door opened and slammed closed. The Wrangler started up and exited her driveway with a screech of tires.

Milada fell back on the couch and covered her face with her hands. Damn, this was embarrassing. Okay, the transition from the sacred to the sensual had been a bit abrupt. But frankly, bringing God into the picture had always been a bit of a turn-on. She'd bedded preachers and priests—she knew damn well that sex and religion were not mutually exclusive pursuits.

A hundred years ago, Mormons were the lechers of the western world. The New York press could not scandalize them enough, Brigham Young and his umpteen wives. Those well-bred men of society—and their mistresses—delighted in being shocked—shocked!—by the *immorality* of it all.

Who knew Mormons were all a bunch of born-again Victorians underneath? Milada paced a line across the floor, met the wall, paced back. *Damn,* she said to herself. Damn, damn, damn, *damn, damn!* She stopped pacing and put her hand on her stomach. She was hungry. She really was. Well-nigh ravenous. When had she last fed? Three weeks ago? That was pushing it. Garrick warned her about getting wrapped up in her work. She should have just taken the boy and been done with it. *Good God, what am I saying?* She hunched over, feeling weak. She wasn't thinking straight.

She headed down into the basement, peeled off her clothes, stalked back and forth. She flung open a drawer, closed it, opened another. There were the BYU sweats Rachel had traded her. Milada held up the top that showed the cougar draped with rapine seductiveness across the block letter Y. She grinned, brushing the tips of her canines against her bottom lip. Yes, this was just right.

She set her wristwatch alarm to four-thirty—always a precaution—and hopped into the Mercedes. The keys were in the ignition, car door remote under the visor. The car glided down the driveway onto Larkspur Lane. She felt extraordinarily good. Her body sensed, anticipated, expected satiation. The adrenaline pumping into her bloodstream gave her an almost giddy high.

She wound her way out of Cottonwood Estates and headed north.

Chapter 20
A faint heart ne'er won a fair lady

THE FIRST TIME MILADA HAD MENTIONED her interest in Utah and Salt Lake City, Garrick asked, "What institutions of higher education are we talking about?"

The University of Utah boasted a highly regarded teaching hospital and computer sciences program with a number of well-known spin-offs, she told him. Division I football, basketball, and women's gymnastics.

All fine and good, but Garrick wasn't referring to the university's academics. He was thinking of the student *body*. Or rather, that's what he wanted Milada to keep in mind. It was a good thing he was over two thousand miles away right then. If he ever got wind of this little fiasco, he wouldn't give her a moment's peace about it for the next decade.

Jane was bad enough. Garrick playing mother hen could get downright annoying. *Don't go hunting in your own back yard,* he always said, and she saw the wisdom in that advice.

But the University of Utah was a *state* university, which meant it should be crammed with libidinous and barely legal young adults eager to get stupid over alcohol and sex, religious convictions notwithstanding. She could get what she wanted with a minimum of manipulation.

It was easier for a woman that way—easier to be seduced than to be the seducer. Even her sister Zoë would settle, in a pinch, for strolling into a bar and letting a man get lucky with her. "Like falling off a log," she'd say, with no little contempt. Zoë had been off men for a century or two, and Milada could see her point.

To seduce was the greater challenge, to consummate the seduction the greater reward. Milada herself hardly missed this intersection of business and pleasure. She could pretend to be above it. But the hunt always thrilled, especially after a long fast. She fell easily into the routines of pursuit. Her long-honed instincts quickened at the thought of blooding the prey.

Which was why her attention this night fell on a comely junior sitting alone at the bar. She was dressed in white cotton and wore about her a practiced look of sophistication. The boys caught up in her scent flitted to and fro about her until she batted them away and they fluttered off, wings and egos bruised.

Milada slid onto the barstool next to her. "Hi," she said, her arm brushing the girl's. "Is this place taken?"

The girl beamed at her. "Not anymore." She tossed her golden locks.

"I just thought—that last boy looked interested in you."

"He might have been. But I wasn't."

"I'm glad you weren't," said Milada.

In her rush, Milada had left her driver's license behind. The bartender wasn't the same one from earlier. To make matters worse, she couldn't remember how old she was supposed to be. She was supposed to start out at twenty-one in each rotation. Or was it every other? What a monstrous annoyance the whole routine was.

"Perrier," she said.

The bartender harrumphed to himself. Yeah, he had her pegged right.

"I'll have another beer," said the girl. She said to Milada, "I'm Teresa."

"Milada."

"That's an interesting name."

"It's Czech."

"Is that where you're from? Your accent is *so* interesting."

"I call New York home these days."

"New York City? Wow. This is really pathetic, but Salt Lake is the farthest east I've ever been."

"Where is home for you?"

"Reno."

The bartender placed two glasses on the counter along with a bottle of Perrier and a bottle of Coors. Teresa took a drink from the Coors. Milada watched her carefully. She guessed the girl had deliberately drunk enough to shut down her superego and relieve herself of any personal culpability should her choices tonight lead her afoul of her desired expectations. This was what college girls called being "liberated."

Teresa said, "You going to school here?"

Milada shook her head.

The girl looked at her sweatshirt. "You a BYU student?"

"What do you think?"

"I don't think."

"I don't think so either. I got it from a friend."

The girl giggled. "Not a bad idea. Kind of a turn-on, especially around here."

"Is there some sport in doing a BYU coed?"

"Next best thing to beating 'em at football, from what I hear."

Two boys came up to the bar, one to the left of Milada, one to the right of Teresa. "Hi," said the boy at Teresa's shoulder. Teresa coolly ignored him. Milada might have enjoyed flirting with them, but she couldn't be distracted now. She scanned the room and picked out a pair of wallflowers next to the jukebox. The boy's hand rested on the bar next to hers. She touched his hand and said, sotto voce, "Those two over there are pretty cute."

The boy picked them out at once. "Hey, Ross, check out those two." He set off across the floor, the other boy on his heels.

"Pricks," said Teresa.

"Not all of them."

"I suppose. If you want it, you always know where to get it."

Milada laughed. "Demand always exceeds supply." She took a drink of the Perrier. "Do you live around here?"

"A couple of blocks." Teresa finished her beer. "How about we get out of here?"

They drove north and then east in Teresa's Honda Acura—her daddy's old car, Teresa admitted. She turned past a lighted sign announcing the campus of the University of Utah. They passed a darkened tennis court, continued down the shaded street. Along the sidewalks the canopy of the trees shadowed the street lamps. Blue moonlight marbled the asphalt.

"What about your roommates?" Milada asked.

"School doesn't start for a couple more days. They're still out of town."

Milada ran her fingers through her short-cropped hair. She flashed a smile at the girl and moistened her lips with her tongue.

Teresa parked in the driveway of a white clapboard bungalow hidden behind a copse of overgrown spruce. Higher up on the university grounds, the rhythmic *swish, swish, swish* of the sprinklers syncopated with the drone of cicadas and Mormon crickets.

Teresa unlocked the door. "Come in," she said.

Milada stepped across the threshold. The interior of the house had been converted to a rabbit hutch of student apartments, killing any charm the early twentieth-century architecture promised from the outside. But it was safe here, shielded by thick plaster walls. And empty—except for them.

Teresa shut the door. Before Milada could turn around, the girl had wrapped her arms around her waist and kissed her sloppily on the back of the neck. Milada relaxed into the embrace, her hands resting on Teresa's before she turned and kissed her back, tasting the alcohol on her breath.

Their lips parted. Teresa cast her eyes toward the bedroom. "You know how to whistle, don't you?" she whispered, her hot tongue touching Milada's earlobe.

"Put your lips together and blow."

The girl giggled. She was not devoid of wit. Or maybe it was a line a boy had used on her once, and she had no idea who Lauren Bacall was. But the girl was enjoying playing the seductress. Or was enjoying the pretense.

Inside the bedroom she darted to the window and yanked down the shades. She returned to the foot of the bed, tugging at her shirttails. Milada caressed the back of the girl's neck with her cheek, the way a cat marks the object of its affections. Teresa fumbled at the buttons of her blouse. Milada undid the girl's jeans, eased off her blouse and bra.

They kissed again. This time after they broke apart, the girl flung back the covers of the bed and cast herself across the sheets. Milada stripped off her sweat bottoms and lay next to her. The girl was not, Milada was sure, a lesbian. This was a dare with herself. A self-indulgent form of payback. If she were clever enough and brave enough, she'd write a paper titled "My First Lesbian Experience" and submit it to the prettiest and most progressive of her assistant professors. And titillate the hell out of the cute boy two desks in front of her when he happened to glimpse the report title as it was handed back.

Milada kissed her long and slow. There was venom on her tongue. No more than a drop. The hollow of the girl's throat invited. She resisted, pressing her cheek against a rising curve. The girl moaned. Milada set to coaxing from her deeper, more passionate exclamations—

Then the girl's rapture subsided, her breathing slowed, grew even, relaxed. Her face glowed with an almost angelic pleasure. There was a slight smile on her lips. Milada knelt beside her. The palatine tendons tightened across the roof of her mouth. She opened her mouth in a half-yawn. The ophidian fangs snapped down into the vertical grooves along the back of her lateral incisors.

Except, her venom should not have acted so quickly.

The girl was fast asleep.

Milada groaned with frustration. It was the alcohol that had emboldened her after all. The girl's warmth radiated up at her, a soft heat rich enough to taste. Milada took a deep breath. She could still take her. The blood would be dulled without the hormonal tempering that came with sex. But prey was prey. Blood was blood.

In the aftermath of those incomprehensible days in Southwark, after Rakoczi had infected her and her sisters and to his astonishment they had not died, the entirety of her life was given over to the hunger. She had taken girls younger than Teresa and far more innocent. She bent them to her will and shared them with her sisters and then handed them over to Rakoczi, who had his way with them and left them for dead.

You shall not be like him. That was the law Michael Daranyi had etched upon their hearts. *Never reveal, never infect, and take only in the consent of the act.* What counted as *consent*—what qualified as the necessary *quid pro quo*—the distinctions she forced herself to make were tenuous ones. But it was in the splitting of these hairs that she created the moral justification for the existence of her soul.

Milada bowed her head, tightening the maxillary muscles in her jaw. The fangs folded back against the roof of her mouth. After retrieving her sweats, she kissed the girl's cheek and whispered in her ear, "It was a dream, now all forgotten." She stroked the girl's cheek, leaving behind the invisible traces that would carry out what she willed.

Milada gathered up the bedding. For a moment, she paused. Propped against the pillows, her left hand draped across her right thigh, the girl was a living portrait of Manet's *Olympia*. The resemblance made her smile.

Yet still so innocent. And so she would remain this night.

Milada tucked her in and shut off the light.

It was a mile back to the bar, maybe two—in either case, a brisk, pleasant walk. The exercise should blunt her cravings. She paused at the corner of First South and University, where the street sloped down from the bench and pushed across the valley toward the lake. At the bottom of the hill, the traffic light turned green. A red 1964 Ford Thunderbird convertible, almost black in the yellow penumbra of the sodium-vapor street lamp, climbed the hill, left turn signal blinking.

A kid stood up in the back seat and waved his arms. "Hey!" he shouted. Hey!" He caught Milada's attention. "Yeah, you! Stay there! Don't move!"

The car screeched to a halt. The kid toppled over. He picked himself up from the back seat. There was a vigorous exchange of opinions between the occupants of the front seat and the back seat. Even from her vantage point, Milada could see the driver rolling his eyes. But he cranked the wheel over, made a wide U-turn, and pulled up to the curb next to her. The kid scrambled over to the side of the car. "Hey," he said.

"Hey," said Milada.

"What's your name?"

"Milly. What's yours?"

"I'm Chad. This is Cole, that's Kevin there in the driver's seat." He reached over mussed Kevin's hair. Kevin tried to look too mature for this sort of horsing around and didn't quite succeed. Chad said, "So what's a nice girl like you doing out at this time of night?"

Milada smiled slyly. "Who says I'm a nice girl?"

Chad and Cole stared at each other with wide eyes. "Whoa!" they both yelled and knocked foreheads.

Milada said, "And what are you boys doing out at this time of night?"

Chad held up two plastic grocery bags, each straining with a pair of six-packs. "Refills!"

"You're going to a party?"

"We're keeping the party *going*."

"Wanna come?" Chad gazed up at her with pleading eyes. He looked like a dog begging for a bone.

Milada laughed. "How about Kevin here? I hope he's not as drunk as you two." Realizing how intoxicated the girl had been aroused in her an extra note of caution.

Chad and Cole shook their heads. "Kevin is our designated driver." Chad spoke like he was narrating a driver-ed video. "He *never* drinks and drives."

Kevin smirked. "Yeah, I'm a real Boy Scout."

"He was, too."

"A real honest-to-God Boy Scout."

She asked, "A Mormon?"

"No, no, no, no, no. Hell, no." Chad turned his puppy-dog look on her again. "Wanna come?"

She felt like patting his head and scratching his chin. "Sure," she said. "Sounds like fun."

Chad yelled, "Bail! Bail!" and grabbed Cole by the shoulders and pulled him out of the front seat. Milada couldn't help laughing. Taking Cole's place, she said to Kevin, "Interesting company you keep."

"Yeah, a pair of regular court jesters."

"Marry, sir," Cole declaimed, "they praise me and make an ass of me."

Milada replied, "Better a witty fool than a foolish wit."

Cole perked up. He struck a dramatic pose. "Foolery does not walk about the orb like the sun; it shines everywhere."

"Ah, this fellow is wise enough to play the fool."

"What are you two talking about?" said Kevin.

"Shakespeare," said Cole. "*Twelfth Night.*"

Two blocks farther up First South, past a row of frat houses, Kevin made another U-turn and stopped in front of a shabby-looking structure after the American Foursquare design: a two-story, brick-faced house with a squat hip roof and broad overhangs. They tramped into the kitchen. From the sound of things, the party was still well underway. Chad and Cole set to work replenishing the alcohol. Amidst the litter of beer bottles and microwave popcorn bags, a haggard-looking boy sat with his laptop and a liter of Diet Pepsi, staring at the screen with bloodshot eyes. Milada peeked over his shoulder. It looked like C++. She repressed the urge to give him a business card.

"A beer?" Kevin asked her.

"I'm not much of a beer drinker."

"How about wine?"

"That might be interesting."

Milada wandered into the living room. The party was a decidedly low-brow affair. She blended right in. An iPod plugged into a stereo amplifier churned through an eclectic collection of Japanese idol pop and German techno MP3 files. Nobody was dancing. A couple lay tangled together by the radiator. Three boys—no, wait, one of them was a girl—crowded together on the couch cradling laptops strung together with CAT5 cable, eyes focused with blazing intensity on the screens, saying nothing except for triumphal yelps when an opponent's character got blasted to bits.

"Wanna play?" Chad asked. He and Cole retrieved their laptops from the coffee table.

"Video games have never been my forte."

Kevin handed her a Dixie cup. "Here you go. The best booze in the house."

She took a cautious sniff. It was a generic red wine, the kind she imagined got shipped from the Napa Valley in tanker trucks. "What vintage is it?"

Kevin laughed. "It's been in the back of the refrigerator for about a month."

Milada took a sip. "Hmm," she said, nodding, "cheap and unpretentious." She drained the cup. The soft sting of alcohol at the back of her throat, the bittersweet taste of dextrose and tannin focused her appetite. She said to Kevin, "What about you? Are you, as they say, a gamer?"

"Only if I want to lose."

She laughed and touched his arm. The MP3 player cycled into another techno dance mix. Milada leaned into him and lowered her voice. "So where does a body go around here to get a little peace?"

Kevin nodded his head toward the stairway. She saw the hot spark in his eyes, the willingness and the desire. Her appetite quickened. She put down the cup and walked toward the stairway, her hand brushing across his arm. It took him no more than a moment to react. As she climbed the stairs, she glanced back at the living room. Nobody seemed to have noticed they'd left.

At the end of the hall, he opened a door and clicked on the light. Milada had to walk almost to the side of the bed so he could close the door. There was barely enough space between the foot of the bed and the wall to access the closet, barely enough space to cram a computer desk into the corner next to the window, barely enough space between the windows and the door to fit a chest of drawers and bookcase. Still, the room did not appear unsanitary. The air was tinged with male sweat and cologne.

Milada said, "You have interesting roommates."

"As Cole says, this ain't a Greek house — this is a *geek* house."

Milada plucked a book off the bookcase. "*Applied Structural Mechanics,*" she read aloud.

Kevin held up his hands in surrender. "Okay, I confess. I'm not a true computer geek. I only use them — I don't live for them."

"The Thunderbird is your work, then?"

He preened. "Yeah."

"I thought you looked a bit out of sorts."

"They keep me around for my charm and good looks."

She smiled at him. Kevin shrugged self-consciously. "Um, want the radio on?" He leaned against her side to click on the boom box perched atop the dresser. The radio was tuned to the university station. The velvet tones of Miles Davis's *Kind of Blue* filled the small room like a rich perfume.

Milada replaced the book. She leaned back against the boy's chest and closed her eyes. The boy wrapped his arms around her. She snuggled into his embrace, tucked her arms under his, pressing his forearms up against her chest. He was remarkably restrained— a modern-day college student trained to not misconstrue even the most suggestive of advances by a woman. But even a civilized man had his limits. Milada drew away from him. Not giving him time to imagine he'd done something wrong, she pulled off her top and then smothered his exclamation of surprise and delight with her mouth.

She fell onto the bed with him, her hands playing across his chest. As their intimacy progressed, she tasted the bite of the venom at the back of her throat. Turning the boy on his back, she parted his lips with hers and dripped venom into his mouth. His heart kicked as the drug hit his bloodstream and his blood pressure spiked. The adrenaline in his blood would soon catalyze the drug. In the space of that transition, she must do her work.

She straddled his waist, leaning forward so he could run his hands along her sides, across the velvety sheen of sweat and oil. He watched her like a child watching fireworks, wide-eyed and amazed, simultaneously falling into a waking dream as the alkaloids took hold. He passed the point of no return.

Her breath rushed out of her lungs in a barely controlled gasp. Her fangs sprang into her mouth. She clenched her mouth shut to keep the razor-sharp fangs hidden. When she could again catch her breath, she caressed his face and kissed him. Giving the venom time to do its work.

Consciousness at last fled his mind.

Milada studied his supple body, unspoiled by age. She smiled at the luster of satisfaction on his face. With cool efficiency, she straightened his body and tucked the pillow under his neck. She turned his head to the left and covered his body with her own, pinning him against the mattress, her left hand across his forehead.

Were he to move abruptly while she fed, her fangs would vivisect his muscles and tissues like a hot scalpel through soft suet. She ran her tongue across his neck, tasting the heat in his veins, seeking the optimal point of penetration. Feeding from the wrist was less carnivorous in appearance, but the slighter volume and pressure in the limbs made it markedly less pleasurable and intolerably more tedious.

She opened her mouth wide. Her fangs extended and sank through the flesh, finding the vein with the precision of a skilled phlebotomist. The blood spouted through the hollows in her fangs and arced across the roof of her mouth. Half a pint would suffice. In her present desk-bound state, her body would metabolize no more.

Stopping the palatine ducts with her tongue, she withdrew her fangs and pressed her lips over the wound, sucking the last of the oozing blood. When the punctures had clotted, she licked the skin clean. By morning, only a pair of slight bruises would remain, hardly indistinguishable from a lover's hickey.

Milada lay on her back next to the boy. The raw plasma burned in her throat. The hemocytes flooded into her bloodstream, disgorging a fresh supply of hemoglobin. Her metabolism spiked as the sudden rush of oxygen surged through her like a hot Santa Ana wind, every cell in her body lighting up in a chain reaction. She arched her back and clenched her fists to keep from crying out.

Her breath relaxed into a throbbing purr. She sank back on the bed exhausted. In this moment, in this silent hour, she was at peace, free from the demons that raged at her out of a dark and wicked past. She drew the covers around her shoulders, laid her head on the boy's chest, and listened to his beating human heart.

In this moment only, she felt sorry for herself. She indulged her loneliness. There were tears on her cheeks when she fell asleep.

Milada's watch alarm chimed.

She awoke. The air touching her face was cool, the boy's body warm. But she could not risk staying longer. She dressed in the darkness. Before she left, she knelt next to the bed. She touched his cheek with the tips of her fingers and whispered, "*Do not remember me. I was a dream. And now I am gone forever.*"

He'd be groggy in the morning. Over the next several days, however, he likely would feel much better for the experience. Such were the palliative properties of her venom.

The television in the living room was tuned to ESPN Sports

Center, volume muted. No one was watching. One of the gamers had crashed on the couch. A faint electronic beeping caught her attention. The programmer in the kitchen had dozed off at his computer, his forehead resting against the keyboard. The screen printed row after row of the letter "Z." Milada eased his head off the laptop and rested it on the smooth Formica. He stirred and grumbled incoherently. "*Shh—*" she said. He complied.

She walked into a dead calm that hung like a curtain over the incipient dawn. By the time she got back to the tavern, the rough edges of the Wasatch Front were painted turquoise blue. She drove home through the gray dawn. She showered and crawled into bed and slept till noon.

Chapter 24
Character is easier kept than recovered

RACHEL WAS STANDING OUTSIDE the Relief Society room waiting for Sunday School to conclude when Charlene Millington rushed up to her with such enthusiasm that Rachel had to restrain herself from pirouetting out of the way like a rodeo clown dodging a charging bull.

"It's incredible!" Charlene exclaimed, seizing Rachel's arm in order to impart added emphasis.

"What is?"

"Andy! You wouldn't believe it!" She released her grip on Rachel's arm and clasped her hands to her ample bosom. "Ever since those bees stung him half to death, his allergies haven't bothered him once! Even dairy, and that was always the worst! Thursday morning Andy got the soy confused with the half-and-half, and how that makes him swell up! So bad he can't breathe almost! Well, I was all ready to rush him to the emergency room, but then I double-checked to make sure of the symptoms and — nothing! Like any perfectly healthy kid. You know, Rachel, I've heard about using bee-sting therapy to treat problems like that. My great-aunt May swore it was keeping honey bees that kept her rheumatoid arthritis at bay all those years. Always thought it was old wives' tales, you know. But I'm beginning to think she was onto something."

Hardly certain of where to begin, Rachel simply said, "So he's all right then?"

"Right as rain. Oh, and that lady you had over—"

"Milada."

"Milada. You really must thank her for me. She handled everything so calm-like. I guess when you live in New York City, nothing surprises you. I was ready to go to pieces." Charlene paused and cast a furtive glance over her shoulder. "Did you hear about her and Troy the other night—?"

Rachel hadn't, but her heart sank. The bell rang before Charlene could tell her. Sunday school let out, and it was time to get ready for Relief Society.

Joan Ellis walked into the Relief Society room a minute later, and Rachel couldn't resist the opportunity to extract information from an unimpeachable source. They exchanged pleasantries. Rachel said, in as offhand a manner as she could muster, "I hear Troy had an interesting date the other night."

"I would say so. Not that he's told *me* all the gory details, but a mother can read between the lines."

"What happened exactly?" Rachel asked with a bit too much intensity.

"What do you expect? A woman like *that*—" Her tone of voice said far more than her words.

Rachel felt a reflexive clenching in her gut. "A woman like what?" But she was guilty of the same thoughts: *not a Mormon, not from around here, not one of us, a* gentile.

"You tell me," Joan shot back. "You seem to know her *awfully* well."

"She's a perfectly honorable woman on her own terms," Rachel replied, even as a nagging voice at the back of her head reminded her that she didn't know Milada well enough to vouch for her character. But she liked Milada and felt protective of her reputation.

"In *my* day there were certain things *honorable* women didn't do on a first date."

"And I'm sure in your day no *honorable* man invited himself into a woman's house on the *first* date."

Just then Sister Garner bustled into the room with the materials for her Relief Society lesson. She practically skidded to a halt, the tension in the room hitting her like an invisible force field.

Joan took a step back and smiled thinly. "I guess I can't exactly blame her. A woman waiting for my Troy to make the first move could get herself awful frustrated. I suppose it's reassuring to know that women still find him attractive."

She laughed, but there was no humor in her laughter. Her son's marital status was a sore point with Joan Ellis. Her opinions on the subject of marriage were a matter of public record. "It's all well and good," she had stated on many occasions, "that Steve Young up and finally got himself married, but I do think the Brethren should have taken him aside and told him to get himself settled down. There's no excuse for a man like that to be single and over thirty."

With that, Sister Ellis made a show of walking over and offering to help Sister Garner ready her lesson.

Rachel's opinion on the subject was that Joan could hurry things along greatly if she kicked Troy out of the house. Or at the least stopped making his lunch and cooking his dinner. Talk about not being willing to buy the cow when he could literally get the milk for free.

But some rhetorical weapons civilized people recoiled from using, if only to spare bystanders the collateral damage.

Chapter 22
A fault denied is twice committed

MILADA SAT IN THE WICKER CHAIR deep beneath the eaves of the porch. Fresh blood coursed through her veins. The flood of oxygen burned like a low fever, making her complexion pinker than usual and leaving her with a contented feeling.

The afternoon sun slanted down the street. The temperature hovered in the nineties. But it was "a dry heat," as they were wont to say in Utah. And measurably more tolerable than the steaming humidity of the Atlantic coast at this time of year. She savored a respectable 1993 Merlot and watched the quiet neighborhood dramas play out in the driveways and front lawns.

The rhythm of people passing up and down the sidewalk told her when services began and ended at the Mormon chapel a block north on Willow Way. She made a game of guessing which of her neighbors were Mormon and which were not. The man in the red shorts washing down his mud-splattered Dodge Ram pickup, probably not. Ditto the two teenagers who'd set up a ramp at the end of their driveway and had been practicing backside one-eighties on their skateboards for the last two hours straight.

The breeze shifted about. She caught the smell of steak broiling on a charcoal grill. From over a fence and across a backyard came the shout and splash of a kid cannon-balling into a swimming pool. A lawnmower started up. The Mormons allowed considerable leeway in their *sharia* as far as the gentiles were concerned. Utah had a paucity of Blue Laws, though obtaining the Merlot had approximated a visit to a twenties-era speakeasy.

The bishop strode down the sidewalk. He was wearing an off-the-rack navy blue suit. It looked like something his mother got for him at Sears. He stopped and talked to the man washing the truck. They both laughed. The bishop slapped him on the back.

So Mr. Red Shorts was a lapsed Mormon.

The bishop waved at the skateboarders. "Hey," the tall one replied, with practiced slacker nonchalance. A lady stepped out of the house opposite Milada's and called to the bishop. He jogged up to the front door, and they spoke briefly. Then he headed across the street, and Milada realized he was coming to visit her.

"Good afternoon, Bishop."

He stepped up to the porch. "How are you doing, Miss Daranyi?"

"Milada," she said. "I am doing quite well, thank you." She set down the wine glass. She took off her sunglasses and hung them on the second button of her blouse.

"You've had a—pleasant weekend?"

"Quite satisfying." She smiled. He was circling an uncomfortable subject. She could imagine what it was and decided to play along. No sense getting in a high dudgeon over her sense of privacy. Besides, she was curious to hear how the other side of the story was playing out in the public imagination.

He got to the point. "Troy does have a tendency to overreact at times, judge situations rather severely. Especially when he's shown to be not as close to perfection as he imagines himself to be."

Milada almost laughed. That made her—what, Bathsheba, despoiler of Christian manhood? She had tried. And if she hadn't been so impressed by the bishop's wife, she might have tried playing the game with him. Troy, though, had proved something of an object lesson in that regard. The payoff was not worth the risk.

He quickly backtracked. "I don't mean to imply—"

The sparkle in her eyes stopped him. "Rest assured, Bishop, I have no schemes on the boy."

"No," he agreed wearily, "I didn't suppose you did."

She could guess at the other questions he'd intended to ask. About how Troy had insisted that what had transpired that night had involved something more than mere temptation. About how she had "overpowered his will," whatever that meant. But she believed the bishop was a man predisposed to see the best in people—especially those he did not know well—and enough of a chauvinist to consider a woman's virtue the man's burden and responsibility.

Chapter 23

Don't look a gift horse in the mouth

DAVID'S CONCLUSION: THE BOY KEPT his pants on, and that's all that mattered in the end. "Why did he even ask her out in the first place?" he asked his wife that night. He sat in bed thumbing through the Sunday *Deseret Morning News*. Reading the Sunday paper was how he unwound from his ecclesiastical duties.

Rachel stared at him as if he were rather dim. "Because she's young and beautiful and rich and successful. And not a little exotic, don't you think?"

"And a nonmember. This is Troy we're talking about, remember. He won't even read the Sunday paper on Sunday!" He shook the newsprint for emphasis. "Can you really imagine Troy marrying someone like Milada Daranyi? Or seriously dating her?"

"Of course not. I think for a brief, silly moment he was reliving his missionary days—dreaming about taming the she-wolf, or whatever he fantasizes about. I haven't the slightest idea. Even Troy is smart enough to know that life isn't like an Anita Stansfield novel."

"So why doesn't he ask out Michelle Montgomery? If that's the type of woman he's attracted to."

"To begin with, Michelle is not the slightest bit interested in going out with Troy. I would be disappointed with her if she did. Troy is definitely *not* Michelle's type. And nothing against Troy, but she can do better."

"Who is Michelle's type?"

"A man not intimidated by the thought of being married to a successful, independent woman."

"I was intimidated by you."

"Really?" She cuddled next to him. "I saw you in my family home evening group that first week at BYU, and I said to myself,

I'm going to marry *him*. My only worry was that one of my roommates might have picked you out first."

"Like I say, the person who knows what he—what *she*—wants always has the advantage."

"And you didn't?"

"I was just off my mission. For two years I'd done nothing *but* think about what I was going to do for the rest of my life. But I was hardly prepared to *do* anything about it." He tossed the sports pages down to the foot of the bed and picked up the financial section.

"That's why I had to. It's a lot easier for a man to find himself if he's got a woman telling him where to look." She thought about it for a minute. "I wonder what Milada wants."

David folded the paper in half. "Apparently, she wants Wylde Medical Informatics." He read aloud, "*Daranyi Enterprises International (DEI) is making a play for Salt Lake City–based Wylde Medical Informatics. The closely-held Wall Street investment banking firm intends to acquire a controlling interest in the healthcare technology company, sources within the industry have confirmed.*"

Rachel read through the blurb herself. "Wow," she said.

"Yeah, maybe we should ask her for a stock tip."

She shook her head. "No. Her company, DEI. *Dei*." She grinned. "Go figure. Milada works for God."

Rachel didn't pick up the dry cleaning until Wednesday. And only then because on her way home from the hospital it occurred to her that it'd be fun to wear Milada's outfit to Relief Society. She'd never quite overcome the impulse to one-up her classmates that had first tempted her in kindergarten show-and-tell.

Ah, vanity.

Mr. Strassel hung four white shirts, the black pinstriped suit and slacks, and Milada's powder-gray outfit on the hook next to the cash register. He punched in the receipt totals at the cash register. "$152.87," he said.

Rachel had handed over her Discover card before the numbers clicked in her mind. She caught her breath and tried not to let it out too explosively. They must have taken apart the seams and washed the lining separately. She shook her head ruefully. Milada had warned her.

Ah, vanity.

David was warming up leftover pizza—Italian sausage, green pepper—in the microwave when she got home. The ward had a stake audit coming up. That plus whatever interviews his executive secretary had scheduled would keep him at church until past nine.

Rachel mentioned in passing that the dry cleaning cost more than she had expected, but he wasn't in a details mode. He was happy enough to have back his "grown-up" suit, as Laura called it.

She and Laura finished off the rest of the pizza. Rachel went upstairs, showered, and changed. To her great relief, the clothes fit. Not perfectly, but close enough. A tad tight around the waist and in the butt—she had to take a breath and suck in her gut to get everything zipped and buttoned. She didn't have Milada's sculpted physique. But neither was she ready to attend the Peter Paul Rubens school of modeling. The ward had a plentiful supply already.

Laura pulled a double-take when her mother strolled into the kitchen. "Hey, neat outfit." A teenage daughter's approval was a rare thing. Rachel posed for her. Laura said, "Isn't that the outfit Milada was wearing?"

"That's right."

"Wow, I bet it cost a fortune."

"It certainly cost a fortune to get cleaned."

"Oh, yeah, that's right. Dough Boy threw up on it. When are you going to give it back?"

"Milada said I could keep it."

"Really? That is *so* cool. Can I try it on?"

"In another three or four years, perhaps."

"Mom!"

Rachel stood next to her daughter. "You need to grow another three inches first. Which, at the current rate, should take you another month or two."

"I can roll up the cuffs."

Rachel gave Laura one of her *I-don't-think-so* looks. "You have any homework?"

"Did it."

"Then finish loading the dishwasher. I should be home by eight-thirty." And because Laura was standing right there and couldn't squirm away, she gave her a hug. She had to take advantage of these opportunities when she could.

Rachel couldn't remember what the topic for enrichment meeting was. "Baby health" sprang to mind, but that was two times ago. She'd developed a surprisingly comprehensive knowledge of pediatric medicine, though not for reasons that anybody around her felt comfortable exploring. She hoped for a benign subject like "How to dry and press your own herbs" or something artsy-craftsy, like macramé.

Michelle Montgomery was finishing a conversation on her cell phone when Rachel walked into the foyer. Michelle folded up the phone and tucked it into her purse. "Nice outfit."

"Thank you." Rachel smiled. An expert's opinion, no less. She was two-for-two for the evening. "I got this outfit from a friend, in fact. Believe it or not, she swapped a BYU sweat suit for it."

You're kidding, Michelle's expression said.

"And I was wondering—well, I was wondering how much an outfit like this cost. Just curious. You know—if I wanted to get another one like it."

"Let me see," said Michelle.

Rachel took off the jacket and handed it to her. Michelle walked across the lobby to where the light was more direct. She checked the label and examined the lining. "The slacks came with it?"

"Yes. And the blouse. Well, I don't know about the blouse—"

"Hmm," said Michelle. She helped Rachel put it on and had her turn around as she eyed the fit.

Rachel admitted, "My friend is a bit thinner than me and broader in the shoulders."

Michelle nodded and did a few more mental calculations. "Fifteen hundred."

"Fifteen hundred," Rachel repeated.

Michelle pursed her lips. "It's not a line I'm familiar with. Not Armani, not this cut. Maybe Helmut Lang or Isaac Mizrahi."

"Fifteen hundred," Rachel said again. "*Dollars?*"

"If I knew who was repping the line, I could probably pick it up for—I don't know—twelve-fifty, maybe."

Rachel suddenly felt as if she were encased in starched crinoline. She couldn't move. Something might break, pull, or tear. She shot Michelle a look of pleading helplessness. Michelle understood her reaction at once and said with a smile, "It's just clothing, Rachel."

"That's like saying a Rolls Royce is just a car."

"More like saying a Lexus is just a car. It's not ready-to-wear but it's not couture. This friend of yours is well off, I assume? What does she do for a living?"

"Corporate finance, I think."

"Then I bet she chooses her clothing mostly on the basis of the cut and feel. A decent Dolce & Gabbana would cost you five thousand."

"Still—it's so generous. Should I send her a thank-you note?"

"You said she swapped a BYU sweat suit for it? Well, think of it this way: I bet she spends a far smaller percentage of her budget on clothing than you do."

Michelle was right. But that didn't change the fact that Rachel was wearing close to the value of her entire wardrobe. When refreshments were served after the meeting, she ate with all the daintiness of the Queen of England.

It was dark when Rachel left the church. As she passed Larkspur Lane, she glanced down the street and saw the big Lincoln parked in front of the former Lindstrom house. She saw Milada step out, speak briefly with the driver, and then walk to the house. The car drove to the end of the block and turned left onto Willow Way, briefly blinding her in the twin beams of its brilliant white headlights.

Rachel stood there, trying to make up her mind. Still not sure how to proceed, she started down Larkspur Lane. She had no idea what she was going to say. As for the fact that she was wearing Milada's outfit, Michelle was right—Rachel was certain that Milada hadn't given the exchange a second thought since.

She rang the doorbell. The porch light came on, the door opened. "Good evening, Rachel," said Milada. "I was not expecting you."

"I'm sorry," Rachel began. Milada hadn't even put down her attaché. "I was on my way home from church, and I saw your car."

That was all she could think to say at the moment.

"Why don't you come in?" Milada said pleasantly.

Rachel had been in the house many times when the Lindstroms lived in the ward. The plan of the house was the same as her own, except turned at a ninety-degree angle. But when she stepped across the threshold, it felt foreign. The living room projected the clean, sterile appearance of a room never lived in. The kitchen was quite the opposite. A multifunction printer sat on the counter next to the phone, along with a cell-phone charger, Salt Lake County phonebook, and framed photograph.

Milada placed her attaché on the kitchen table. The table was cluttered with sheaves of printouts, manila file folders, and FedEx envelopes. She took note of Rachel's attire and said, "It looks quite sharp on you."

"Thank you."

Rachel's attention was drawn back to the photograph. Family portraits had that reassuring sameness about them that made them recognizable anywhere. Three men standing, three sisters sitting. The man in the middle must be their father. He didn't look so much older in age as in bearing and demeanor. The other two men were brothers, perhaps. Or uncles? Two smaller photographs were set behind the glass on either side of the frame, wallet-sized photos printed in sepia tones.

"Is this your family?" Rachel picked up the frame. The small photograph on the right showed the same man who stood on the right in the portrait, a handsome man dressed in a frock coat and bowler hat, a half-smile on his lips, a wink in his eyes. The other was of Milada and her father, Rachel guessed. Milada was seated, the man stood behind her with his hands on her shoulders, and both wore Victorian-style clothing.

"Garrick," said Milada, pointing to the man on the right. "He is a—friend." More than a friend, the way she said the word—but not a lover either, Rachel felt. Pointing to the man on the left, Milada continued, "And Uncle Frank."

Again, Uncle Frank looked less like an uncle than like a cousin, and bit of a bounder at that. Milada lightly touched the glass and confirmed Rachel's thoughts: "A man never content with what he has. And without a thought in his head of what to do with it when he gets more." Her fingers strayed. "And you can see that Zoë was going through one of her gothic phases at the time."

Zoë was the girl with dark hair. From her complexion, it was obvious that the hair was dyed. Now that Rachel looked more closely, she saw that they all shared the same fair skin and silver-white hair. It was obvious even in the black-and-white photo of Garrick.

"And this is Kamilla."

Rachel said, "The doctor."

"Yes. A pediatrician."

"And your father."

"My stepfather, Michael."

So he was her stepfather—and yet all so similar. Rachel set the picture down on the counter. Milada made a point of adjusting it, just a half-inch or so. "Was there something you needed to see me about, Rachel?"

For a moment, Rachel was stymied. Then she said, "The boy, Andy—the boy who got stung by the bees. He's doing quite well. His mother wanted me to thank you."

"That is good to hear."

"In fact, Charlene tells me his allergies don't bother him at all now." Suddenly Rachel knew the reason she had come here. "Last Monday, when you found Andy—I know it sounds strange, but I really can't remember what happened."

Milada gave her a slightly amused look of measured forbearance. Rachel went on relentlessly. "I—I remember telling Laura to run and get David and Brother Millington, and then I think you started CPR, but after that—and then, and then David and Brent came running up and you gave me your cell phone, yes, that's right. But in between—"

And that was when Milada put her hand on Rachel's shoulder, her fingers brushing the back of her neck. Rachel stopped talking. The words simply refused to leave her mouth. She felt ridiculous. Her face grew hot with embarrassment. "It is not important," Milada said. She walked her to the door, Rachel dumbly letting herself be guided. Milada said again, "It's not important, Rachel. Go home."

A minute later, Rachel stood on the sidewalk outside her own house, feeling abashed.

"Rachel?"

The bishop came up behind her. Rachel spun around, startled. She was standing in front of their house. "How—?" she started to say.

"Forget something?"

"I—I was thinking—"

"Where were you?" He sounded curious, not inquisitorial.

"I was—I was at church."

"I didn't see you there. When I came down the walk, you were crossing the street."

"I had to—um, drop something off at Arlene's . . ." Her voice trailed off uncertainly.

Rachel knew what she said wasn't true. But it wasn't a lie. It was simply the most rational explanation she could think of at the time. She had been at the church. Twenty minutes later, she was here. The in-between vanished into thin air.

The puzzle kept her quiet as she undressed for bed. David said, "Brent tells me that Andy's doing quite well."

"Yes, that's what Charlene says too. She thinks it might've been the bee stings. Her great-aunt claimed that bee stings cured her arthritis."

"Well," the bishop said, and he spoke without any trace of irony in his voice, "by next fast Sunday I'm sure she'll see the hand of God in it."

"Some of his ways are more mysterious than others." Rachel closed the closet doors and sat on the bed. "So why does Andy Millington get this little miracle, and—" She stopped herself from saying, *and we don't*. "And the Bromleys didn't?"

David smiled and shook his head.

"What?" she demanded. She playfully threw a pillow at him. "You always do that!"

"Do what?"

"You smile whenever somebody mentions the Bromleys. It was a terrible tragedy!"

"Yes, it was." He sobered up. "A terrible tragedy. But the whole thing started out so absurdly. I mean, Doug gets LaRita pregnant and then goes on his mission as if—what, nobody was going to find out? I can only imagine what his companion must've thought when he got sent home."

"Maybe she didn't tell him."

"And what a way to find out! Congratulations, Elder, it's a girl! Now, about that lesson on the law of chastity—"

"So is that why they died?" Rachel didn't think so, but she had to ask.

"They died because a drunk driver ran a red light. It certainly wasn't because of what they did. Not when you've heard what I've heard, people doing things—people doing things *in this ward*—upstanding members of the community and all that. If anybody's going to hell for their sins, I can promise you it won't be Doug and LaRita Bromley. Jesus told the woman to go and sin no more, and that's what they did. Some shotgun marriages do work out for the best. I had faith in theirs."

"Then why them?"

"I don't know. For all we know, that drunk driver was going to run somebody down that night, and if not them then some other unlucky couple. I could even believe that at that moment they were as perfect as they were going to get in this life. They'd started over and were headed in the right direction. Not everybody completes the circle like that. People die all the time, for all the wrong reasons. But that's the whole point of the gospel, isn't it? Having faith in Christ, believing in the atonement and eternal life. Or deep down, do we cling to mortality and fear death the same as everybody else?"

He stopped talking. They were both silent. It was a rhetorical question.

It struck Rachel that in many ways Carl and David weren't all that different, Carl relying on theology to explain his good fortune, David relying on theology to explain their bad luck. That's the way men's minds worked: they coped with life by explaining it. But the explanations didn't make life hurt any less. The explanations didn't solve anything, really. Forget logic. Maybe pitching a fit now and then, having a real temper tantrum, was what it took to get God's attention. After all, Jacob wrestled with the angel, and Jacob came away with the blessing.

Rachel rested her head on her husband's chest. "But I still want a miracle."

Her husband kissed the crown of her head. "So do I."

Chapter 24
Discretion is the better part of valor

AT THE FRONT DESK, THE BRILLIANT SMILE on Cindy's face told Milada that the good news had nothing to do with work. "Something came for you this morning," she said.

Milada answered with a look of practiced insouciance and continued on to the conference room. The *something* had been placed at the end of the table where she usually sat by the phone, arranged—by Karen, undoubtedly—to catch the muted light from the curtains on the gold foil of the long, slender box.

Karen waited anxiously while Milada put aside her parasol and attaché and took much longer than necessary to get around to opening the box. She untied the ribbon and lifted off the cover to reveal a single long-stem white rose, resting against burgundy velvet. *A casket for a relationship,* Milada thought.

"How pretty!" Karen leaned forward to examine it. "It smells so nice. What does the card say?"

Milada slit open the envelope. As she suspected, the gift had come courtesy of Troy Ellis. On the card he had written in a careful hand: *The symphony deserved a better encore. Lunch at the Garden?*

She smiled to herself. She still harbored some guilt about the clumsy manner in which their date had ended and was not averse to concluding it on a more proper footing.

Karen said, "It's from Mr. Ellis, isn't it?"

Amazing that Karen remembered who he was. But there was no arguing with a person's true priorities. "The Garden is a restaurant?" Milada asked.

"It's in the Joseph Smith Memorial Building, the old Hotel Utah. It's a really nice building, right over on South Temple."

"Oh, yes." Steven had pointed it out to her in one of their many jaunts past Temple Square. Milada retrieved her phone and dialed the number Troy had included on the card. He picked up on the second ring.

"Milada!" he exclaimed, obviously startled that the gift had been deemed an acceptable recompense.

"The rose is lovely," she said. "And Karen informs me that the Garden is a respectable establishment."

It took him a moment to parse her language. "Yes, yes, it is."

"Would a one o'clock lunch fit your schedule?"

Some rustling through papers. "Not a problem. Why don't we meet by the statue."

"The statue?"

"The Joseph Smith statue in the lobby. You can't miss it."

"But of course. One o'clock."

By the time she hung up, Karen had found a vase. The rose did make a pleasant addition to the conference room. Around noon she extracted from Karen more precise directions.

The heliocentric city center that was Temple Square evidenced a devotion not so much to art or even piety but to meticulous grounds keeping and a persistent wanting to be liked. These folks would not kindly countenance the Baptist whirling in from the desert on the breath of God and crying repentance from the city walls.

Not unless he got himself a permit first. And kept off their property. And took a shower.

The Joseph Smith Memorial Building, though, had originally been built for no more noble cause than to comfort the wearied traveler and please his eye in the bargain. Milada could see that the lobby harkened back to the era of Grand Central Station and the New York Public Library, late echoes of the Greek revival of the early 1800s. The marbleized pillars and the towering reach of the glowing art-glass ceiling made the expansive inner space into a kind of cathedral.

She folded her parasol and entered the foyer. Her eyes were drawn to the statue at the center of the room. Troy was lounging at the prophet's side. After greeting him, she returned her attention to the building's namesake.

"Brother Smith, I presume." She removed her sunglasses and stepped back to examine him further, this young man who had ignited a religious order now ruled over by old men. "A pity I never met him. Was he ever in England?"

"No. But Brigham Young was."

"Yes, I do recall his followers causing something of a stir at the time, though I suspect the idea of a new America was as intoxicating as a belief in the new God." Her analysis amused him, she could see. "And what other purpose does this building serve?"

"There's an IMAX theater and a genealogical library. The rest is church offices."

"And restaurants."

"Yes. On the tenth floor."

Milada bid the prophet good-bye. They set off to the elevators.

The sky had clouded over, a gauze drawn across the sun. Still, she insisted on being seated away from the mezzanine windows. A comely waitress attended to them with cheerful deference. Clearly Nordic in her ancestry, her bright, blond face radiated that well-scrubbed look of Panglossian satisfaction with this best of all possible worlds. *They must breed them in a laboratory somewhere.* Milada often glimpsed them posed in ever-present twosomes inside the Temple Square gates, shepherdesses waiting for the lambs, ready to reach out with their staffs and snatch souls away from the brink. She found their individual selves more fascinating than their gospel. But she was a wolf dressed in beguiling white, and the thought of sheep only made her hungry.

She ordered the shrimp cocktail, Troy the cold-poached salmon. The restaurant served no wine.

The waitress retreated with the menus, and a pensive look returned to Troy's countenance. He sat back in his chair and studied the table settings. "About the other night—" he began. "The bishop thought maybe I overreacted."

Milada shook her head as if to dismiss his concerns. "A clash of cultures," she suggested.

Troy picked up on the idea. "When I was on my mission in Japan, I think the hardest thing to get used to was that people weren't automatically Christian. Most people didn't even know the difference between the Catholic church and any other Christian church. They thought we all worked for the pope."

"I guess you all do look alike."

Troy grinned. "Yeah, I suppose so." He relaxed noticeably, now that the worst of his confession had been accomplished.

Milada said, "I think perhaps your Japanese friends were right. We are really not so different. Because, you see, Rome never fell. We are her children and have inherited all that she was. Her language, art, architecture, politics and governance, her coliseums, her entertainment. Her religion and her gods. Only streamlined, made more efficient, and given new names."

The entree arrived, making it unnecessary for Troy to conjure up a response.

The menu boasted *large shrimp on a bed of house greens*, but the greens were buried beneath the sauce, and if the shrimp were indeed of a large variety then they had been harvested before their time.

But it was palatable fare. The meal curtailed conversation and gave her time to think. She wondered about what indeed the bishop had thought. And what did his wife think? Milada hadn't wanted to hear her pleas the night before. She could guess where they might lead. The bishop's wife had noticed things, had started to connect the dots. Where would the dots lead her? A fervent belief in God could hem in the realm of the possible, channel it along the narrowest of lines. Or expand it to an infinite degree.

"Tell me, Troy, does your religion believe in faith healing?"

Delighted to be asked, he sat back to form an answer. "We believe in blessing the sick, and we believe in miracles, yes."

"So at what point do you yield to God's will?"

"Brigham Young once said, when asked if prayer was enough to heal, 'I might as well ask the Lord to cause my wheat and corn to grow without my plowing the ground or casting in the seed.' As our scriptures say, by grace you are saved after all you can do."

"So Paul meets the Pelagians. Well." Perhaps it was a religion that frowned on the fanciful. That reassured her.

They both refused dessert. The pressing demands of work proved as good a reason as any to curtail the outing. Down in the lobby, Troy gestured to his left. "I've got to jog over to the Church Office Building. I hope to see you around, Milada."

"I'm sure you will."

Troy smiled. Her eyes hidden by her sunglasses, Milada winced. What an unfair thing to say while he still kindled hope. After all, his gut reaction to her advances that night had reflected her true nature. His innocence *had* tempted her, *had* tasted sweet and inviting. She knew to the core of her being that she could pretend to be exactly what he imagined he wanted and what he expected of this untried acolyte, as he imagined her in all his shattering naiveté. She could make herself into the vision that lived in his mind's eye, make of the lion a lamb, and kneel to discover — or so he would think — the truth at his hands. Taste the true word on his lips. And in the process ruin him utterly. Take that trust and turn it and draw him into a world he believed was of his making until he discovered, too late, that it was populated with her ravenous kin.

She knew where her own gullibility had once led her. That was the lesson Rakoczi had taught her: how longing becomes the tool of slow torture. All that wanting, and no question of what was being offered to sate her desire. *We must,* she had told her sisters, because she *wanted*—wanted a father, a husband, a lover—she couldn't remember what, except that the nuns at the orphanage couldn't provide it. She *wanted.* Rakoczi had offered what she wanted. And then it was too late. She only wanted more.

Personal enmity was the ultimate price of undisciplined desire.

And so she compensated, strove to make of her life something that grew and changed, a substitute for the progeny she would never have. Were the processes of her mind so simple, so obvious? After all this time, shouldn't she have garnered the attention of more daring and inventive demons?

The iridescent ceiling told her the clouded skies above remained nevertheless shot through with sunlight. She raised her parasol and walked into the bright day.

Milada's last stop of the day was Wylde headquarters. Dr. Brickey met her in the reception area and escorted her to a large desk tucked into the back of the computer room. The soft, indirect lighting and blast of air conditioning that cooled the server racks reminded her of an autumn evening at the Hamptons.

"Your sister is a remarkable young woman," Dr. Brickey said. "An M.D. and Ph.D. at her age!"

Milada detected a slight put-down in the latter half of the remark. In other words, a mere Columbia MBA didn't quite measure up in the company of physicians.

"This is Kamal Nath, our head DBA."

The Indian man seated at the desk in front of the three large LCD displays glanced up and nodded. Kammy stood at his left shoulder. She was wearing her green hospital scrubs. Milada wondered if she ever took them off. She'd look quite striking in a nice dress.

Kammy turned and saw Milada and smiled. Milada almost stopped in her tracks. This wasn't Kammy's wry or weary or knowing smile. She was *beaming.* "Come and look at this," she said, motioning impatiently with her hand.

Milada joined her, standing behind Kamal's right shoulder. Kammy didn't wait for Dr. Brickey or Kamal to start things off. "This is the Utah Population Database," she said, indicating the screen on the left. "Eight million multi-generation pedigrees, including family and medical histories."

She pointed to the screen on the right. "This database hooks directly into the Agilent sequencing and microarray platforms, and the Amersham Lucidea array controls for hybridization, scanning, data capture, and analysis."

"It also tracks the DNA, RNA, and peptide synthesizers," Dr. Brickey added.

Kammy gestured at the display in the middle. "This is the biostatistics database. It ties everything together in a clinical and epidemiological framework. In other words, gene mining across the board in a real-world context."

"What about privacy?" Milada wondered, her business-oriented mind focusing on the most likely liability issue.

Kamal explained, "The hashes linking the genealogical and genome sequencing records are indexed to encrypted personal information in a separate database. That database can be unlocked only with a 128-bit private key escrowed by a third party."

Milada nodded. That sounded good to her. "So I take it you're impressed with the technology," she said dryly.

"Hell, yeah." Kammy grinned again.

A small smile came to Milada face. She didn't understand half of what her sister was saying, but she completely comprehended this rare burst of enthusiasm. *You see, Troy,* she thought to herself, recalling their conversation at the Japanese restaurant. *This is what a business can do.*

And to keep on doing it, it would have to make money. That was something *she* could do.

Chapter 25
The bishop's always the last to know

Rachel closed the book and placed it on the stand next to the hospital bed. Most times when she came to see her daughter, she read aloud to her. It was Veralee's suggestion. The book she'd just finished was *Anastasia, Ask Your Analyst* by Lois Lowry. It was a funny book, and funny was a prerequisite. Everybody lived at the end. She wasn't about to read *Charlotte's Web* or *Bridge to Terabithia* any time soon, thank you very much.

In *Anastasia, Ask Your Analyst,* Anastasia acquires a pair of gerbils for a science project. In no time at all, the two gerbils become eleven and then are set free from their cage by her little brother's classmate. Making matters worse, Anastasia's mother has a phobia of the vermin. Frankly, Rachel had never been keen on the whole rodents-as-pets concept herself, not since Carl's lab rat breeding project back in high school, when pretty much the same thing happened.

Carl's rats met a more gruesome fate when his project turned into an experiment in building the better mousetrap—the ones who didn't escape into the Logan Valley countryside, that was. Being at the age at which she could easily imagine her own personal actions holding sway over the fate of the universe, Rachel fretted that loosing lab rats upon the world was going to tip some delicate ecological balance.

Uncle Warren, the herpetologist—it had been his idea in the first place—scoffed at her concerns. "Naw. Snake and coyote food like the rest of them. And pretty bland fare at that. I imagine your typical free-range rodent provides a more succulent meal."

Her mother's reaction: "You can sure see what side of the family Carl gets it from." *It* being whatever made Carl do the things Carl did.

There was a lot of *it* in her too, Rachel thought. She just did a better job of hiding it. She worked and played well with others. She always tried to walk a mile in another person's shoes before criticizing them. And then when she did criticize them, she was a mile away and had their shoes — the old Steven Wright joke.

On the other hand, maybe this was all a façade: denial and repression, the two big self-help/feel good/psycho-crap no-nos. Maybe she was *that* close to taping aluminum foil to her head and hauling her daughter off to Mexico and cramming her full of apricot pits and snake venom.

Snake venom. A cold knot tightened in her stomach. Like when she cracked a joke in class and the teacher glared at her and said, "That wasn't funny, Miss Cameron."

Why wasn't it funny? This was the same feeling she'd had the night Andy got stung by the yellow jackets and she couldn't remember what happened. She still couldn't. That wasn't funny either.

"Do you think I'd be mature enough not to mind?" Anastasia asks her mother at the end of the book. "Why don't you ask your analyst?" her mother replies, meaning her daughter's bust of Sigmund Freud.

Rachel never considered going to an analyst. She'd never thought of herself as depressed. Having bad things happen to you didn't mean you were depressed. Job wasn't depressed. He was grouchy and ill-tempered and put out about being covered with open sores and having everybody in his family bumped off and then constantly lectured by a bunch of self-righteous know-it-alls.

And who wouldn't be? Even if she was depressed, taking antidepressants struck her as cheating. How profound would the old patriarch's tribulations be if the scripture read: *And it came to pass that Job went to his shrink and got a prescription for Prozac, and the old man really mellowed out after that.*

When Joseph Smith was locked up in Liberty Jail, God didn't get him a lawyer. God told him, "All these things shall give thee experience, and shall be for thy good."

Rachel wasn't so sure about the *good* part. But all this *experience* had better add up to something meaningful pretty soon.

"Oh, I see you're reading Lois Lowry. The children do enjoy her books so much." Veralee bustled into the room to record Jennifer's vitals. "Keeping the box scores," was how David described it. Veralee and Rachel had gotten to know each other well over the last six months — too well. Veralee said, "And how are you today, Sister

Forsythe?" Not waiting for an answer, she directed the sum of her attention to Jennifer.

Veralee believed that the comatose were aware of their surroundings and kept up a constant chatter with her charge. Reading aloud was only the half of it. "It's a wonderful day, isn't it, Jenny? Too bad you've had to stay out of school so long. You'd be in second grade, this year, isn't that right? I bet your classmates all miss you. They'll be so glad when you're all better."

Veralee believed in showing a positive mental attitude. She put Jennifer's charts down on the bedside table and bustled about checking IV lines, oxygen tubes, the electrodes that measured heartbeat and blood pressure.

Rachel glanced at the chart, more of a reflex action. Her attention was drawn to a bright yellow Post-It note stuck to the cover of the folder. *Remember,* the note said. The word was underlined twice.

Remember what?

More writing was visible beneath the double lines. Rachel craned her neck to read it, a jumble of numbers and letters, a filing number of some sort.

"I think she's doing just fine, Sister Forsythe!"

Rachel's attention snapped away from the folder.

Veralee beamed at her. "She's such a brave little girl."

Rachel nodded mutely.

Veralee said, "Bye, Jenny." She picked up the folder. She patted Rachel on the shoulder. "You need anything, you let me know."

I need a well child.

Sharon Sundwall called shortly after Rachel arrived home. Sharon asked if the bishop was home. It was the middle of the day—what did she think? Calling now was an excuse to bend Rachel's ear, the bishop's wife possessing a certain authority by proximity.

The subject was Derek, the eldest male child in the Sundwall clan. Now well into his thirteenth year, Derek was *not* well on his way to becoming an Eagle Scout. Derek was a good kid, but he was setting a bad example in the Boy Scout department, what with three younger brothers coming up behind him.

"Tammy says she won't let her boys get their driver licenses until they've earned their Eagle rank. But I don't see how that helps in Derek's case."

So Sharon was seeking second opinions.

Rachel didn't see how either. She also didn't see how these creative forms of bribery and blackmail aligned with the ideals of Scouting. Then again, she didn't come from a Scouting family. Scouting was way, *way* up on Carl's don't-get-me-started list. David had been an Eagle Scout. But even for David it was more a matter of duty than devotion, something good Mormon boys did.

Besides, questioning the righteousness of the BSA in this church was something akin to heresy, way, *way* up on Rachel's if-you-can't-say-anything-nice list. So she mostly listened, interrupting with the occasional "Yes, of course," and "Uh, huh," and "Really?" which, as she paced from room to room collecting laundry, was interpreted by Sharon as deep empathy with the nature of her plight.

Laundry was not for Rachel a disagreeable activity, once the children were potty-trained. She found something sacramental about it, a restoring of the environment to a higher state of purity. Besides, it gave her a good excuse to go through her daughter's room without a search warrant. She limited her examinations to the honest pursuit of dirty clothing. She didn't pry, though she did make the occasional mental note. She figured Laura could start doing her own laundry if she didn't want her mother peeking into her closets.

Rachel hauled the laundry basket down to the basement and loaded the whites into the washing machine. Back up in the family room, she collapsed on the couch. Sharon finally hung up, off to get a third or fourth opinion, no doubt. Rachel relaxed to the rhythmic drone of the washing machine. She listened for sounds of an unbalanced load in the spin cycle. She felt the cat jump up onto the couch, the soft pad of paws on the cushions, the animal turn around and nestle next to her thigh.

Remember, the note had said. The note on Jenny's chart.

She remembered standing on the street in front of her house after Relief Society, David coming up behind her. Where had she been? He hadn't seen her at church. She was coming home. Home from where?

She'd been to see Milada. About—about the outfit? Maybe. No. About—

Rachel heard a faint buzzing, the washing machine timer going off. She opened her eyes. The cat stirred and yawned, ivory canines flashing against its pink mouth.

An electric shock shot through Rachel's chest, her mind lighting up with the flashbulb illumination of a memory, suddenly before her eyes and then gone. She sprang to her feet as if to pursue it. Or to escape it. She didn't know which. She was frightened but without anything to be frightened of. Her heart thumped in her chest. The cat gave her an annoyed look, an expression that said, *Stupid human, now I'm going to have to find someplace else to sleep.* It jumped down from the cushions and pranced up the short flight of stairs to the living room.

Rachel stood still, breathing hard, not moving, trying to let the dull reality of her life settle back around her. She went downstairs and took the wet laundry out of the washing machine and put it into the dryer and returned to the family room. She unlatched the sliding glass doors, stepped onto the warm patio, and walked across the lawn to the property line. The furrow was still there in the grass where she and Milada and Laura had trod out to the lone apple tree in search of Andy. Almost without thinking, she began to retrace her steps.

Late in the afternoon, the work site was winding down. Men were loading up pickups and parking the backhoes. The screech of a circular saw biting into particle board rang out like the cry of a raptor, interrupted by the rhythmic thumping of a solitary air hammer pinning shingles to tarpaper and plywood.

"Don't worry, ma'am. It's plenty dead."

Rachel started, and then she saw both the man and the snake at the same time, the man's sweat-stained tank top and bright yellow Caterpillar hard hat, his muscled arms streaked with grease—

The rattlesnake draped over the low limb of the tree, hanging limply, swaying in an unfelt breeze.

She recoiled. But at once she knew that the man was right. The snake was quite dead. She leaned toward it. She'd handled dead rattlers before, bigger ones than this. Its head was crushed, probably with a shovel, its jaws frozen open at the moment of anger and death, fangs extended, biting into empty air.

With a jolt of recognition that struck her with the force of a physical blow, the raw images rushed into her brain like a surging flood tide. She almost staggered. The Caterpillar operator held out his hand as if to steady her. "You okay, ma'am?"

"I'm fine, I'm fine."

"Like I said, dead as a doornail. Ain't gonna bite nothing no more."

She smiled gamely. "Yes, thank you." She mustered about herself a sense of resoluteness and headed back to her own property, her own house, her own life.

Her own secrets. When David was first made bishop, it killed her with curiosity not knowing what he knew about people they had known for years. "The thing is," he told her, "as long as I'm the only one who knows, even if the whole rest of the congregation could make a good guess and figure it out, they aren't committed to the *fact* of it. But when they confess it to somebody else, that's when it becomes *official*. That's when there's no going back."

He had a point. Last April she was driving back from the Relief Society session of general conference with Amber Boyce when Amber told her, "I'm divorcing Randal." Just like that. Rachel already knew from the ward gossip. And she'd seen the referrals to LDS Social Services on David's desk. But once Amber told her, once Amber *went public,* Rachel knew it was a done deal. There wasn't going to be a reconciliation.

So now she knew. Rachel sat down at the picnic table and stared out into space. Is this what Jennifer wanted? What God wanted? Was there a difference? Did God take a neutral stance on inspiration, on miracles? Maybe Milada had done her a favor by making her forget. Maybe this was one of those things she wasn't supposed to remember. The same reason human beings forgot about their premortal lives when they were born into this world. The veil of forgetfulness. Mormons didn't believe in original sin. Everyone started life with a clean slate.

Laura's voice interrupted. "Earth to Mom—" Her daughter was standing at the sliding glass doors. "The dryer's done."

"Thanks."

Laura glanced around the yard. "What are you doing?"

"Thinking."

Laura shrugged. Being a teenager meant that the odd behavior of her parents did not demand exhaustive explanation as long as it didn't personally involve her. "I'm going to Heidi's."

"Be home by five."

"Yeah."

In the basement, Rachel emptied the contents of the dryer into the hamper. The clothing was fluffy with static and smelled of fabric softener. She folded the clothes, a simple, repetitive chore that left her mind open to a storm of thoughts. *So what do you do when you know? When you know, you act.* That was the whole point of an evangelical church: acting upon the word. But to what end? What was the grand design in her life that dictated her next move? Where was the instruction manual?

Nowhere, Carl would have told her. Believe enough in a grand design and she'd find one. If necessary she'd make one up and then find *that*. Life was God's cosmic Rorschach test: here's a blob, now find the pattern. If she had the will, she could make it so. Anyway, who didn't want to be Jean-Luc Picard at the helm of the *Enterprise,* captains of their own souls, as William Ernest Henley put it?

Even if Carl was right, Rachel was not above holding firmly onto two contradictory beliefs at the same time. She had carved out of her personal philosophy plenty of room for the special cases, the exceptions to the rules. There was—there had to be—a cause, a reason for it all.

The reason it pointed to—and the result that would follow—were crystal clear in her mind.

Chapter 26

A bad cause requires many words

AFTER DINNER, LAURA AND HER FATHER went to the church to play basketball. Two or three times a month, a handful of fathers and daughters in the ward got together on Friday night to play four-on-four. In Rachel's opinion, it was the best idea he'd had as bishop. And it was such an endearing sight, the two of them in matching purple and gold Jazz T-shirts, Laura's hair tied back in a bobbing ponytail. It strengthened Rachel's resolve. Jennifer too should have the privilege when Laura started finding better uses for her Friday nights.

Rachel finished clearing the table and started the dishwasher. She didn't think Milada would be home until after eight, if then. She turned on the television and blankly watched whatever was playing on PBS.

At the conclusion of *Washington Week*, Rachel turned off the television. She went to the kitchen and ran a glass of water. What if she was wrong? But she was sure she wasn't. *This* memory and *this* recollection she trusted. She glanced at the clock, not wanting to leave too early. Yet she didn't want to be here when David and Laura got home and have to explain where she was going. Better to be early.

She left the house, walked down the sidewalk, and crossed the street onto Larkspur Lane. She tried not to hurry. Someone in the ward would see her. Someone would wonder where she was going. And when it became clear where she was going, they would wonder why. All the necessary antecedents had been established — that disastrous family home evening barbecue two weeks ago — but it was an odd thing for the bishop's wife to be doing, odder on a Friday evening, odder still at this time of night. And by now everybody had heard a version of the date with Troy.

She repeated to herself Christ's rejoinder to Peter in John, chapter 21: *What is that to you?*

Rachel rang the doorbell. Nobody was home. She sat in the wicker chair on the porch. She watched the darkening street and rehearsed to herself what to say, the reasoning to employ, the arguments or denials Milada would raise and she would decisively counter. She could be positively erudite when she was alone with her own thoughts, a brilliance that rarely measured up when she had to open her mouth and say the words.

The limo pulled up to the curb. Milada emerged from the car. The flash of her silver-white hair made her appearance unmistakable. The dusk was growing heavy, and Rachel was sitting far back under the porch awning, but Milada saw her at once. She tilted her head to the side as if to say, *What? You again?*

The car drove off. Milada strode up to the porch. She said politely, "Good evening, Rachel."

"I need to talk to you."

Milada didn't reply. She retrieved her keys and unlocked the door. Rachel said, "It's important." She bit her lip. She was already pushing, betraying her anxiety, blurting instead of speaking calmly and rationally.

Milada considered Rachel for a moment. "Then come in and talk."

Entering the dark house was like walking into an empty cave. Milada switched on the swamp cooler. A refreshing draft wafted through the rooms.

"What did you need to talk to me about?" She placed the attaché on the kitchen table, folded her arms, and faced her.

Rachel took a breath. "I remember."

"You remember?"

"I remember what happened, what happened last Monday—I mean, the Monday before last—when Andy got stung, by the bees, the yellow jackets . . ."

Milada did not react as Rachel expected. No, she reacted exactly as Rachel *should* have expected. Her expression betrayed no worry, no concern: the dispassionate, half-amused look a cat gives the small animal it has trapped with outstretched claws.

Shall I kill it? Let it go? Play with it a while longer?

Milada crossed the kitchen to the refrigerator and retrieved the bottle of Sparkling Catawba. "It is nonalcoholic," she said. "Though I fear that at the rate I am consuming it, it won't be so for long."

Rachel declined and immediately regretted it. But it was too difficult for her to be polite and keep focused at the same time.

Milada shrugged. She poured a half-glass, sat on the barstool at the counter island. She sipped at the Catawba. "So tell me, Rachel. Tell me what you remember."

"You bit him." It sounded absurd when she said it. But she said it anyway. "You bit him on the wrist." She raised her right arm to illustrate.

"And why would I do that?"

"To make him better—" It came out like a timid question. Her confidence failed her. Her practiced rhetoric abandoned her mouth.

Milada's face grew stiller. She stood up and approached Rachel, reaching out to her as if with compassion, reaching out to a friend. "Rachel, would it not be better if you went home and thought it over?"

Rachel recoiled, jerking her arm away. Milada's fingers barely brushed her skin. *Go home.* An outward-directed gravity pulled at every muscle in her body, toward the door, to the sidewalk, up the street. *Home.* The intensity of the desire was almost painful. She retreated to the foyer, to the edge of the carpet, but not yet onto the flagstones. She stopped and planted her feet and clenched her fists, digging her fingernails into the skin of her palms.

She closed her eyes. "No," she stated, a command to herself. "*No.*"

A step behind her, Milada said, "The boy, did he not recover?"

"Yes."

"Then why trouble me further in this matter?"

"You cured him!"

"That was not my intention."

"How was it not your intention? His allergies are gone! Charlene told me herself. You did cure him!"

Milada paced back to the kitchen. Rachel followed on her heels. "You felt sorry for him. You wanted to help. You did. Somehow you did. What is so wrong with that?"

Milada's response was emotionless. "Yes, I felt sorry for the child. Pity overcame judgment. Clearly it was a mistake to try."

"How could it be a mistake?"

Milada's voice lowered practically to a hiss. "Do not look in me for what is not there, Rachel. You will not find it."

"I know what I *saw.* What did you *do?* It wasn't *normal,* what you did!" Rachel realized too late that she was shouting. She couldn't stop herself. "What did you do? *What are you?*"

Rachel bit her tongue, but she could not call the question back.

Milada stared at her, eyes widening, until Rachel averted her gaze out of shame.

"What do you think I am?"

Rachel felt the word forming on her lips but couldn't bring herself to say it aloud.

Milada smiled. "Kammy hates that word too." She added with a shrug, "As for myself, I get called far worse on a regular basis."

Hearing her darkest suspicions so blithely confirmed left Rachel too stunned to reply.

Milada continued with blank disinterest. "There is a substance in my venom that under certain conditions mimics the properties of epinephrine. What any doctor would have given the boy in his condition."

"But his allergies—"

As Kammy would tell you, evolution is not sentimental. It speaks to the self-interest of the parasite to keep the host alive."

"Your sister—"

"The doctor. Understand that I am only repeating what she has told me. Unfortunately you met the wrong sister."

"I don't think so."

"Rachel, I cannot help you. I can't cure cancer. That's what this is about, isn't it?"

Rachel closed her eyes and nodded.

"Call me a hopeful monster if you wish, but I am no miracle worker."

"Why didn't you—why didn't you infect him as well?"

"It doesn't work that way. There is no virus in the venom. Kammy says it is bound to the hemoglobin. I don't understand it well enough to explain the reasons why, except that blood must touch blood."

A sudden insight illuminated Rachel's thoughts. "It's not the cancer. It's the transplant. My bone marrow. It's like an allergic reaction, only different in degree. Her immune system—"

"As I said, the effect is unpredictable."

"What would make it less unpredictable? What would your sister say?"

"What, indeed? She would say it was unproven and inadvisable, a breach of family law. More than that, she would call it a violation of established medical protocols. She is traditional that way."

"And after that, what would she say?"

For a long minute, Milada refused to respond. "The venom affects certain antigens in the host. Apparently there is a benefit to keeping small the circle of our prey, something we do not always take advantage of."

Rachel's brow furrowed in thought. "So the immunologic properties of your—*venom*—should react according to a specific blood type."

"I suppose so. But necessary only to condition the blood for *our* consumption."

"And you can introduce—inject—the venom more directly—more deliberately—as you did with Andy—"

Again, hesitation. Then, "Yes."

Rachel straightened. She took a deep breath and looked straight into Milada's almost-transparent eyes. "It was *my* marrow they used for Jennifer's transplant. I was the closest HLA match. If your venom follows upon blood type, taking *my blood* should condition it to suppress the antigens triggering Jennifer's GVHD. Just as you did with Andy—"

Milada's soft laughter interrupted her mid-sentence. "Do you know who you remind me of? Sister Gertrude. Mother Superior of the orphanage in Szeged. My God, how we used to argue. Like a pair of Greek philosophers. And she thrashed me every time through sheer force of wits. I guess that's why you surprise me, Rachel. I would have thought you too level-headed to allow your own logic to lead you to such fanciful conclusions."

"Now you're being cruel."

"I meant it as a compliment. You are familiar with what Chesterton had to say about God and belief? But that would be cruel." Milada took a longer draught of the Catawba and set down the glass. She leaned back in the chair and recited in a sonorous, sing-song voice, as if to mock some long-dead preacher: "*And when Saul enquired of the Lord, the Lord answered him not, neither by dreams, nor by prophets.*"

The words twisted like knives into the softest parts of Rachel's soul. She shut her eyes tightly and finally brought her hands to her face to cover her ears.

"*Then said Saul unto his servants, Seek me a woman that hath a familiar spirit, that I may go to her, and enquire of her.*"

A long moment of silence followed. When Milada spoke again, she quoted from the Book of Luke, answering her own soliloquy: "*So must I avenge her, lest by her continual coming she weary me?*"

"*Hear what the unjust judge says,*" Rachel echoed, dropping her hands and opening her eyes. "I'll do whatever you want."

"Really?"

Before Rachel could react, Milada strode across the room to her side, standing so close that their cheeks almost touched. Rachel reflexively shrank away until she was wedged into the corner of the kitchen dining nook. Milada planted her left hand against the wall like a bar across her breasts. Her lips touched the back of Rachel's neck, sending a shiver down her spine. She tried raising her hands to ward her off, but Milada pressed her into the corner, rendering her immobile.

Low and husky, Milada's voice resounded in her ear, "I sleep with my prey first."

Rachel hunched her shoulders and twisted her head defensively, her heart pounding inside her chest with a force she knew Milada could feel.

"Sex tempers the blood and heightens the response. A kind of catalyst. I believe that is what Kammy would say. And she is a doctor, after all." Milada's voice took on a playful, impish tone.

Rachel did not respond at once. A sudden weight of guilt descended on her mind—that she would even *contemplate* the possibility. But she did. Her only question was: *What do you mean by sex?* The desire for clarification only served to damn her conscience. And yet—if this was the sum of the cost—

Milada's right arm circled her waist. She pressed her forehead against Rachel's left temple, tipping her head back, her lips closing gently on her earlobe—

"No—no—*please*—" Rachel drew a deep breath that shuddered through her body. She pressed her face against the wall, hiding her own hopelessness and shame. Tears stung the corners of her eyes.

Milada took her left hand off the wall and, with a gentle caress, brushed the tear from Rachel's cheek. "Don't worry, Rachel. I would not do to you what was done to me."

She stepped back and let her go.

Rachel opened her eyes and turned apprehensively to face her. Milada watched her with that same feline expression, an impassive mask of faint amusements and small curiosities. She again leaned deeply into Rachel's personal space. Rachel inhaled the musk of her natural perfume, the hint of raw vanilla, the scent of her hair and skin. It left her flushed and light-headed. She gained a measure of admiration for Troy in that moment—that he'd been able to resist.

This time their cheeks did touch. "You have made me hungry, Rachel. Make love to your husband, and I will take your blood — tonight, before I change my mind, whilst I am still curious to taste you."

Rachel nodded her head. "Thank you," she said, in a gesture of purely involuntary politeness.

Milada replied severely, "Do not thank me, woman. I have promised you nothing."

But these were terms Rachel could live with. Because this once in her life, she had no choice.

Chapter 27
Near is my shirt but nearer is my skin

DAVID WAS IN THE SHOWER when Rachel got home. "Is that you, honey?" he called out after Rachel opened and closed the bedroom door.

"It's me, dear."

She began undressing. The shower turned off. He poked his head around the jam. "Hi, hon. Where were you?" He ducked back into the bathroom to dry off.

"I went for a walk." She hung her blouse in the closet. "I went to see Milada."

"How is she?"

"She's — an interesting person."

David emerged from the bathroom wrapping the towel around his waist. "You know, I've been thinking about her."

"You've been thinking about her?" she teased. "I can imagine what *you've* been thinking about."

He gave her a comically annoyed look. "What I was thinking was, we all want to believe that everybody is the same under the skin. But meeting a person like her makes me think some people really *are* different from you and me and the guy next door. Not *bad* different. Just different."

"In ways you would never guess."

Rachel wrapped her arms around his waist, leaned against his chest. His skin was hot and moist against her cheek. She smelled the faint redolence of his deodorant, Old Spice. She felt herself relax, the tension melt out of her muscles. She was tired, exhausted — yet vibrantly alive. So she said the dullest thing she could thing of: "How was the game?"

"Pretty good. That Trisha Garner really impresses me. She's only fifteen, but I can really see her playing for BYU or the WNBA, even. She's got a jump shot I never had."

"Ego a little bruised?"

"Nah. Anyway, she was on our team. I pretended I was John Stockton and concentrated on making the assist."

"You're good at that—making the assist."

He brushed the hair away from her face. "Is that a compliment?"

"I think so."

He kissed her. Lightly at first, lips brushing lips, a restraint that kindled desires too long dormant. His hands played across her back. She clung to him, catching her breath as he bent her across the bed and kissed her neck. She wanted to kiss him in turn, but she did not want him to stop either. She tugged at the towel. It dropped to the floor. He lay her down on the bed, undressed her, and with his hands and lips wrote sonnets on her skin.

She fit herself to him, tongue and groove, the arch of her back pressing the curve of her flesh against his torso. The physical response of her body to his always surprised her, like the unexpected bloom of a desert flower, the shock of sudden beauty on the plain stem. Sex wasn't something she spent a lot of time thinking about—nowadays, even less often than she ought to—but the act of lovemaking never failed to conquer her completely.

The verses from Proverbs rang in her heart and in her head: *May my breasts satisfy you always. May you ever be captivated by my love.*

Her pulse quickened in her throat, and she panted hot against his shoulder. Her hips rose without bidding to meet his, pushing herself into the hot thrum of pleasure, desperate for release. Her inner core shuddered in taut ecstasy, a rapture almost too much to bear.

"Rachel—" He spoke her name like a caress, an intimate touch welling up involuntarily from within the deep and subtle parts of his being. She let her body respond in full, held him with all her strength, as if to fuse their bodies together, as if to make their molten spirits one.

Rachel stirred. She had fallen asleep naked, tucked into the crook of her husband's arm. It was not something she did often, not when a child was likely to burrow into the marriage bed at any time of night. She sat up, suddenly aware, her attention tensed, her mind reaching out through the silent house, making a count of present souls. She caught her breath, recognizing the faint scent of vanilla.

She eased off the bed, pulled her bathrobe around her shoulders, and stole out of the room. There was something unearthly about a still, silent house at this hour. The hallway was a catacomb, the walls turned to cold, mottled stone. She paused at the door to Laura's room and then continued on, finding her way by touch.

In the kitchen the digital numbers of the microwave clock glowed a dim fluorescent green. A faint, distant light shone through the curtains. As her eyes grew accustomed to the darkness, she descended to the family room. Milada stood there in her BYU sweats. The woman turned, and her eyes shone. As with any other nocturnal animal, Rachel knew it was only the reflection of incidental light off the back of her retinas. But the sight froze her with an instinctive fear, speaking to her primate mind of that primeval fear of predators that rule the night.

Milada approached her, breathing in the fragrance of her sex. Their temples almost touched. "This time I really must kiss you."

Rachel closed her eyes. "Don't make me forget—"

Milada promised her nothing. Her mouth met hers, warm and insistent. Her tongue wet her lips. There was witchcraft in this kiss. Rachel was not aroused, but neither was she repulsed. She was lost as to how she should react, aware only that she was losing her awareness, losing her ability to react to whatever Milada might wish to do to her. She had never been so vulnerable in all her life.

I would not do to you what was done to me. What a terrible and reassuring thing to say.

A tingling sensation pricked her lips and tongue, followed by a creeping numbness. Then the sudden thump in her chest, as when the dentist's lidocaine courses through the bloodstream and hits the heart. The room spun slowly. She floated off the carpet. Milada lifted her effortlessly in her arms and set her on the couch, slipping a pillow under her neck and turning her head to the side, exposing the curve of her neck. Milada's left hand pressed firmly against her forehead, further immobilizing her. Rachel harbored one last thought: *Don't make me forget.* Then the deep, sharp punctures, and she was swept into oblivion.

Rachel was conscious but not awake. Or maybe it was the other way around. She tried opening her eyes. Her heavy lids opened. Yes, she was awake. The bedroom was bright with filtered sunlight. Where was David? He was up and about. It was Saturday morning, time to get things done around the house.

She pulled back the comforter. She was loosely wrapped in her bathrobe. Why? When had she put on her bathrobe? She pushed herself into a sitting position, groaned, and fell back on the bed, staring up at the ceiling. *Milada,* she said to herself. And then came that sense of quiet victory: *I remember.*

Rachel sat up again and collected herself. Planting her feet on the floor, she stood, keeping the expanse of the mattress behind her. Black spots swam before her eyes. She held out her arms to keep her balance and filled her lungs with air. *There, that's better.* She did a quick inventory of her body. Everything was okay. Except that she was thirsty. And she was ravenous.

She shuffled into the bathroom, leaned on the sink, and peered at her reflection in the mirror. She looked better than she felt, that was for sure. She touched the left side of her neck, fingered the delicate pair of bruises. She did remember everything. And now some of Milada was inside her doing heaven knew what.

She pulled up the collar of the bathrobe and snugged the sash tight. On her way down the stairs, she made good use of the banister. Laura and her father were in the kitchen, Laura trying to negotiate an afternoon at the mall with Heidi. At the bottom of the stairs, Rachel pushed off and managed to approximate a casual, relaxed gait until she reached the kitchen table and sat down.

"Morning, hon. So you're up."

She yawned. "I decided to sleep in for once." Well, not exactly *decided.*

Laura gave her a suspicious look. Rachel was pretty sure she had something of a languid, self-satisfied grin on her face. And she was bathed in enough afterglow to light up a small auditorium. But she was too exhausted to try and hide it. Sometimes the facts of life just presented themselves as a *fait accompli,* kiddo.

Laura glanced at her mother, at her father, and back at her mother. Her mother knew exactly what she was thinking: *They didn't really – did they?* Oh good grief, they had! *Sheesh.* Gamely ignoring the obvious, she said to her mother, "Can I go to the mall with Heidi this afternoon?"

"What did your father say?"

"He didn't."

Her father said, "It's not so much the going as the taking." He handed his wife a steaming mug. She took a sip. Orange spice. She smiled warmly at him.

Laura said, "You know, this won't be a problem once I get my driver's license."

The girl was already thinking ahead, priming the pump. Her mother said, "That's something we can all look forward to."

"Can I or can't I?"

"What time?"

"Two-ish."

"Two-ish to what-ish?"

"Six."

"What in the world are you going to do at the mall for four hours?"

"Mom!"

Her mother shrugged. "Whatever. I'm sure I can arrange to do my shopping at two or so."

"That's all I needed to know," Laura exclaimed, stomping out of the room. "You guys always have to make such a big deal out of stuff."

David sat down at the table next to his wife. "I'd almost swear you enjoyed that little exchange."

"I might have. A bit." She kissed him, a kiss that deepened. She stroked the rough stubble on his chin. "What's on your schedule for today?"

"Mow the lawn, for starters."

"Then you'd better go mow the lawn, husband." She didn't let go of him right away. She considered inviting his hands inside the robe, but common sense overcame temptation. Heaven knew that a teenager wanted to believe that her parents' knowledge of the facts of life was purely hypothetical. It would not help at this point to provide any more evidence to the contrary.

When Rachel left church Sunday afternoon after welfare meeting, the bishop was still busy with interviews. Sharon Sundwall and a couple she didn't know were seated in the little alcove outside the bishop's office. The matter of Derek and the Boy Scouts remained unresolved.

Located directly across from the clerks' office, the alcove was something like a doctor's waiting room. She knew her husband's regulars, ward members for whom the bishop was cheaper than a psychiatrist, less demanding than Dr. Laura, more reliable than Ann Landers. But as for the others—she couldn't help seeing people there and wondering, *What does* he *need to see the bishop for? And what about* her? Maybe just the equivalent of a flu here, maybe cancer there.

Rachel liked to believe she possessed a special divine insight into the human character, an adeptness at spiritual phrenology. But perhaps what she was really attuned to was a particular way of speaking, a style of grooming, the mannerisms unique to their culture. That new couple sitting there — the bishop always met promptly with new members in the ward — he could be a mass murderer, she a high-class call girl. And would the ward know otherwise? No. Just as no one looked at Rachel Forsythe and could begin to imagine the depth of the confluence between herself and Milada Daranyi.

When Rachel reached Milada's house, she found the woman sitting at the back of the porch, hidden behind her sunglasses and her mask of porcelain stillness. Rachel understood why she sat and watched as the gods must sit and watch. Mortals must amuse her so, scurrying about in a constant tizzy, hastening with every skipped step toward the end of their too-short lives.

"How are you feeling, Rachel?"

Rachel stepped onto the porch deck. She was afraid that a sudden sense of intimacy, as one finds in a friendship too quickly formed, would dampen any real friendship that might exist between them. "Quite well, thank you. Saturday morning I was a little woozy — "

"A perfectly normal response." Milada said, "I do not imagine, Rachel, that you have discussed this arrangement with your husband?"

Rachel shook her head. "I prefer not to have to lie, but no."

"I agree. I hire people to lie for me." Her thin smile almost became a grin. "Shall I meet you tomorrow at the hospital then? Around eight o'clock?"

Rachel's heart skipped a beat. The substance of their relationship rushed into the forefront of her thoughts. She nodded. "Deseret Children's Hospital, room 3209."

"Very well. You could give me a ride home. Spare my driver the journey south. He's a remarkable young man, my driver. Twenty-three, married with two children, determined to enter medical school."

"I was twenty when I got married."

"And in my youth, girls were married barely out of childhood. What our elders expect of us we come to deem as natural, even right."

There was more to that statement than she said. Rachel shifted the weight off her right foot. She meant to bid Milada good-bye, thank her again, step back, and take her leave. Instead she stepped forward. "How did this happen to you, Milada? Who are you really?"

Milada turned her head to look at her. A long moment passed between them. When she spoke, she quoted from a text Rachel felt she should know but couldn't recall: "*And how he fell from Heaven, thrown by angry Jove sheer over the Crystal Battlements.*"

Rachel knew the context, the Book of Revelations: *The great dragon was cast out into the earth, and his angels were cast out with him.* She said, "Those fallen angels were condemned to never be born into this world, to remain spirits forever. You could not have been one of them."

Milada smiled at her reassurances. "But I fell softly."

Chapter 28
No man can serve two masters

GARRICK'S MERGERS AND ACQUISITIONS TEAM arrived Monday morning to ramp up for the Wylde Medical Informatics takeover. Milada was confident that a deal was in the offing. The accountants from KPMG had already rented the suite next door. Milada directed the troops from her command post in the conference room at Loveridge & Associates. She was the coach taking her college squad into the final four.

They were at that point in the game when things were getting interesting. They'd been running up and down the court for forty minutes, the score was all tied up, and if something important was going to happen, it was going to happen now. Seconds left, a three-point shot arcing high over the basket.

The constant press of the players was for Milada a necessary evil. She preferred to work alone, to reach out through the proxy of her aides, Jane in New York and Karen Talbot here at Loveridge. Even Garrick, as relaxed on the floor of the New York Stock Exchange as she was in her empty West Seventy-Second Street brownstone, preferred to retreat at the end of the day to his subterranean cell, to his solitary self.

Den dwellers like the lycanthropes mystified her. The behavior ran in the genes, she supposed—that primeval affection for the group, that inherent desire to belong that made *homo lupus* ultimately more human than *homo lamia,* despite the more monstrous and undisguisable nature of their metamorphosis. Wolves lived in packs, far from the madding crowd. She lived alone, but alone among many. It amounted to more than the simple utilitarianism of keeping her food close at hand; that incalculable need to maintain the illusion of her humanness kept her at once insulated from the teeming city, yet cheek by jowl with the peopled world.

Karen sidled up to her. "Mr. Burke is on the phone."

Milada plucked the receiver off its cradle. "Good morning, Garrick."

"Milly, turn on CNBC."

The television was set into a bookcase behind a pair of cabinet doors. Karen found the remote. She clicked through the channels, finally landing on CNBC.

Milada said, "Quiet, please!"

The room immediately shushed. On the screen, CNBC news anchor Bill Griffeth was saying, "The run up in WMI stock over the most recent quarter has been widely attributed to substantial positions taken in your company by DEI."

The camera switched to his guest, a white-haired man with sunburned cheeks and heavy jowls. He leaned slightly forward in his chair. His tweed sports jacket scrunched up at the back of his neck. A polished agate bolo tie fastened a plain white shirt at the collar. The graphic along the bottom of the screen said, DARREN WYLDE, CHAIRMAN & CEO, WYLDE MEDICAL INFORMATICS. The photograph in the annual report was kinder to him. But then, this was the face of a man who didn't care what he looked like.

Darren Wylde said, "We're aware of that."

"Then you're also aware that over the past decade DEI has pursued a strategy of buying into small high-tech companies, replacing the boards, and taking them private."

A twitch of annoyance flicked across the man's face, that of a bull bothered by a horse fly. He swiveled his chair around so that he was looking into the camera. His eyes were as sharply defined as his worn features were not. "We're not interested in market valuations. Let the speculators and day traders worry about that. Our corporate goals haven't changed. I have every intention of keeping this company true to the principles it was founded upon."

"Are you saying you have no interest in negotiating a takeover bid from DEI?"

"I'm saying we're not going to be swayed by outside influences. As far as I'm concerned, there's only one way of running this company. And as long as I'm in charge, it's my way."

Garrick whistled softly at the other end of the line. "I admire that attitude. Home, home on the range, and get along little dogies. Maybe you and the old man should just have it out with six-shooters at a dozen paces."

On the television screen, Bill Griffeth was thanking Mr. Wylde and announcing his next guest. Milada said, "So who do you think he was addressing there at the end?"

"You don't think he was talking to you?"

"No. I think that little performance was about mustering the troops. I suspect discontent in the ranks."

"At these price levels, I'd be dying to cash out too. How do you want to play this?"

"Give me half an hour. I'll call you back. In the meantime, check the most recent 144 filings. See what insider trading has been going on." She said to Karen, "Get me the stockholder list. Oh, and clear the room, please."

Karen shooed everybody out of the room with the temperament of a schoolmarm calling recess. She returned with the folder Milada had requested, looking concerned. She didn't quite understand the game, but no doubt she sensed that the other team had scored an important point. She waited until Milada had paced back from the curtained window before asking, "Is this bad?"

"The interview with Wylde? Maybe, maybe not. It depends. Have you ever seen King Lear?"

"You mean, like Shakespeare?"

"The best analysis of how *not* to run a family business ever written. It starts with Lear, president and CEO of his clan. The old man wants to retire. He comes up with this great idea of dividing the company equally among his three daughters. The youngest, Cordelia, immediately sees where this is headed and objects. So he disowns her. But once Goneril and Regan get their hands on the goods, Dad is sent packing as well. From that point on, it's a bloody game of king-of-the-hill."

"Is that what's happening here?"

"Combined, his kids and relations are the majority holders, and he has *not* picked a successor. It must keep him awake at night. Having an overvalued stock makes it that much tougher. All those dollar signs dancing in their eyes. But stock is not money. The only thing you can buy with it is more pieces of paper. There is no cash in the bank. Still, we act as if it *is* money. And when it goes away, oh, does it hurt."

A secretary came into the conference room and handed Milada a fax. It was from Garrick, a copy of an SEC 144 report listing the insider trader declarations. Milada scanned down the list and nodded. "The friends and relatives are cashing in. Now we shall make them eager to sell out, regardless of what Mr. Wylde wants or doesn't want. That's what his little performance on the telly was about: dressing down the kith and kin. But we shall see how much sharper than a serpent's tooth are a child's greed and ingratitude." She dialed Garrick and hit the speaker button.

"What say ye, Milly?"

"I say dump the stock. Hold as much of our current positions as you can, but kill the support levels, kick the legs out from under."

"Oh, boy," chortled Garrick, and Milada could imagine that mischievous grin dimpling his cheeks.

"The rumor is that we're reconsidering our stake in the company. The interview prompted a reevaluation."

"The cover story isn't a problem. How far, how fast?"

"Let's finish it off with a flourish, but keep the cat from bouncing too high."

After Garrick hung up, Karen asked, "Cat bouncing?"

"Even a dead cat will bounce when it hits the sidewalk. Bargain hunters buy up an oversold stock hoping to stake out a position based on momentum alone."

"That doesn't sound very nice."

"It's not nice at all. But that's the way this game is played."

"Mr. Burke seemed very happy about it."

"Ever since Garrick got stung in the South Sea Company fiasco, he's made it something of a divine mission to punish speculators. When the day traders bid up a stock he's trying to corner, he takes it personally."

Karen was satisfied with the answer. She didn't know enough to know that when the stock bottomed and the margin calls kicked in, otherwise decent and well-meaning people with their car payments due and second mortgages on the line and tuition checks in the mail wouldn't be able to cover those calls and were going to lose a lot of money they could not afford to lose.

As Garrick liked to say, *Serves them right.* When a market-maker was working a stock with a stratospheric price-to-earnings ratio, the amateurs should stand aside. The rain falls on the just and unjust and especially on the reckless and the greedy and the stupid. It wasn't Garrick's or her problem. Obsessing about the short-term suffering only guaranteed long-term pain.

"Karen," Milada said.

Karen stopped at the door. Milada busied herself at her laptop. She didn't look up. "If that accountant friend of yours is holding Wylde stock, he might want to consider some sell options."

Karen looked blankly at her for a moment. "Okay," she said.

Milada swore to herself, but not harshly. Knowing Karen, though, it would come to no harm. Karen was not Jane. Jane knew everything. Jane knew that the South Sea Company failed in 1721, the apocalyptic financial scandal of the time. That was why Jane was so important to her. Jane was a person she could tell things to.

In the end, that was what Milada needed human beings for. Once every generation, she must find a confessor and bury her secrets in the vault of a mortal soul.

Chapter 29
Action is the proper fruit of knowledge

LAURA AND HER FATHER WERE WATCHING FOOTBALL for family home evening. David bounded up to the kitchen at the end of the first quarter to get a pop and popcorn refill. Rachel said, making a point of retrieving her purse from the counter as she spoke, "I'm going to stop by and see Jennifer."

A factually awkward statement. She'd have to drive halfway across Salt Lake to "stop by" Deseret Children's Hospital. She could have said, "I'm going to see Jennifer." It wasn't the *going* she was dissembling about, but the *why*. There was no way she could explain the *why,* and lies had a way of piling up like a house of cards.

"Do you want me to come with?"

"That's okay. I won't be long. Stay with Laura. Be a dad." She touched his arm and smiled.

He grinned and nodded. "Give Jenny my love."

She waited till she was seated in the minivan to sigh mightily in relief.

Rachel thought about the *why* as she drove north. What she was doing—what she'd asked Milada to do—was beyond bizarre. Mormons believed in faith healing. How bizarre was that? They just didn't believe in the Pentecostal, Bible-thumping brand. But holy books written on golden plates, angels and visions, God appearing to a boy in a grove of trees—nothing wrong with all that, though.

So it was no great shakes for her to believe six impossible things before breakfast. *She* believed them. She looked inside herself and found no doubt at all. And if she'd come to believe as well that the albino lady down the street was four-plus centuries old and could perform a miracle on her dying daughter that no doctor could? Why not exercise that faith?

Yes, this was *peculiar,* a word Mormons had once used to describe themselves, back when different was good. *A lot of the things we do are strange,* she thought. The temple, for starters. Any given fast and testimony meeting. If they were romping around a Brazilian rainforest dressed in coconut palms and surrounded by *National Geographic* photographers speaking into microphones in hushed, reverential tones, they'd be an ethnographic curiosity pored over in anthropology journals.

Was doing strange things a sign of faith? Doing what was out of the ordinary? *Faith without works is dead.* By which Mormons meant: faith without *work* is dead.

She was working as hard as she could.

Chapter 30

Hard cases make bad law

STEVEN DROPPED MILADA OFF at the main entrance to Deseret Children's Hospital. "A friend of mine, her child is in the hospital," she'd explained when she'd given him the directions.

"Do you want me to wait?"

"I have a ride," she said, and sent him home.

The DCH lobby was a pleasant surprise. None of the grim, bleach-white, sterile spaciousness of the modern general hospital. It had a friendly, almost intimate, air about it, the walls finished in pink and purple and green pastels. The numerous donor plaques were stenciled in the shapes of toy blocks.

In the center of the lobby, a wishing pool, its blue tiles scattered with copper and silver coins, surrounded a wire-and-metal sculpture. *A Child's World* it was titled, a collection of intricately designed Rube Goldberg contraptions: wheels and gears and engines and paddles and wings and sails, all commanded by their child pilots, small forms cast in patinated bronze.

Etched in gold leaf into the wall opposite were the words, THE CHILD FIRST AND ALWAYS. And next to it a captioned black-and-white photograph of the original Deseret Hospital Board of Directors, dated July 17, 1882. All women, several of them wives of Brigham Young, two of them holding medical degrees from the Women's Medical College in Philadelphia and the University of Michigan.

In the late nineteenth century, Milada understood, the most progressive social and political institutions on the American continent could be found in Utah among the Mormon polygamists. *Go figure.*

Milada took the elevator to the third floor. In the waiting room outside the bone marrow transplant unit was a surgical scrub basin. A sign instructed visitors to wash their hands before entering the unit. She stopped at the water fountain. She rinsed her mouth and spit the water into the basin. She stood at the sink and washed her hands and examined herself in the mirror.

You are out of your mind, said the needling voice in her head.

She shook the thought away.

You are out of your bloody mind.

She'd been out of her mind before. She knew what *that* was like. If there was any justice in this world, she would have hung until dead from the Tyburn gallows. Unlike Rakoczi, she wouldn't have had the courage to kill herself first.

Kammy's going to catch you.

That brought her to a dead stop. Rachel's question came back to her. *What would your sister say?* Kammy would be curious, but she would never go along. She had too many principles—where had she gotten *them* from?—and she took too many precautions. She used her connections to get fresh blood from the blood bank instead of picking up men. *How did she end up so normal?*

It was Zoë, who had too few principles and took too few precautions—Zoë who'd discovered the relationship between venom and allergies from a girl who was cured of her debilitating allergies after Zoë slept with her and took her blood. One of the odd side benefits of having a sexually adventurous sister.

And Michael? He would disapprove categorically. *Give when you take; never infect; never tell.* Those were the rules of the family. *Never tell.* She had crossed that line and crossed it with a woman bound to her not by money or power or fear but by compassion. Of all things. She'd paid the ferryman, and there was no shoreline in sight.

Chapter 31
Needs must when the devil drives

THE STATION NURSE, CAROL LINDLEY, GREETED RACHEL when she arrived on the unit. "Good evening, Carol," Rachel replied. Rachel was on a first-name basis with all the critical-care nurses. What would they think if they knew what she was about to do? Another Munchausen's Syndrome by Proxy nutcase. They'd cluck with sympathy as they pumped her full of antipsychotics and locked her away.

Rachel set a chair at the head of the bed and combed her daughter's hair with her fingers, brushing the silky strands away from her face. "It's going to be all right, Jenny. A friend of mine is going to help you get better." She took her daughter's hand in hers and saw, as if for the first time, the marks in the skin from the countless needles and IVs.

My daughter the junkie.

Through the large window along the interior wall of the room, Rachel watched Milada approach the nurse's station. Milada spoke briefly with the nurse. The nurse left and returned a minute later with a set of charts. Milada flipped through the papers, examined one or two of them, nodded, handed them back. Rachel noticed the casual way her fingers touched the nurse's hand as she thanked her. The nurse did as Milada asked. With no reason to resist, it would not occur to her to question why.

Could she really overpower the will, Rachel wondered, or only make people do what they really wanted to do beneath the ever-present veneer of self-righteous civility—or were eager to do before they calculated the consequences? At what point did temptation trespass into coercion?

"So this is Jennifer."

Milada stood in the doorway. The sky-blue jamb framed her china-white hair and pale features. Milada's young face and old eyes looked as an angel's must. She lacked only a pair of wings folded against her back beneath her gray Armani jacket.

She took in the rest of the room. "I see your point about the dragons," she said, sitting down across from Rachel. "She is a beautiful child."

Rachel nodded. She looked at Milada and, for the briefest of moments, saw a depth of emotion she had never seen before in a human being: a longing, a desire, an unearthly connection to a life lost and destroyed at some point in her distant past.

Milada touched Jennifer's cheek with her fingertips. A look of tenderness passed across her face, then a spasm of guilt that she just as quickly erased. She cradled the child's left arm against her right arm, her thumb resting at the crook of Jennifer's elbow. She glanced at Rachel, her eyes asking, *If you wish to say no, now is the time.*

Rachel did not say no.

Milada remained still for several long minutes, her gaze focused on a point far beyond Rachel's left shoulder. Then she raised her chin slightly, tightening the tendons in her neck. Her pupils dilated. She narrowed her eyes against the light—eyes no longer human, filled with an animal curiosity that asked, *What are you to me?*

Her lips parted, the slender white tips of her fangs clicked against the back of her incisors. There was an almost delicate beauty to them. She pressed her thumb against the soft tissue at the crook of Jennifer's elbow, compressing the vein. Her head dipped, and her mouth closed over Jennifer's wrist. The child's body jerked once. It hardly took more than a second, and every move she made was so subtle—so *practiced*. This was something she was good at. Something she had done many times before.

Milada raised her head, her expression blank. She craned her neck again, and Rachel observed the ripple of muscles along her jaw as the fangs pulled back and up against the roof of her mouth. Rachel tore her gaze away. The two pinpricks in Jennifer's wrist closed to a pair of dots. Rachel remembered the punctures in her own neck and that there were no bloodstains on her pillow.

Just another track in her daughter's veins.

Milada placed Jennifer's arm gently beneath the sheets, and everything returned to exactly how it was before she came into the room. She pushed the chair back, stood, and left the room.

Chapter 32

The child is father to the man

FOR SEVERAL MINUTES RACHEL DID NOT and could not move. She stared at her daughter, waiting for the sudden miracle. She blinked and sat back in her chair. She had somehow expected something more: Latin incantations, a ring of burning candles, black-hatted witches. No, she had done it because it *made sense,* her reasoning was so *scientific.* Andy Millington was proof that Milada's venom — and it seemed so ordinary now to think that a person should have *venom* — could suppress the autoimmune response. Should it not act the same on the chains of proteins working such ruinous carnage in her daughter's body?

Rationality begot only more rationality, and what was logical ultimately failed to inspire.

She found Milada in the lobby, standing in front of the large windows that looked west across the city. The city lights sparkled in the late twilight, like the reflecting pool of the universe. Milada said, "This will not work. This will not make a difference."

"Then why did you come?"

"Because you asked."

The minivan wound down North Campus Drive, headlights glowing in the falling dark, a firefly lost on the face of the broad expanse of the towering mountains. Fifteenth East ran along the East Bench, the narrow streets shrouded with trees, the leafy branches closing out the sky. It was one of those almost-otherworldly parts of the valley. More like Massachusetts than the Rocky Mountains.

The Mormons who first came to this high desert valley had ventured forth from New England, sailed from Great Britain and Scandinavia, trudged through New York, Ohio, and Illinois and across the Great Plains. They came and irrigated with a vengeance until the green memory of their ancestral homes sprouted from the ancient sandy shores of Lake Bonneville.

Rachel said, if only to break the silence, "Getting your driver's license renewed must be a curious experience."

"A small annoyance. Garrick has a retired Treasury Department engraver on retainer. He prepares all our identification papers. Garrick convinced him that working for the family was a less risky and more rewarding hobby than passing the odd hand-drawn C-note at the 7-Eleven."

"Should you be telling me things like that?" Rachel asked lightly.

"Who would believe you?"

"I suppose you're right." Rachel shook her head. There was no *suppose* about it. She began again, "The story you told about being named for the abbess—was that really you?"

"I was named for the abbess, as I said. Boleslaw and his kin lived in the tenth century. I was born in the sixteenth." She paused, reaching back into the past. "In 1566, the year Transylvania fell under the suzerainty of the Ottoman Empire. When I was ten, my parents died. Kammy believes it was cholera. We were sent across the river to an orphanage in Szeged."

"Oh," said Rachel, remembering. "You said Michael was your stepfather."

"Yes. As I remember it now, the orphanage was not a bad life. But ten-year-olds are such indomitable creatures." This time she did smile. Her cheeks came close to dimpling, a smile that vanished as soon as she resumed her narrative.

"Two years later, a man arrived to claim the meager remains of our parents' estate, ourselves included. He was from the provinces, he said. A distant relative. He had only recently heard of our parents' deaths. He produced papers to the effect and a sufficient amount of money to convince the powers that be. He called himself Rakoczi, a count of some sort or another. I was certainly impressed."

Rachel glanced at her. The casual tone of her narration did not mask the tone of ambivalence in the statement *I was certainly impressed*.

"But you said that Michael—"

"That came later." Her brow furrowed. "Except for the Mother Superior, the sisters were quite happy for us, so rare it was for a child, let alone three, to be rescued from rags to riches. It only happens in fairy tales." She conceded, "It was an adventure to experience so exciting and vast a world. So beyond our small imaginations. He took us to Budapest, Vienna, Paris. I had seen most of Europe by the time I turned fourteen."

"You speak with a British accent."

"I've spent most of my life in London. We came to America shortly before the Great War. Michael takes the long view of things, and he's usually right."

What are you leaving out? Rachel thought as she pulled up to the curb on Larkspur Lane.

Milada opened the car door. Rachel reached across the armrest and grasped her arm. She said, and she did not speak out of any reflexive social obligation, "Thank you."

Milada again showed that small, self-deprecating smile, in which Rachel had begun to see the whisperings of a long-buried childlike sweetness. "You have your angels to answer to, Rachel. I have my demons." She got out of the car. "And I do hope yours have the ear of a kinder God than mine do."

Rachel watched her walk up to the porch and disappear into the house. She drove home and sat there in the dark garage for a long time before getting out of the car and going into the house.

She told her husband as they got into bed later that night, "Milada came to the hospital to see Jennifer."

"Milada? Really?"

"While we were driving home, she told me something of her childhood. I'd assumed she was born into money. But her parents died when she was ten. It was a number of years before she and her sisters were adopted by that well-off family."

"Still, happily ever after, no? And you think it only happens in fairy tales."

"Maybe it does." She rolled over on her back and laid her head on the pillow and spoke to the ceiling. *"Therefore I have uttered what I did not understand, things too wonderful for me, which I did not know."*

He sat down on the bed beside her. "I get worried whenever you start quoting Job."

"Don't be. Things are getting better after this. I just know it."

"You've never been this sure before."

She raised herself up on her elbows. "Because I have reason to believe," she said and then kissed him.

It did not occur to him to ask why. As much as his wife might rail against God, she was the optimist in the family, the one who steadfastly refused to accept the bitter consignments of fate.

Chapter 33
Any burden's heavy if far borne

MILADA SAT NEXT TO THE BED, where Rachel normally sat. She retrieved the WMI proffer from her attaché. It was a rough draft, full of estimates, talking points, trial balloons. Another month to finish the preliminary audit and put together a proposal. Another month after that to negotiate stockholder compensation and golden parachutes. By the end of the year, she hoped.

A nurse poked her head into the room. SUANNE LANE, R.N., her name tag said. She said, "Ma'am?"

Milada looked at her, threatened a glare, and then cocked her head to one side, innocently, quizzically. "Is there a problem?"

The nurse returned her look with equal severity.

Well, then?

The nurse nodded and backed out of the room and continued down the hall. Milada watched her through the glass. She might have to speak to that nurse alone. She returned her attention to the proffer. She took out a pen and circled a number she didn't agree with, another she knew was wrong. Her pen hesitated on the paper, numbers and tables blurring together.

She rubbed her eyes, blinked hard, but her mind kept running away from the subject at hand. Or rather, it kept running to the girl beside her.

Milada had vaguely begun to understand the darker reasons for her attraction to the child and her irrational willingness to respond to Rachel's pleas. She knew what it meant to be the last, best hope. She'd hunted for her sisters as the lioness hunts for her cubs. They could not have survived without her. And how she'd enjoyed tracking the prey, seducing them, cutting them away from the herd. Making them follow her, obey her — making them *like* her before delivering them to their fate.

"Sometimes I think I'm turning into him," she'd told Kammy once. Kammy didn't speak to her for months afterward. But Milada relished being the one who provided for them, the one *Rakoczi* depended on. She would allow *nothing* to stand in her way.

She'd been in charge then and was now. Michael played the godfather role well, to be sure. He made and enforced the rules. He condoned or endorsed her decisions. And brooded in his Central Park West manse and carried on like a young Howard Hughes cast in *The Picture of Dorian Gray,* everything growing old around him while he remained the same.

DEI's success was her success. It was enough, she told herself. *It was enough.* She hadn't deliberately injured another human being in three hundred years. Not since Rakoczi died. Not in a blood lust and not in anger.

And before Rakoczi died? Yes, she had known what would happen to Rakoczi's victims. She understood why he did what he did and what he wanted: eternal companions to share the same lonely, eternal dusk. And so she had inured herself to a world in which a nasty, short, brutal life was the lot of common humans.

Even now, as removed from the temptation as she had become, as far removed from the instinct and inclination that had occasioned the sin, she still could not forget that she had once been tempted, that once she fell. There were stains on her soul that did not fade.

She could not change the past. But this child's future she could change.

When Milada got back to Sandy, Kammy was sitting on the porch reading a journal by the glow of the porch light. Her Camry was parked next to the mailbox. Kammy could afford any car in the lot, and she always chose a Camry.

Milada parked the Mercedes in the garage and ducked out before the door closed. She checked her watch. Ten-thirty.

Kammy said, as she came up the walk, "You said to stop by sometime."

Milada realized that Kammy was wearing her scrubs. They could have passed each other in front of the hospital and not even known it. She reminded herself again: *Kammy doesn't work pediatrics.*

"I hope you haven't been waiting long. You should have called first."

Her sister shrugged the way she always did. "Your cell phone wasn't on. I left a message."

Milada got out her phone and turned it on.

Kammy gave her a funny look. "Milly turning her phone off? The thin mountain air must be getting to you. Garrick will never believe me. Anyway, I was at Wylde, and it's not that much farther to here."

Milada breathed a quiet sigh of relief. She unlocked the front door. Kammy followed on her heels.

"You're certainly not cramped for space," she observed. "Your kitchen is bigger than my flat in New York."

"My limo's bigger than your flat," Milada said, getting the bottle of Sparkling Catawba from the fridge.

"What's that?"

"A ginger ale and grape juice concoction."

"I'm game."

Milada filled two glasses. Kammy sat down at the counter and took a sip. "Doesn't suck. Rather bland, though. A wine spritzer sans the alcohol."

"Sort of a metaphor for this place."

"The mountains are nice. In the mornings I don't have to mess with my Indiana Jones outfit."

"At least you don't mind wearing your Indiana Jones outfit."

"When it's a hundred degrees outside? Yeah, I do." She drank a little more of the Catawba. "How's the Wylde deal going?"

"A few critical variables are still up in the air. It'll all shake out soon enough."

Kammy nodded. "I'm for it."

Milada made no effort to hide the surprised look on her face.

"Hey, I'm not agreeing to any of this running-the-company business. I'm only saying that there are a whole bunch of cool things we could do with the resources they've got there. I wonder if St. Jude is tied into their databases." She got out her cell phone. "Sending myself a memo," she explained, thumbing the keyboard pad.

Milada said casually, "I've been thinking that Wylde presents a good opportunity to analyze the properties of the virus."

"The virus?" Kammy snapped the cell phone shut and looked up. "Oh, *that* virus."

"You have to have the mutation to survive, right? What if a way could be found to mitigate that condition?"

"Hypothetically the mutation could be engineered with a retroviral vector," Kammy said. "Nobody's got it to reliably work yet, but let's pretend. So a significant fraction of the population gets to live forever, farming the rest of the human race for their hemoglobin. Wow, talk about your haves and have-nots."

"I don't mean that."

"Even if the CCR5 barrier could be engineered around, then what? We're sterile, remember? Humanity would die out. Pretty much the definition of a Pyrrhic victory, no? I mean, there's a reason for the rules."

"The rules Michael made up, you mean," Milada said.

"Be serious. That's like saying gravity's just a rule Newton made up. Try stepping off a tall building and see if you don't go splat. We can't go around infecting people willy-nilly. I for one have no desire to end up on a slab at the CDC being puzzled over by a bunch of epidemiologists."

"No one said anything about willy-nilly."

"There's always a price," Kammy said. "You know that. We paid it. Do you want to pay it again? Do you really want to make somebody else go through *that* again?"

"Conditions can be mitigated."

"What, like an existential epidural?"

"You're the doctor. Explain why any woman would have a child more than once."

"Hormones. Sex. Endorphins. Family. Love. Progeny." Kamilla's eyes narrowed. "What are you getting at?"

"I'm not getting at anything." Milada said, a bit too defensively. "What about killed virus? Blood to blood, not enough to infect but enough to generate the necessary antibodies and attenuate the immune response? I recall you mentioning that the infection threshold is fairly high."

"In a normal, healthy human." Kammy nodded. "What immune response?"

"Say, organ transplantation."

An amused look flashed across her sister's face. "You've been doing your homework, Milly." She thought about it for a minute. "You've got a point. That's the one thing that really cripples quality of life even in successful transplant patients."

"What about the venom? Its immunological qualities. Remember that girl Zoë slept with?"

"Yeah. Good thing her parents weren't keen to nose about the exact nature of the relationship." But she shook her head. "It's pretty weak tea. Even concentrated. A mild allergic response, yes. It's not going to touch a real autoimmune disease like lupus."

"Graft versus host?"

"GVHD? Not a chance."

So it was back to the virus. "What about the genome? The genes that keep us living?"

Kammy laughed. "My God, Milly. You really are keen to monetize this investment of yours."

Milada answered with a nonchalant shrug. "It's what I do."

"You know," Kammy said slowly, "you might have something there." She rested her elbows on the counter and tilted her head to the side. "Yes, that just might work. Sneak random samples into the database tagged as anonymous donors."

She stared vacantly off into space. Milada could practically hear the gears turning inside her head. "Allergies. IgE-receptor interaction. That's a good place to start. Specific to the genome but abstract in the application. Start with the nuts and bolts, not the whole bloody car. Build from the ground up. Go for the universal applications. And no trail of breadcrumbs to backtrack from *there* to *here*." She poked herself in the chest. "That way we can reference it as public data. Can't exactly run around calling it some magical Romanian elixir from the old country. The FDA's funny about that."

She got out her cell phone and keyed another memo to herself. "And there is a cancer angle," she said, as much to herself as to Milada. "Dendritic cell immunotherapy. A long way down the road, but worth exploring."

"How much farther down the road?"

"A decade."

Milada stared at her sister for a long moment. She couldn't keep the thought out of her head: *Jennifer can't wait that long.*

Kammy tucked her phone back into her waistband and spun around in the chair. She peered down at the family room. "Hey, you got cable?" She slid off the stool and skipped down to the family room and found the remote. The television came on to CNBC. Kammy sat back on the couch. That was when she saw the Triple Combination sitting on the coffee table.

"What's this?"

"Mormon scriptures. Troy gave it to me. He was my date, if you recall."

"How'd that turn out?"

"Not exactly a disaster, but close enough. He's a rather charming young man in his own naïve way."

"In other words, he had no intention of sleeping with you."

"Most definitely not."

Kammy laughed. "See, Garrick's never wrong about stuff like this. Two cheers for strong moral fiber."

The late-night repeat of the Donny Deutsch show came on. He was interviewing Eric Schmidt of Google. Kammy said, "You hear about Uncle Frank's latest business scheme?"

Milada groaned. She hadn't, and she didn't want to know.

"Some green-energy investment business he's starting with Alan Ridgeway."

"Frank is a never-ending train wreck in slow motion."

"You're the one always harping on us to do something *productive* with our lives. Frank finally took it to heart. Monkey see, monkey do."

"Exactly."

"I don't know. Maybe being a fun guy to be around counts as leading a productive life."

"Maybe."

Kammy flipped through the channels until she found Letterman. They sat there and watched the last half-hour of the show. It occurred to Milada that since coming to Utah she had seen more of Kammy than in the entire year before. Being strangers in this strange land together had made them sisters again. She didn't want the relationship to end.

Chapter 34

It's always darkest before the dawn

RACHEL SAT IN THE HOSPITAL ROOM watching her daughter. She'd brought along another Anastasia book, *Anastasia's Chosen Career*. In a moment of honest introspection, she would admit to liking the books because she pictured Anastasia and Sam, Anastasia's precocious little brother, as she wished to picture Laura and Jennifer: alive and well in a better and safer world.

Veralee strode into the cubical on her morning rounds. Seeing Rachel with the book, she said, "Oh, don't stop on my account. I'm sure Jenny's looking forward to it. Aren't you, Jenny?" She set to checking the lines and monitors and recording the data for the day's charts.

Sufficiently goaded, Rachel opened the book and began reading. She completed three chapters before having to leave in order to get home before Laura did.

"A moment, Sister Forsythe," Veralee called out, catching up with her in the lobby.

"What is it?" Rachel said. Almost automatically she checked for her purse, thinking she had left something behind.

"I'm sure it's nothing," Veralee said. Yet she lowered her voice and drew Rachel aside with an air of professional discretion. "Suanne on the night shift says that a woman's been coming up to the unit the last couple of nights and sitting with Jennifer."

"Sitting with her?"

"I never saw her before this week. She brings work with her, like from the office. She always asks how Jennifer is doing. She'll sit in the room for several hours, sometimes till very late. I figured she must have the doctor's permission to stay after visiting hours. I guess no one's thought to question her. But I thought I should ask, just the same."

"Do you mean an attractive young woman about my height, well dressed, platinum blonde, very light skin—"

"Why, yes, that's how Su described her. Do you know her?"

"She's—a friend of the family."

"It seems she cares about Jenny very much."

"Yes," Rachel said, and she was surprised to hear herself say it. "Yes, she does."

And yet she also felt a flurry of fear in her heart.

Wednesday afternoon Rachel received the call she had been waiting for. The call came from the High-Risk Leukemia Clinic at the Huntsman Cancer Institute, asking if she and her husband could meet with Dr. Ingebretsen at the hospital the next day. There was nothing unusual about the request. They regularly met with the good doctor for progress reports on Jennifer's condition.

Thursday at ten, the doctor found them at Jennifer's bedside and led them back to his office. He seated himself behind his desk, a judge shielded behind the great bar of medical justice. He examined Jennifer's charts, raising his head to peer through the bottom lenses of his bifocals. Then he put the charts down, adjusted his glasses, and cleared his throat.

"Jennifer rallied there for a few days."

Rachel closed her eyes and opened them. The past tense in the statement flashed in her brain like a neon warning sign. She clenched her hand in David's grasp.

"Her FDP levels are rising again. Her absolute neutrophil count is below five hundred. The latest bone marrow smear was not promising." He stopped and cleared his throat. "At this point, I'm not convinced—"

"Another transplant," Rachel offered, her voice trembling.

But the horrible man insisted on completing the sentence he'd started. "At this point, I'm not convinced that another transplant would help."

Other than his solemn, practiced gravity, no hint of emotion shadowed his voice. He delivered Jennifer's death sentence like a black-robed judge.

They'd driven to the hospital separately. David had to get back to work. What he really had to do was get away from the hospital, Rachel sensed. He had to get away from *her*.

"I was sure she was doing better," Rachel said.

He agreed without words, dutifully. She knew it was out of duty. He kept a stiff upper lip as well as any of his stolid British forebears. Whenever Laura got into a rage he'd remind her, "Comes from your side of the family. Those rambunctious Celts."

The wisdom in her husband's silence said that there were better ways for a child to leave mortality than in this half-comatose state, her tiny body ravaged by cancer. And then the chemo. And then the radiation, the bone marrow transplant, and doses of methotrexate and steroids that would have brought a full-grown man to his knees. Was it any wonder that her daughter chose to remain in this twilight of sleep?

But failure was not an option. "We should get a second opinion," Rachel said.

"A second opinion?" David repeated in an incredulous tone that she hadn't heard before but had been a long time coming. "We're into *double digits* when it comes to second opinions!"

They had been of one mind through the worst of it. They had borne the burden together. In his own way David had mourned when she mourned, comforted her when she stood in need of comfort. He had never mentioned the cost financially or emotionally, had never complained or protested.

He was getting to the end of that rope.

"We can't give up!"

"There is a difference between giving up and facing reality."

Rachel followed him down to the parking garage. David's voice echoed with uncharacteristic force in the cool, gray catacombs.

"If there's something more we can do—"

"Rachel, that's not the point. There will *always* be something more we can do. Jenny's not a *plant*. We're not winning points for simply keeping her *alive* another day."

Rachel glared at him. "*I'm* the one who's been with her every day." Meaning that his job and bishopric duties were more important than his own flesh and blood. "She's still our daughter. She's still Jennifer. She still *here*. It's *our* job to sacrifice for her, not the other way around."

That's not what he meant, of course. When he got to the end of his rope, she'd be there to hang him with it.

"But when is enough enough?" David asked plaintively.

It was the one question Rachel could not answer. Instead she said, "Milada's sister."

"Who?"

"Milada's sister is a doctor at St. Jude Children's Research Hospital in New York." Miraculously this tidbit of information came back to her now. "We could ask her. Maybe she knows about new, experimental treatments."

"Rachel—" David threw up his arms in frustration and laced his fingers across the top of his head. He had run out of words, she sensed, to express the futility of these suggestions without deliberately wounding her. Finally he turned and asked, "Does she even *work* in oncology?"

Rachel didn't know.

That was how the argument ended, how their arguments usually ended: with sufficient doubt raised in her mind and sufficient wordless frustration clouding his. A perfunctory kiss and he drove off, probably with a great sense of relief.

Rachel returned to Jennifer's hospital room. She was so accustomed to the aberrant world in which their daughter existed that she no longer felt comfortable in reality.

Chapter 35

She knows how to play rough

WHEN MILADA ARRIVED AT LOVERIDGE & ASSOCIATES on Friday morning, a thin nine-by-twelve envelope was waiting for her. The envelope label said LIGHTNING EXPRESS COURIERS, a local messenger service. The return address said WYLDE MEDICAL INFORMATICS. She placed it unopened in her attaché case and continued down the hallway to the conference room to watch the final act of the little Off Broadway melodrama she and Garrick had orchestrated.

WMI had been losing steam all week on the New York Stock Exchange. Today was the day Garrick intended to deliver the coup d'état. The show would close with a bang.

And yet she found herself somehow sad — or perhaps regretful — about what they were about to do. Garrick, her Henry Higgins, had taken this flower girl of a security and turned it into a grand duchess. But the gulf between the company's valuation and its fundamentals had become unbridgeable. The girl was loveable because everybody loved her. Now the midnight hour approached, and it was time for the horse-drawn carriage to turn back into a pumpkin.

The girl's jealous suitors, when the object of their affection had lost favor in the others' eyes, would regret they ever knew her. And thus would they miss the deeper qualities the modest lass possessed. So it was not *schadenfreude* that prompted a small smile of reassurance on Milada's part.

Garrick's strategy was a simple one: he would come to a sudden realization, throw up his hands in disgust, and stalk off the trading floor — or rather, do their digital equivalents. But he'd been practicing for several centuries and had gotten adept at throwing financial temper tantrums when it suited the goals of DEI.

The NYSE was bullish that morning, but Garrick treated WMI

like the scariest of bears. The more experienced market makers soon took notice. They were bearing down on a sizeable iceberg, and three-quarters of it was buried beneath dark, cold water. They took a hard look at its PE and started to sell.

Every time the stock hit a support level, Garrick rotated his orders to sell at market, a move interpreted in the pits as a move of pure desperation. The Damoclean sword fell. Day traders used to treading in shallow waters at once found themselves in the deep end of the ocean. The price and volume curves took off in a V-formation.

At two-thirty New York time, the stampede seemed to ease. The charts leveled off. In the boardroom at Loveridge & Associates, Milada brought up the real-time price/volume graphs on her laptop. She smiled to herself. The stock had hit an air pocket. Sell volume had outstripped buy volume. There were no bids, the worst possible thing that could happen to a stock. The market makers, day traders, elves and technicians, the portfolio managers, anybody with a position in the company—including a great many people who had no idea what the company did but had bought heavily in the run-up—perched in front of their NASDAQ Level II screens and held their collective breath.

They could only hold their breath so long. They all gasped together. WMI dropped like a rock. A thrown rock, to be sure, gliding down in a gentle curve, sinking slowly at first and then accelerating under the growing grip of gravity. Now the margin calls started kicking in, and the real carnage began.

Wylde bounced to the top of the most-active charts, a foreboding achievement for a small-cap stock. When the markets closed at four-thirty Eastern Daylight Time, it had bottomed out at 11 and recovered to 12.125.

Milada waited for the West Coast satellite feed of the *Nightly Business Report* to call Garrick. WMI led both the NASDAQ Actives and Big Movers charts. As the graphics flashed on the screen, the anchor provided commentary with the manner of a sports announcer running through the box scores: "Wylde Medical Informatics lost two-thirds of its value this week, dropping from forty to a tick over twelve. The sell-off is widely attributed to comments made late last week by CEO Darren Wylde, rejecting a possible takeover bid by DEI, one of Wall Street's consistently underrated high-tech investment firms."

Garrick was at dinner when he answered the phone. She could hear in the background the chime of silverware on fine china, the reverent, dignified commotion of waiters and busboys at work. *La Grenouille* on Fifty-Second, she guessed.

"Hi, Milly," said Garrick. He said to his dining companion, "It's Milly."

"Hi, Milly," said Jane.

Garrick said, "You enjoy our little performance today?"

"I've been watching the Wall Street wrap-up. You could have been a tad more subtle, Garrick."

"I tried, I tried. But that's what makes this economy such a wonderful thing. You get to go bankrupt with such speed and expedition. No helpless flopping about. I'd hate to be that Wylde chap right now. His board is going to have him for breakfast, lunch, and dinner."

"Especially when you consider that the board consists mostly of his kids."

"You can be mean, Milly."

"What is our position in the company?"

"I bought in heavily at the end, moved us to just over half of outstanding."

"What about capital gains?"

"Did my best to break even."

"Good. I don't want you getting arrested on me."

"Hey, not a worry, Milly. The Feds love me. I never make money except when I'm supposed to. Where do we go from here?"

"Twelve is a generous market valuation. The stock should lose a few more points on momentum next week. But that's where we'll start the negotiations."

"Will do."

"Let me speak to Jane."

Garrick passed the phone across the table. Jane said, "Hello, Milly."

"Jane, when's the last time we asked for a meeting with Mr. Wylde?"

"Last Wednesday, if memory serves."

"So he knows where to find us."

"He certainly does. Anything else?"

"What's Zoë been up to?"

"Hasn't gotten herself into trouble. Recently."

"Good. How about Frank?"

"Still jazzed about this green energy thing he's got going with Alan Ridgeway. Ethanol and fuel cells are where it's at these days."

"Is he serious about that? A little learning is indeed a dangerous thing." Milada sighed. "And Alan Ridgeway? What's in it for him? God, I thought it was all talk, another one of Frank's phases. At any rate, make sure Muriel signs off on the books before anybody at the SEC starts asking for them."

"Sure, as soon as she can *find* the books. Oh, Garrick wants to say something."

She handed back the phone. Garrick said, "It's been a good day, Milly. Go get yourself something to eat."

Milada laughed. "I had a very interesting repast this past weekend."

"You must tell me all about it."

"I'll think it over."

"You do know how to keep a man intrigued."

"You'll have to settle for Jane in the meantime."

"I'm intriguing her right and left."

She heard Jane laugh. A pang of loneliness struck hard at Milada's heart. In that moment she wished more than anything she were back in New York, sharing the table with Jane and Garrick, her two best friends in the world.

"Take care, Garrick."

"Cheerio, Milly."

Milada hung up the phone, took off the headset, and hit the intercom button. "Karen, call Executive Ground Transport and have Steven sent over. Hold my calls. I'm done for the day."

Chapter 36

Women are like wasps in their anger

RACHEL STOOD AT THE DOOR to Jennifer's hospital room, waiting for Milada to glance up and see her. She felt a pang of guilt in her heart for having burdened a complete stranger with her own family's tragedy. She'd been expecting drive-by charity. Milada actually *caring* hadn't been part of the equation. But now that empathy seemed like the single remaining thread of the lifeline keeping Rachel's head above water.

Rachel sat down across the hospital bed from her. Milada casually retrieved a nine-by-twelve envelope from the side table and returned it to her attaché. Something to do with her business, no doubt. Milada had fewer qualms about revealing the impossible things about her life than the mundane.

Rachel was no different. The more impossible her beliefs, the more bold she was in her beliefs and the more willing to claim a knowledge of *things not seen*.

But now a black tide of doubt spilled into her thoughts.

Again, in a moment of honest introspection, she would admit that Laura was right about her sister: *She just lies there.* What drew her time and again to this sterile room, what kept her in the uncomfortable plastic chair by her daughter's bed, was a daydream, a hope, a fantasy that in the next moment Jennifer was going to open her eyes and recognize her and say, "Hi, Mom."

And she would be there to take her in her arms and comfort her. The thought alone brought tears to her eyes.

When that moment didn't come, there was the next moment, the next moment in which everything would change, and then the moment after that. It was pure hope, it was faith without works. But it kept her more alive than anything else she knew.

She said to Milada, "Do you need a ride home?"

• • •

Rachel couldn't think of anything else to keep the conversation going. She really did need to learn more about business and finance. There was no telling when such knowledge could come in handy.

When she pulled into Milada's driveway, she put the Odyssey in park and turned off the engine.

"Thank you for the ride," Milada said with perfunctory courteousness.

Rachel hesitated a second and then got out as well. As she came around the front of the car, Milada gave her a disconcerted—even annoyed—look that Rachel pretended not to see. She hated presuming on other people. But desperation was a powerful thing. It drove Saul to Endor, and it drove her here. The briefest memory of Jennifer lying comatose in her hospital bed eviscerated any second thoughts.

The last straw. This was it. She would seize it and let it go and let the wind carry the chaff where it may.

The air inside the house was still warm from the heat of the day. Rachel closed the door behind her. Milada turned on the kitchen light and then the cooler fan, filling the dark, empty quiet with soft incandescent light and hushed white noise.

"Jennifer was doing better for a while."

Milada didn't answer.

Rachel could no longer be bothered with subtleties. She said in a pleading whisper, "If Jennifer were like you, she wouldn't die—"

"The infection alone would kill her."

"The cancer will."

"Does your faith thrive on failure, Rachel? Pascal's wager is the rationalization of gamblers everywhere. God plants the seed, and we do everything in our power to make it grow. He gets the praise if it lives. We take the blame if it dies. How is that fair?"

Rachel stared back at her. She didn't know the answer.

"You asked me before, so I shall tell you: I am the creation of a virus. A carrier, a host, or perhaps I have become the parasite itself. Genetically speaking I am hardly human. A medical curiosity. There is nothing miraculous about me."

"Then why do you care?" Rachel asked desperately.

"Do you want the truth? Then let me tell you about my family. I have three fathers—the man who gave me life, the devil who gave me eternal life, and the *paterfamilias* who forced upon me a life worth living. If Jennifer became like me, whose blood would flow in her veins? Whose daughter would she be? Tell me that is something you could live with."

She pushed Rachel out of the way and descended the stairs to the basement. But Rachel knew how to deal with recalcitrance. She had a teenager in the house, for Pete's sake. Most of her life her brothers had been bigger and stronger than she was. She was the eldest, and she could goad them into doing things her way. She could be insistent when she wanted to, stubborn to the point of belligerence. It was not something she was proud of.

"What do you want, Rachel?"

The tone of indifferent exasperation in Milada's voice only stoked Rachel's fury. "*Jennifer wouldn't turn out like you!*" she shouted, the words erupting out of all her shattered dreams and wounded pride.

Milada whirled about, eyes blazing, the tendons in her neck tight with fury. Rachel quailed. She retreated to the hallway, retreated until her heels clicked against the baseboard and her head thumped against the sheet rock. Milada's right hand flew to her throat, pinning her like a butterfly to the wall. Rachel did not doubt that if Milada closed her fingers her spine would snap in two.

The flesh between Milada's thumb and forefinger pressed so evenly against Rachel's larynx that she was not conscious of the force Milada was exerting until her lungs convulsed from lack of air. Instinctually she grabbed at Milada's forearm. She might as well have been grasping an iron rod.

The pupils in Milada's pale eyes dilated, widening into ovals. Her lips parted, revealing the tips of the needle-sharp fangs behind her white incisors. Rachel felt the raw scream of anger coming. She tried again to push the hand away. Black splotches bloomed in the borders of her vision.

At the last moment Milada held back, her voice emerging in a strained shout, still loud in Rachel's ears. "That man came from going to and fro in the earth, and from walking up and down in it. *I was twelve years old.* When did I fear God for naught? I did as I was told and did it well. Tell me, where are my fourteen-thousand sheep and my six-thousand camels and my seven sons and three daughters? *Where?*"

Milada's voice broke. The ferocity in her countenance faded as suddenly as it had appeared, replaced by a softer expression, hurt, almost, by what she had been driven to do. She walked away.

Rachel slid to the floor, gasping for breath, her limbs twitching, the blood pounding in her veins. Her hand went to her throat. Milada had not, she was sure, even bruised the skin. A storm of emotions kaleidoscoped through her mind. Rachel started to laugh and then to sob.

She pushed herself off the floor. When she got to the top of the stairs, Milada was sitting at the kitchen counter staring at a glass of red wine. She didn't look up. Rachel steadied herself. She took a breath and let it out.

"You may have her."

After all you can do. It would be impossible for her to do more or to offer more. Had Milada asked for her life in exchange, she would have laid her own body on the table. But Milada didn't want her life.

Now Milada looked at her.

Rachel said, "Hannah asked for a child, and when she was blessed with a son, she took him to Eli to raise as his own."

Milada looked away. Bitterness filled her voice. "*Therefore I have sworn unto the house of Eli that the iniquity of Eli's house shall not be purged with sacrifice nor offering.*"

"Please. Surely the Lord forgave Eli for the life he gave Samuel."

"Do I look like a mother to you?" Milada smiled wryly and shook her head in disbelief. "Christians claim to believe in eternal life. So why are you so afraid of death, Rachel?"

The question rocked her back on her feet. Her heart reacted before her mind could respond, before her mouth could answer. Rachel clenched her hands and teeth but couldn't restrain the tears coursing down her cheeks. The reason was so very simple, and yet she had never articulated it aloud before. "Because I'll miss her when she's gone. I'll regret all that she could have been." She drew a great sobbing breath. "I'm sorry, Milada. I shouldn't have—" She turned toward the front door.

Milada came to her feet. "Rachel, stay. Don't go home like this. Sit, have something to eat. I'll order out."

"No. I'm sorry. I shouldn't have in the first place. It was my fault." She took a deep breath and somehow managed to maintain her composure until she'd made it back to the car and driven the hundred yards up the street to her own driveway.

She sat numbly in the driver's seat, staring through the windshield at the back of the dark garage. A few minutes ago Milada could have killed her. She wouldn't have, Rachel was certain, but she could have. Rachel had come close to bodily injury before in her life. She could think of a dozen times as kids when one of Carl's stupid stunts could have put them all six feet under. But she had never looked at death directly, stared into its eyes, and seen embodied there the raw power and will to extinguish life.

"Rachel?" said David. His voice brought her back to her senses.

He opened her driver's-side door. As she climbed out, her limbs gave way. David reached out and caught her. The dam broke. She collapsed in a flood of tears. His arms encircled her, bearing her up, protecting her, promising her eternal refuge against the storm.

Rachel wept until she had cried herself out, and then she rested her head against his shoulder for a long time. "I just guess everything finally hit home," she said, and he nodded. *Many are the plans in a man's heart, but it is the Lord's purpose that prevails.* He understood. He was a very understanding man, and she loved him for it.

Walking back to the house, his arm firmly about her waist, she felt the weight lifting off her shoulders and rising into the night sky. After all that anguish, she somehow felt better about the world and her place in it. And much worse about Milada.

Chapter 37
Hell is paved with good intentions

Milada had never before asked herself why she had never wanted a child.

She'd never asked because the answer was so obvious. Because the hands of her biological clock turned no more quickly than she aged, no more quickly than a year every century. Because by the most precise measurement Kammy could devise—the length of their chromosomes' telomeres—she was twenty years old, and twenty-year-olds did not quit power-suit careers and empty out their savings accounts at fertility clinics. Because it was impossible for a twenty-year-old to believe that she'd ever turn forty and that at forty she would give anything to have gotten knocked up at twenty.

And because she could not. Simple as that. Because her eggs were all dead. Dead as doornails. Dead for centuries. The virus had seen to that.

She could adopt. Michael had no opinion on the matter, if only because the matter never came up. She'd informally adopted Jane. Jane was *almost* a member of the family. When Milada first hired her, they had looked the same age. Now Jane was in her late thirties, an older sister. Soon, she would become like Milada's mother, then her grandmother. Duffy, Michael's manservant, was heavily into late middle age, graying, paunchy. And because she saw him and Michael less often these days, with every encounter came that shock of realization that humans changed so much over time, grew old, and eventually died.

It was a hard-enough fact to face between employer and employee. Between immortal parent and mortal child, it would be intolerable. So what explained her attraction to this child?

The elevator doors opened on the transplant unit. Milada

approached the nurse's station. "Good evening, Doctor," the nurse said.

Milada smiled. She hadn't said she was a doctor but had allowed a casual touch and a practiced air of authority to dissemble for her. "The charts for Jennifer Forsythe?"

The nurse delivered them to her. Milada flipped through the folder. She had studied up on the subject enough to know what the numbers meant: FDP up, ANC down. She nodded and returned the charts.

The nurse offered hopefully, "Dr. Ingebretsen still thinks there might be reason to hope."

Milada nodded. Rachel was right. They were all quietly hammering nails into her coffin.

She sat in Jennifer's hospital room feeling enormously depressed. What was the real reason Kammy would not see patients? She wouldn't risk accidentally exposing children to the virus in her blood. No, not by accident. The dangers of infection were simply not that great. Or perhaps she felt the tug of the same temptation — the temptation to do what Rakoczi had done and what Milada now thought of doing.

Milada turned Jennifer's gene survey over in her hands. The single-page printout was worn and wrinkled from being repeatedly taken out and stuffed back in, but she read it yet again: *Jennifer was positive for the CCR5-D32 mutation on both alleles.* Milada knew she had to destroy the printout and forget it existed. But she held onto it like a talisman, as if the paper and cardboard would speak to her and tell her what to do next.

Her faith in the intangible was as foolish as Rachel's.

If I'd only acted upon this information the first time, Jennifer might have been strong enough —

She shook her head. *No.* That was Rachel's sense of desperation insinuating itself into her rational mind. Milada knew what it was like to act in true desperation.

And yet — Jennifer was going to die anyway. *I cannot change the past, but this child's future I could.* Milada ran her hand lightly along the child's fragile arm, her fingers coming to a rest at the bend of her small elbow. She had never infected another human being, but she knew how it was done, having observed Rakoczi's failed efforts often enough: drive the tip of her fangs down into her gums, wait for the capillary action to draw the blood into the hollow channels, then find the vein and —

"Milada."

Startled, Milada glanced up, her heart pounding madly, tasting Jennifer's blood on her tongue, mingling with her own. There was nobody else in the room. Her body trembling unnaturally, she stole to the door and peeked out. The hallway was quiet and dusky, the only occupant at the nursing station absorbed in a novel.

Milada returned to her seat. A child's voice said again, "Milada."

Her gaze fell on the hospital bed. The child looked at her, her eyes wide and clear. Young eyes, yet eyes banked with ancient fires. Something like her sisters' eyes, yet pure. She knew the difference. Her sisters' eyes, her own eyes, had long since been defiled.

"Jennifer—" Milada gasped, grasping the bed railing so tightly it began to deform under the pressure.

"What did my mother ask you to do?"

Milada shook her head.

A note of severity crept into Jennifer's voice. "Don't hide from me what she said."

"She asked for you to live."

"And so you have done what is good in your eyes."

The question didn't sound like a question to Milada, but the reality of what she was saying suddenly overwhelmed her. "*Oh, God,*" she moaned, covering her face with her hands. "*Oh, God.*" A plea, or a statement of horror. She *didn't*—she was sure she hadn't—but when she looked again, the two needle pricks on the child's wrist had already closed, blending in among all the other wounds she had suffered.

"Why?" the child asked.

"You were going to die."

"Is that what troubles you? Why life is given to the bitter of soul—"

"—whose way is hidden and whom God has hedged in."

"If he wills that you tarry till he comes, what is that to thee?"

"What is it to me?"

"Perhaps a time to prepare to meet God. Perhaps you need more time than most. Perhaps you needed some help."

Milada almost laughed. "If God exists, it is not a meeting I look forward to. And neither should he."

Jennifer smiled. "Perhaps if you spent less time trying to atone for the past and more time trying to do right by the present." The girl turned away, as if listening to a person speaking to her on the other side of the bed. She turned back, her eyes sparkling. "The old man—there's no need to fight him any more. Give him what he wants, and he will be happy. And so will Kamilla."

She smiled again, a friendly, reassuring smile, as if they had known each other for ages, and settled her head on the pillow. "I'm glad we finally got to meet, Milada." She closed her eyes. "God never walks away from an honest wager. Tell my mother that. And remember what you said in turn, Milada."

And then she was still. Very still.

Milada blinked. "Jennifer," she said. The child did not respond. "Jennifer!" Her voice tore from her throat.

The desk nurse leaned over the counter and peered through the glass at her. A candy striper paused in the doorway. "Is something the matter?"

"Is something the matter? The child was conscious!" Milada gesticulated wildly at the comatose body. "She spoke to me!"

The woman stood there like a post, stunned.

Milada roared, "Do something!"

Suanne Lane rushed into the room and scanned the monitors. "Who's on call?" she barked, taking her stethoscope from around her neck.

"Dr. Cheng."

"Page him and Dr. Ingebretsen." She said to Milada, "Ma'am, you're going to have to leave. *Now*."

Milada nodded. She wandered out into the lobby and stood there, not knowing where to go, not knowing what to do.

Chapter 38

Sorrow is always dry

RACHEL AWOKE. THE BEDROOM WAS DARK. She felt a draft. The bedroom door was open. "David," she said. He stirred beside her, and she raised herself to a sitting position. She opened her eyes wider and looked again for what she thought she had seen in the first place.

Laura. It was not a dream. Laura stood at the foot of the bed, wisps of her hair backlit against the window curtains. "Laura?" said her father. "What—"

Rachel put her hand to his mouth. Laura never sleepwalked, but her mother could tell she was not awake. Her eyes stared. Her mouth opened and closed, as if she was trying to say something but had forgotten how to speak.

Rachel whispered, "What is it, honey?"

Laura's consciousness latched onto her mother's voice. Her body stirred to respond. "It's Jennifer. She was in my room. Just now. She says she loves all of us very much, but she has to leave us."

The glaze left her eyes. She saw her mother and ran to her. Rachel swept the sobbing child into her arms. She could not remember the last time her daughter cried.

Down in the kitchen, the phone rang.

The traffic light flashed to yellow, to red. David stopped well before the crosswalk. Rachel bit her tongue. *There's nobody here! It's four-thirty in the morning! Run the damned light!* But that wasn't David. Five minutes, ten minutes, what difference did it make? Would her being there make the doctors any more brilliant? *Yes, it would.* Being there always made the difference. As long as she was there, they could raise Lazarus from the dead.

You want to see your daughter, or you want a chauffeured visit to the

ER? That's what David would tell her — if David was Carl, that is — and Carl would be right. Finally, they were on West Medical Drive. David let Rachel off at the main entrance and turned to park.

Rachel charged through the reception area. She ran up the open staircase. She burst into the bone marrow transplant unit. She didn't stop to wash her hands first. Jennifer's room was empty. She whirled on the desk nurse. "Where is she? Where's my daughter?" Her voice came close to shrieking.

She was intercepted by Suanne Lane. "Jennifer's in critical care." She took Rachel by the arm. "This way."

Back down the hall, through the two sets of pneumatic doors, into the Critical Care Unit. Into the machine. It was a machine, a living machine, and her daughter was caught in the center of it, in the web of an enormous mechanical spider, her body lit up in blue-white light, tubes and wires running in and out of her as if she were some kind of disassembled robot, some half-human android. Small throw pillows were strangely packed around her body, and medical personnel swarmed around her.

The nurse left her there, just inside the doors. Where was she going? *Come back!*

A woman stood outside the cubicle. Milada. She turned, her face almost transparent in the halogen light. She grabbed the hand of a passing intern, spoke tersely to him. The intern nodded and waded into the press of doctors and technicians around Jennifer's bed and found Dr. Ingebretsen. Dr. Ingebretsen looked and saw Rachel. His face grayed. He nodded to the intern and worked his way around the gurney and toward her. He was not in a hurry.

Laura and her father came through the doors behind her, arriving at her side the same time the doctor did. Dr. Ingebretsen said, "Her temperature spiked about an hour ago. Most likely an opportunistic infection, a risk equal to GVHD in cases like this. We're doing our best to cool her down."

"Ice packs?"

Dr. Ingebretsen nodded. "Low tech but effective."

Rachel closed her eyes and held her breath. But nothing would change. The chaff caught the breeze and whirled away, dust in the wind. When Rachel opened her eyes and glanced over her shoulder, Milada was still there. She had not moved in all that time. Their eyes met. Milada tore her gaze away.

"Milada—" Rachel called.

Milada pretended not to hear.

Chapter 39

Work is love made visible

MILADA HEADED FOR THE ELEVATORS.

After four hundred years, the seemingly infinite depths of human sentiment still perplexed her. To truly understand human suffering was beyond her. It was safer not to tempt feelings she had never felt. The safest response was to ignore everything.

Ignore what I have just done. In her lifetime she had broken every commandment in the book. But never before had she tempted God. She felt His eyes upon her and had to get herself anyplace else but here.

Her phone hummed in her pocket. Jane. At this hour, it must be important. Over the past four centuries, if nothing else, she had learned the business of business. What she'd told Troy was the truth. This was her higher purpose, her righteous calling, her contribution to human civilization. The one thing she could leave behind when and if her time ever came.

Not answering the phone, she took the stairs at a brisk pace, almost running, her shoes tapping against the skid-resistant concrete steps. When she reached the main entrance, she switched her phone off standby and autodialed New York.

"Finally!" Jane exclaimed. "I was beginning to wonder where you were."

"Beg pardon, Jane. I've been away all night."

"I know it's an awkward time to call. But we just got a message from Mr. Wylde. He says he's going to be at his farm in Wallsburg. I gather it's not too far from Salt Lake. If you want to see him, he'll be there today. He's returning to his ranch in Idaho this evening."

"Did he leave a number?"

"Nope. Either you show up or you don't, that's the gist of things. I'll fax directions to your home number."

"Then that's what I shall do."

Thanks to daylight savings time and the approaching fall, morning hadn't broken by the time she got back to the house. She reached Steven and told him to pick her up at eight. Did he know where Wallsburg was? Not a problem, he said.

She showered and dressed. Then stopped dressing. Wylde was going to be at his farm, or so Jane had said. She should not go there in business attire. Mr. Wylde would measure a man by his work and by his manner when surrounded by other men at work. He'd want to see if she tiptoed around the cow patties and balked at the sight of an untethered horse. Knew a prairie-dog hole from a fairway divot. And didn't go all Greenpeace on him when he took out the trusty Winchester and blew the little critter away.

What kind of a farm was this, anyway? He had definitely given himself the home court advantage.

Jeans and a white shirt—that worked. A white shirt by itself provided too little protection from the sun. She added a denim jacket. A pair of tan Fieldstones—it paid to keep a few stereotypes salted away in the back of her mind. A Stetson? No, that'd be trying too hard. The fedora—it said she would go along, she would conform, but she would not condescend.

She examined the results. She looked like a dude ranch tourist, but she didn't look stupid.

Lastly, the sun block. If she were lucky, he'd show her the spread from behind the double-pane windows of his palatial—she hoped—cabin. In case not, she'd better use SPF 60. It went on like Elmer's glue. Not too thick, or she'd end up looking like a lifeguard.

And her gloves.

She clumped up to the kitchen in her Fieldstones. Where was the Wylde file? Where was her attaché? *Damn*, she'd left it in the hospital room. What did she have in it? Mostly the Wylde Medical papers. The attaché would be turned into the lost and found, not the SEC, thank goodness. She took a deep breath and let it out.

The doorbell rang. That'd be Steven. She checked the fax for the directions, as Jane promised. Steven was waiting at the door. She said, "Where is this Wallsburg, again?"

"Off Deer Creek Reservoir before you get to Heber."

She nodded, as if she knew what he was talking about.

Steven drove west on 209, picked up I-15 going south. Milada sat in the back seat, primly composed. The jeans were not exactly comfortable. She felt like a girl going on a date. She'd worn herself out getting ready, and the date had yet to begin. On top of that, she'd had hardly any sleep thanks to the damned kid. *God, that was a mistake.* She had known it going in. The whole Wylde deal would have been wrecked if Jane had missed her.

The highway curved up the shoulders of the bluff at the south end of the valley, past gravel pits and cement factories. Point of the Mountain, they called the bluff. The point was slowly being gnawed away by backhoes and conveyer belts. Down into Utah Valley. Hang gliders, their bright nylon wings catching the first slanting rays of sunlight, sailed off the lee edge of the bluff. Utah Lake lay ahead at two o'clock.

Steven took the North Orem exit, highway 189 east. A hospital on the left, school on the right, used car lot, grocery store, strip mall, block after block of residential housing. The steeples of the ubiquitous Mormon chapels poking up among the trees.

Down into the river bottoms. The banked four-lane highway swept into a jagged V in the mountainside. The highway followed the river up the canyon. The mountains rose up around them like skyscrapers, the canyon floor still shadowed, a slash of sunlight bright against the high northern walls.

Milada rolled down the window. The wind whipped against her face. A sign flashed by:

VIVIAN PARK
SOUTH FORK
HISTORIC RAILROAD

"Steven," she said, "pull off here."

The car bumped over a railroad crossing. Steven pulled into the parking lot. The tires crunched on loose gravel. "I'll be a few minutes only." Milada let herself out of the car, walked up the path, and found herself in a grove of trees at the edge of a pond.

What did the child say? *Give the old man what he wants.*

What did the old man want?

She leaned back her head, trying to remember. *He doesn't want to sell out.* Not the company. *His ideals.* All the reasons that had kept him going all these years, all the reasons that enough was never enough.

Milada opened her eyes. All around her the gray canyon walls shot up in vertical columns. A great calm descended upon her, like the calm she'd first felt at the manor house in Cheapside. She'd hid herself within the heavy stone walls, within the deep, damp darkness where God would never find her.

In that solitude she had shaped her atonement. It was there that she'd come to understand that the name Daranyi and its wealth were the only inheritances she could ever bequeath. Only this enterprise would grow with her, yield to her guidance and direction. She would ensure that her child would never die. The great estates of England would crumble around her, meet all the prosaic ends their founders feared. But Daranyi—*Daranyi would live forever.*

Wylde had sons and daughters, two dozen grandchildren. Fecundity that could found a nation. Or disperse a fortune to the four winds, grind diamonds into dust. What he wanted—more than any heavenly reward—was to know that his life just wasn't about the money. His death wouldn't just be about the dissipation of assets.

It was always about the money. But more than the money, what he did with it made all the difference. He had bought power, influence, and reputation and did what good he could in the world the best he knew how.

Now in his twilight years the old man had gathered his family around him, felt their love, and welcomed their affection. Yet he knew that none of them really understood what he had built or why it was so important to him. They wanted for nothing, including passions of their own. Had a son or daughter pursued some high-minded, impractical, or pointless cause, exhausted a fortune in pursuit of a political seat even, he'd willingly have let the coin spill through his fingers.

But he feared that all they really cared about was *comfort*—a bigger house, a better car, a higher standard of living. Liquidate his life's work for that? *Look at the roots,* Milada told herself. Look at where the tree took hold. The engineer was still at work on his Sistine Chapel, digging the foundations by hand. When he was gone, he wanted his life to say: *I made something, I created something, I left something real behind in the world.*

That assurance she understood, and that assurance she could give him.

Past the turnoff to Robert Redford's Sundance Resort, the road narrowed and serpentined along the northern wall of the canyon. Every mile or so along the route, the parking lane was crowded with SUVs and pickups, men in hip waders hauling fishing equipment from the trunks of their cars.

Fall descended as they climbed up through the Wasatch Range toward Heber Valley. An early frost had already painted the foothills with pointillist daubs of neon red and electric yellow. The highway turned across Deer Creek Dam, hugged the south rim of the reservoir. A sign pointed off the right: WALLSBURG.

The rolling brown hills were dotted with juniper and sagebrush. Farmhouses surrounded by thousand-acre spreads. Horses standing in open fields, a feed silo sheathed in corrugated tin.

It was like they had driven into western Oklahoma. A Mormon chapel stood on the left. They came to a crossroads scattered with a handful of houses and trees and sheds. The Round Valley Market, the post office, another chapel. Steven pulled into the church parking lot and examined Jane's instructions. He nodded to himself. Back on the road, he took the next right, a left, and a right. The road bordered a long rectangular field for almost a mile. Left onto a particular road.

"This is the place, I think."

He turned into an unpaved driveway and parked behind a Ford F-150 pickup with Idaho plates. Milada put on her hat and sunglasses. The sky overhead was a pure transparent blue. The sun itself seemed only an arm's length away.

The driveway ran alongside a simple A-frame cabin. A rusted-out Escort was parked on the lawn next to a GMC Sierra. An older Chevy sat on blocks in front of the garage, a hay tedder on the ground next to it.

Milada came around the corner of the house. A herd of—not horses—in the north paddock. In the field east, a good hundred yards off, a tractor hauled a hay rack. The man on the tractor saw her and waved, jumped down off the tractor. She might as well meet him halfway. Good thing she wore the Fieldstones.

She stepped into the raw sunlight, unfiltered by smog or haze. Her skin tingled. She lowered her head against the angle of the sun, as if striding against a driving rain. Chaff drifted up into her face, bringing with it the smell of earth and the last of the dew burning off the scattered hay left behind in the windrows.

She straightened as they met. He reached out a big hand. "Miss Daranyi."

"Mr. Wylde."

"Got to finish up these couple of rows. Then we'll have our meeting. That okay with you?"

"Perhaps it might go faster if I helped."

He didn't hide the dubious look in his eyes. "We're stacking hay, here. It's some heavy lifting."

"I did my share of field work when I was growing up."

"Well. Never would have guessed."

She smiled. "Most people don't."

She fell into step behind him, taking out her cell phone. She felt faintly ridiculous making a hundred-yard phone call. But it was preferable to turning around and marching all the way back. Or having Steven sit there blocking the driveway.

"Steven, we're going to be a couple of hours. If you've got someplace to go—"

"BYU's only a half-hour from here. I could go there to study."

"Do that. I'll call you." She folded up the cell phone.

They walked up to the hay rack. Darren Wylde said, "This here's Terry Lang."

A burly man in his early forties heaved a hay bale onto the bed of the hay rack. Milada stepped forward and shook his hand. He nodded, put his hands on his hips. "And his son Blake." The teenage boy waved from the bed of the hay rack. "Terry's got the hundred-fifty acres starting at the north road, leases another hundred of mine."

Milada assumed he'd already told them who she was. Darren Wylde climbed back on the tractor. "Blake, you got another pair of gloves for the lady?"

The boy reached down and tossed her a pair of heavy work gloves, stiff and creased across the palms. She put them over her gloves. Wylde jammed the tractor into gear. The hay rack lurched forward and then clunked along at walking speed.

Milada observed Terry Lang out of the corner of her eyes. He'd catch the baling wire, his hand even with the heel of his right boot, and lift as he stepped forward, letting gravity swing it forward, heaving the bale onto the bed of the rack, where Blake was stacking them.

She figured out the motion after a few tries and fell into step just behind the elder Lang. Darren Wylde watched her over his shoulder. He raised an eyebrow and nodded. She'd made an impression—the right one, she hoped. At the end of the row, he said, cranking the tractor around, "You might want to take off that jacket, Miss Daranyi. You're gonna give yourself sunstroke."

The sun was blazing down by now, all the more reason to leave on the jacket. Not taking the man's advice would require a suspicious amount of prevarication. Taking the man's advice would put her in good stead. So she took off the jacket and handed it to Blake, who hung it on the top spike on the rack.

They worked down the next row. "That should do it," said Wylde. He wheeled the tractor around and drove to the edge of the property line, marked by a line of oak and box elder. They offloaded the bales onto a round slab sheltered by a concrete umbrella.

"What you got there is a stressed rebar frame," explained Darren Wylde. "We poured her the same time we did the footings for the cabin. Hoisted her up with a hydraulic jack. Textbook structural engineering. Did it for my senior thesis." He said to the Langs, "Thanks, Terry, Blake. You need anything, let me know."

Father and son walked back to the driveway and drove off in the Sierra.

"Miss Daranyi—"

"Milada, please."

"I go by Jack. I guess you did grow up on a farm."

"The sisters at the orphanage believed we should earn our keep by the sweat of our brows."

"Where was that? You don't sound American. Sorry if that's not a good way to put it."

"Hungary. But I've been an American for at least a lifetime."

"We're all immigrants one way or another. C'mon, I'll show you the burros."

He stopped at a weeded-over garden. "Here we go. A few old carrots." He knocked off the dirt, gave her a bunch. When they approach the paddock, the burros came trotting over to the fence. "You can't ask for a better pack animal." He patted the muzzle. The huge ears swiveled from side to side like radar dishes. The other burros crowded in to get their fair share. Milada was glad she still had on the heavy gloves.

"We lend them out to the scout troops. Good camping in these hills here."

The carrots gone, they retreated to the porch. The old man shadowed his eyes and stared up at the sky. "Looks like a front's moving in."

Milada followed his gaze. A towering column of cumulonimbus advanced on the valley from the south. Not quickly enough. A wisp of cirrus momentarily dimmed the sun. Milada felt the refreshing shadow on her face.

Darren Wylde lowered his gaze and gestured expansively at his property. "We bought this land while we were going to the Y. Started off with a hundred acres. Had it in mind to build some equity, graduate with something in the pocket other than a diploma. Took us that long too. Dug the foundations, did all the framing ourselves. Then we liked it so much we couldn't bear to let it go."

Milada recalled her biographical notes. "You studied mechanical engineering."

"That's right. But when my dad died I took over the funeral home. There was just one at the time. I taught myself what I needed to know and grew the business. Then I ran into an old classmate of mine, Clayton Reid, about twenty years ago. He had a startup going out of the University of Utah School of Medicine and was looking for venture capital. Clayton knew the biology, I knew the tech, so we leveraged the business and here we are today."

He checked his watch. "Look at that, half past eleven. I caught some rainbow trout this morning. Thought I'd fry it up with a little rice. Come on in." He got up and opened the sliding glass doors.

It was pleasantly cool in the cabin. Wylde could not resist commenting on that fact. "Yep, these mountain valleys heat up fast and cool down fast. You see twenty, thirty below in the winter on a regular basis. I got high-R insulation in here"—he smacked the closest wall with the palm of his hand—"and double-glazed windows. I can heat her year round for a hundred dollars of Carbon County anthracite."

With that bit of show and tell, Darren Wylde disappeared into the kitchen.

Milada paused to take in the interior of the cabin. It was the definition of what antique dealers meant by "original condition." Nothing tattered, but well worn.

Wylde called from the kitchen, "If you need the bathroom, it's up the stairs and at the end of the hall."

The floor plan divided the cabin along the frame of the A. The living room faced north. The kitchen faced south. The staircase wound up to an open hallway, the bedrooms over the kitchen. A basketball hoop was nailed to the banisters. It'd probably been there forty years.

In the kitchen, Wylde had gutted and filleted the trout. A daub of butter melted in the frying pan. He tossed in a handful of mushrooms and sliced summer squash. A pot of rice bubbled away.

"Plates in the cupboard there," he said, with a nod of his head. "Silverware in the drawer next to the sink."

So Milada set the table. When the rice was just about ready, he fried up the trout, a few minutes on each side. He placed the frying pan on a hot pad on the table next to the rice. He couldn't find any napkins, so he tore a couple of sheets from a roll of paper towels.

They sat down. He said a quick grace and then served the trout. "Got yourself a bit of a sunburn there," he said. "On a clear day in these high, dry valleys, it's easy to overlook the UV."

"I don't get out much." Milada took a bite of the trout. "This is quite good."

"Keep it simple, and you can't go wrong." Then he said, "Seems you did some profit taking the other day."

"Do you believe your stock is worth forty dollars a share?"

"Of course not! But better if some people found out more gentle-like, not with an uppercut to the jaw. I've got too many relatives who think a stock certificate is money."

"My broker says we lost almost as much as we made."

"And acquired another ten percent of outstanding shares in the bargain. By my calculations, you could acquire us outright. You don't need me at this stage of the game. So I have to wonder what you're doing here."

"There's more to running a company than electing the board," she said with a small shrug. "And it's not always the CEO who's the problem."

"In any case, this CEO's not going to be around forever."

"My sister would run the company, meaning the primary WMI assets."

"Your sister?" Then he nodded. "She made quite an impression on Dr. Brickey."

"Kamilla has an M.D. in pediatrics and a Ph.D. in biochemistry."

"Impressive. But that's not all the company does."

"I've looked over the numbers. For a mortuary business of its size, you should be netting a good fifty percent more."

"There's no easier way to make good money in a bad way than with a funeral home, guilting people with a lot of grief in their hearts into burying a goodly part of their inheritance six feet under."

"I can respect that. Frankly, I have no plans of interfering with the operations of Wylde Funeral Homes as long as it earns its keep. I'm more interested in the potential of your genealogical database technology. The problem is, you're undercapitalized. The informatics business pays its own way, but there isn't enough left over to fund R&D without leveraging the mortuary business. You push one at the expense of the rest."

"I'm not arguing with you about that," said Wylde.

"So this is what I propose. We split off a tracking stock, call it Daranyi Medical Informatics."

"Like selling off the division."

"Yes, but not quite. It will still fall under our corporate umbrella. The Daranyi name will give you considerable leverage in the financial markets when it comes to raising new financing."

Wylde sat back in his chair and folded his hands on his stomach. He nodded. "Yes, I can see how that would work." He leaned forward. "You realize that what makes the data so valuable is its homegrown roots. Public domain genealogical records aren't enough. Getting the rights to the gene surveys requires a delicate touch and a lot of personal trust, the kind of thing easily lost in a business acquisition. Turning the hearts of the fathers to the children and the hearts of the children to their fathers, that's the way people around here see their genealogy."

"That's from Malachi, isn't it?"

Wylde smiled and nodded. "Every good Mormon knows it by heart."

Milada smiled as well. She'd made exactly the impression she'd intended. "I don't see a problem with that."

"Then I think we have something to negotiate about."

Chapter 40
Everything has its price

It was past three when Steven picked her up. She and Darren Wylde had spent most of the afternoon discussing this child they had given birth to: Daranyi Medical Informatics. He felt enough enthusiasm that she thought it might warrant incorporating as a separate entity. It was something to think about, the sight of this old man, at threescore and seven, so invigorated at the prospect of initiating a radical change in his life. Michael would do himself some good to spend time around a man like Darren Wylde.

"Miss Daranyi."

She opened her eyes. They were back in Sandy, on Larkspur Lane, in front of her house. She'd fallen asleep.

"Thank you, Steven." She got out on her own accord and stopped at the driver's side window. "I'll not be coming into work on Monday. So I shall see you on Tuesday."

The sun was well gone, hidden behind the roiling charcoal sky. A hot sirocco coursed along the Salt Lake Valley, churning up a dirty yellow curtain of dust. Virga fell like veils across the horizon. In the house, Milada turned on the swamp cooler. But the wind whipped at the curtains, and she tasted the grit in the air. So she turned off the cooler and closed the windows.

She took two hundred milligrams of fexofenadine to retard the histaminic reaction to the sun, then stripped off her clothing and took a long, cold shower. Besides washing off the dust and sweat and oil, the water fixed the reaction in the skin, kept the burn from spreading. In a few hours any pressure on her skin would become unbearable.

Milada examined herself in the mirror. *What a mess.* Darren Wylde was right about the incidental ultraviolet. And her shoulders — she should have kept on the jacket — were just as bad. It would look like hell soon enough, and her skin would hurt even worse until the damaged flesh scabbed over. And then another twenty-four to thirty-six hours until it shed.

She showered, toweled off, and tied her *yukata* loosely around her waist. She gathered up her collection of drugs—antihistamines, codeine, ibuprofen, cortisone cream—that she always kept handy just in case. With her metabolism, it was a trick to take any drug with the right timing and in sufficient amounts to be effective.

In the kitchen she filled a liter bottle with warm water. She had to keep hydrated as well. In the family room, she spread out a bath towel and lay down. Then she called Jane.

"Are you okay?" was Jane's first question.

"Do I not sound okay?"

"You sound—stressed. You're sure you're okay?"

"I'm okay, okay?"

A suspicious tone crept into Jane's voice. "Did you get sunburned up there?"

"A little."

"A little?"

"Okay, a little more than a little. I shall recover."

"Do you have enough codeine and cortisone on hand?"

Milada sighed. This was why Jane needed to get married, so she could have a child of her own to bestow all her mothering instincts upon. Jane took the cue and moved on. "How'd the day go?"

The day had started with her sending a kid into the ICU. *Aside from that, Mrs. Lincoln.* She composed herself before she spoke. "The meeting with Mr. Wylde went better than expected. We are going to have to pull a few rabbits out of a few hats, but I am optimistic."

"Anything you want me to relay to Garrick?"

"No. I shall write up a memo and e-mail you tomorrow. I'll call the two of you Monday."

"From home or the office?"

"Home, most likely."

"So you got burned pretty bad then."

"Jane—" Milada said with tender exasperation.

"Someone has to watch out for you girls."

"I appreciate it, Jane. I promise to lie very still and think calm thoughts and take lots of drugs."

"If you promise."

"Good-bye, Jane."

"Good-bye, Milly. And take care."

Milada clicked off the phone and tossed it aside. She uncapped the water bottle and washed down two codeine tabs and a thousand milligrams of ibuprofen. Then she lay very still on the floor and thought calm thoughts. Spinning off Daranyi Medical Informatics as an independent company could prove quite lucrative. No debt financing, a pure intellectual property play. She would have smiled if it didn't hurt so much.

Chapter 41
A sin confessed is half forgiven

RACHEL WATCHED THE LINCOLN **turn the corner, cruise down the street and out of sight. She wondered how long she should wait. She'd gotten into the habit of bursting in on Milada and was reluctant to do so today, even when she had a good excuse.**

"Aren't you going to take her attaché back?" her husband asked.

"Maybe after dinner."

After a light meal eaten in uncomfortable stillness, Rachel picked up the attaché case and walked down the street to Milada's house. Milada didn't come to the door when she rang the doorbell. Maybe she was napping. Milada didn't strike her as someone who napped. She tried the doorknob.

The door was open. She called out, "Milada? It's Rachel Forsythe."

She tiptoed into the kitchen and glanced down through the banisters into the family room. Milada lay on the floor on a bath towel, her head resting on a small throw pillow. The louvers across the sliding glass doors cast lines of light across her waist and legs. Her robe was pulled down from her shoulders. Next to her on the carpet were a water bottle, several prescription pill bottles, a cell phone.

Milada's eyes followed her as she came down the short flight of stairs. "Hello, Rachel," Milada said. Her voice was stiff and muted. She did not lift her head.

"You left your attaché case at the hospital."

"Thank you," Milada mumbled.

Rachel set the attaché case next to the staircase and stood there, trying not to stare at the pill bottles, trying not to wonder what the drugs were, because it was none of her business. But then she looked closer and gasped. "Milada! What happened to you?"

"A sunburn. Don't you know your lore, Rachel? We do not fare well when exposed to the light of day." She tried to smile. "You needn't worry. A temporary setback. What do you want? You always get that look on your face when you want something."

Abashed, Rachel retreated a step. "There's something I have to ask you."

"Then ask me," Milada said, the resignation clear in her voice.

"What happened in London?"

Milada turned her eyes toward Rachel, a pair of diamonds shining out of a pool of soot. "You know what happened there."

Rachel did. She felt the touch of evil and forced herself not to imagine what she knew from that simple statement.

Milada spoke without prompting. "I understand now what Rakoczi wanted. He wanted a family, companions to share the long night of eternity with. But he was in no way prepared to be a parent. When we alone survived, he had not the slightest idea what to do with us. Yet he did it over and over. Perhaps it became the only way he knew how to connect to women with any semblance of passion, as perverse a passion as it was."

"But how did your stepfather—" Rachel pressed in a whisper.

"Garrick found us. He was a sheriff's bailiff, his way of staying one step ahead of the Puritans. He recovered the body of a girl near London Bridge. He recognized the marks as being what only one of our kind could make. Such careless violence imperiled all of us. He ferreted out Rakoczi, arrested him, and turned him over to the Royal Court. The three of us he sent to Michael's estate at Cheapside. We took his name and became his daughters. Years we spent isolated inside those walls. We were quite mad at the time and each of us unique in our madness."

"And Rakoczi?"

"He confessed to the murders. Better that than be condemned a warlock, with the Witchfinder General prosecuting the cases. He spared himself the torture. But he never reached the gallows. He died at Newgate Prison—he stopped taking blood. He could have survived. He could have pled benefit of clergy. He could have escaped. He had the power, and I know what that hunger is like. A death by hanging would have been kinder punishment."

"You think he deserved kinder punishment!" Rachel exclaimed.

"No. And yet—I believe that all his life he rationalized his predilections by telling himself he was an evil man in the thrall of an evil passion. But in the end he was not evil. He was a pathetic man who led a pathetically lonely life that made him desperate to ruin everything he touched. I felt sorry for him. The Stockholm syndrome, isn't that what they call it—when the captive falls in love with the captor? But as I said, I was by then quite mad."

Rachel bit her bottom lip. "How many?" she asked faintly. "How many girls?"

Milada didn't answer. Rachel could not leave the stone unturned, could not leave without knowing the mundane, ordinary horror of what had happened. *What did you do?* she'd asked Milada at the beginning. And now she needed the answer, a death she could understand. If not her own daughter's, then someone else's. She said, "You killed them. Not that—that Rakoczi." When Milada didn't answer, she repeated the question: "How many?"

"The last one, the one Garrick found, was the only one I killed to further my own ends. The rest for—" She paused. "For mercy. They would have died anyway, after what he did to them. The fever burns. The blood boils in your veins. You think you will kill yourself before it kills you. *I* got better. But you never are better. Those girls never would have gotten better. They would have suffered for nothing."

"Not all of them. You don't know that."

"Mathew Hopkins and his witch prickers had the run of London. Cromwell and the Roundheads ran everything else. You prick us, and we do not bleed. It is written in the Bible: *Thou shalt not suffer a witch to live.* I wanted us to live. That was the only way I knew how."

"And Garrick?"

"I learned the routines of his watch. I left the body where I knew he would find it, the key to Rakoczi's strongbox in her hand, and in her pocket a locket identifying another of the missing girls. As if she had stolen, fled, and died."

"Because Rakoczi raped you and your sisters?"

"*He never touched them in that way.*" A quiet fierceness crept into her voice. "I was responsible for my sisters. I was responsible for the fate that befell us. If he would not have me, then I would procure the necessary surrogates. Yet I knew he would betray us eventually. Through incompetence or willful self-destruction. I was sure I could care for my sisters on my own. We had lived almost five decades with him. Alas, five decades had not made me wise. Only cruel. Wisdom does not come with time, Rachel. Wisdom comes with age. Wisdom must be worn into the soul. And we Daranyi age very slowly."

The sun settled in the west, the bands of light slipped across her face, illuminating her chin and cheeks and the bridge of her nose. The skin was charred, almost blackened.

"Are you sure you're all right?"

"It is less severe than it looks. It only feels that way." She tried to smile. "I met today with a gentleman farmer. He also owns a company I wish to buy. We spent the morning stacking hay. Such are the lengths I will go to. This is an allergic reaction. I am allergic to sunlight. Ironic, don't you think? The one thing I cannot cure is myself. Or your daughter—"

Her voice caught in her throat. She closed her eyes and fought to retain her composure. Rachel knelt on the floor next to her. Despite all that the woman had confessed, Rachel wanted only to somehow comfort this terrible, fallen angel. But she could see the stripes on her shoulders and didn't know how tender the rest of her body might be.

"You don't know that. I asked impossible things of you. I put you in an impossible position. It wasn't right, and it wasn't fair."

"You worry about being fair to me? And yet how your God harries me." This time she did manage a smile.

"I don't know who you were, Milada. I don't even know who you are. I'm in no position to judge you or judge your past. But I know what you were willing to do for me. You didn't have to, but you did. And that is enough." Rachel got to her feet. "Is there anything I can do for you? Anything I can get you?"

"No. I will be fine. By Tuesday I should be as good as new."

Chapter 42
You can't go home again

THE DRUGS AT LAST LULLED MILADA to sleep. The narcotics freed her dreams. Dreams that flew her halfway around the world. Dreams that loosed the restless past from its sepulchral moorings. The rain fell, the hurricane roared, and the doors of the manor house shook with heavy reverberations.

Milada awoke with a start. Her breath caught in her throat. The shock of realization raced through her veins and struck hard at her heart: the consummation of her own design, sooner than expected and hostile beyond expectation.

She parted a slit in the heavy curtains. The street below her window was painted with the flickering orange glow of fiery torches, the dancing gray and black shadows of the jostling throng. She crossed to the door, cracked it open, and peered out. She heard the swift padding of small feet behind her, turned and caught Kammy by the shoulders.

"No," she whispered in their native tongue. "Leave it be."

An awful crash below made them both jump, the battering ram at last deployed. Across the room, Zoë's wide, frightened eyes stared, aglow in the dark. Milada spun her sister about and pushed her toward the bed. "Stay with Zoë till I return."

She looked once more to ensure that Kammy did as she was told, and then she stole down the hallway. The way was clear. She darted to the balustrade and crouched low behind the banisters.

The Master staggered from his bedroom. "What? What?" he exclaimed, his mind confused by sleep. "Robbers!" he shouted. "Brigands!" He twisted his head, the movement almost a spasm, toward the narrow staircase.

Milada ducked her head, overcome by guilt and fear.

The final assault splintered the jamb. The door fell inward and crashed onto the flagstones. The Master shrieked and stumbled backward. A phalanx of uniformed men swept through the entrance hall, an angry tide drowning the Master in a rain of pummeling fists and kicking feet. Furniture broke under the force of blows, as did glass and bones. The Master was as strong as half a dozen men; half a dozen more surged into the breach. Milada heard the harsh clank of chains, the muffled roars and curses as the bolts were locked and hammered into place.

She smelled blood in the air. The rich odor of steel and salt brought out the prickle of sweat on her skin. A casualty supported by two compatriots hobbled to the shattered entranceway. Another man followed, hand clasped to his bloody forehead. The clutch of constables came next, dragging the bound Master. They needed no more violence. Terror had numbed his faculties to the point of paralysis. They dragged him out of the house, onto the cold, cobbled street. Then came the thud of a body cast hard onto the bed of a wagon, the rattle of irons against rough wood.

The horses unhitched. The shake of reins. The creak of wheels on the stones. *Leave,* Milada urged them in her mind, *and leave us alone.*

Just as suddenly, the storm subsided.

She waited until she believed they had gone for good, until she believed her plan had worked. She stood to return to the hall just as a man walked into the quiet house. He was different from the others. He wore the colors of some official rank. He stepped carefully over the fallen door and surveyed the damage.

"M'lord?" A constable bearing a lantern joined him. "Shall we search the house, sir?"

The man shook his head. "On the morrow. A devil such as this—this *Rakoczi*—he might have lain traps for us to stumble upon in all this darkness." He reassured the man with a friendly push on the shoulder.

The constable was only too eager to agree. He departed, leaving the man once again alone in the dark.

The man made ready to leave as well. But he hesitated. He glanced back over his shoulder, eyes focused on the stair head, then to the left. For an infinite, horrifying second, his eyes met hers. He was the man from the White Hart. She knew at once that he'd recognized her, even in the dark.

Milada shrank back from the balustrade and pushed herself across the floor to the opposite wall. The man approached the staircase. His boot heels clicked on the worn steps. He did not rush. Milada finally picked herself up and fled down the hall. Kammy stood outside the bedroom door. "What's going on?" she demanded. Her eyes narrowed. "What have you done?"

Milada shook her head—in despair, not in denial. "Someone is coming." Kammy lunged forward. Milada caught hold of her and dragged her into the room and shut the door behind them. She sat on the bed. She could think of nothing else to do. Zoë clutched her arm. Back then, Zoë always stayed close of her own accord. Milada closed her eyes. This she had not counted on. She only *suspected* what he was, only *knew* that he was the law. She had not dreamt of rescue. She had dreamt of freedom, the freedom to rule their lives as *she* saw fit.

The iambic rhythm of his footsteps came closer. The knob turned. The door opened. The three sisters drew breath simultaneously.

The man stepped into the room.

The glow of the moon glinted on the shrouded windows. Yet they saw him plain as day. He removed his hat, a strange courtesy to them. He stepped forward. He was young, yet his hair was a silken mane of silver and white. His eyes clear as glass. His skin like porcelain.

Kammy gasped and whispered, "But he is one of us."

The man smiled. The first genuine smile any man had given them in half a hundred years.

Brilliant light exploded in her face. Milada flinched awake. She heard the pelting rain, the rolling crash of thunder from the lightning strike. She got to her feet, pulled aside the curtains, and opened the sliding glass doors. The air smelled of rain, cool and fresh and wet, sweet with the electric taste of ozone. Flashes of blue-white illuminated the mountains.

The storm cell drifted north. The echoes of thunder died into the distance. Milada closed the doors and descended to her subterranean chamber. She slept till morning. The sun once again rose into a shocking blue sky, shining across the clean, new day.

Chapter 43
To err is human

MILADA DRESSED IN HER BYU SWEATPANTS and nothing else. When Rachel stopped by after church, she donned a shirt for the sake of modesty. Rachel did a poor job of hiding her shock and concern. Milada's once-white cheeks were the color and texture of worn shoe leather.

"It feels much better at this point," Milada reassured her. "It only looks worse."

"The damage isn't permanent, is it?"

"The skin will shed soon enough, like a snake's skin. Uncomfortable, but neither permanent nor life threatening." She asked, "And you? How are you doing, Rachel?"

Rachel flashed a chagrined smile. "At any rate, the Relief Society's taking good care of me." She held up the brown paper back she was carrying and placed it on the kitchen counter. "Lasagna," she explained. "Sister Millington made it. It's quite good. When it comes to parceling out sympathy, your average Relief Society puts the welfare state to shame. At the current rate, I won't be making a meal by myself for the next month."

A small thing, it seemed, but not having to worry about dinner did take a great weight off her mind. If she were shameless enough, she could get out of doing most of her housework as well.

"How is Jennifer doing?"

"She isn't doing any worse, which I count as doing better." Rachel added, "You must come over for dinner sometime. Laura thinks you're cool."

I'm cool, Milada murmured to herself, but did not say one way or the other.

She spent the rest of the afternoon writing up Saturday's meeting with Darren Wylde. She e-mailed Jane, Garrick, and Michael, and

CCed Darren Wylde as well. The success of the venture depended on them staying on the same page, on Wylde believing that he'd sold her on his vision of the company's future.

This was not a problem, because he had. She had not seriously considered it before the trip to Wallsburg. But the DEI *keiretsu*, she now argued, needed a biotech R&D center. It was the one remaining piece that would make everything fit.

The Wylde Medical Informatics acquisition would provide the necessary impetus for a more substantial reorganization of DEI. She envisioned three interlocking circles—finance, services, research—combining in a shared sphere of mutual concern. She did not include any of this in the memo. For the time being, Wylde must see his brainchild as the only jewel in the crown. But she liked the possibilities.

DMI would be Kammy's company. For all her sister's contrariness, Milada knew all along that Kammy would succumb to curiosity once she made the pitch. That and the opportunity to get away and be on her own. Yet not so far away and not so entirely on her own. Milada remained the lioness, wary of—jealous of, suspicious of—her sisters' independence. When they wandered too far from her reach, she sought any way to bring them back within the pride.

Monday morning in the shower, Milada shed the skin from her face and shoulders. She promptly flushed the glob of flesh down the toilet. It was quite disgusting. Her freshly exposed dermis was tight and raw, as if she had just had a facial chemical peel.

She had hardly dried off when Jane rang her. "I was going to call you later," Milada reminded her. "Have you had time to read my memo?"

"Something's come up. I don't know if it's hit cable news yet, but I wanted to make sure you found out first. Didn't want you to get blindsided."

"If *what* is on cable news yet?" She found the remote and turned the television to CNN.

"Frank's been arrested."

"He's been *what?*"

"Arrested. Securities fraud."

"Damn! That business scheme of his."

"Yes, and that's not even the half of it."

"Alan Ridgeway too?"

"The Feds hauled in the both of them."

"Muriel?"

"The last I heard, the marshals had taken her into protective custody. Milly, it's much bigger than the three of them. Our contacts in the U.S. Attorney's office say they're handing down a dozen indictments, charging over a hundred people, including a number tied to organized crime."

Milada swore again. "What has Frank gotten himself involved in? And why did none of us see this portentous of a downside?"

"You think Frank knew? Not to be mean, but the word *patsy* comes to mind."

"The word is accurate in this instance. He may perchance plead sheer stupidity as he is wont to do." She paused. "Hold on a second. Something just came on CNN."

Jane said, "I see it too."

Milada clicked up the volume. The reporter was doing a live remote from the U.S. District Courthouse in Manhattan. "Sources within the FBI confirm that members of four New York City organized crime families were involved in the stock market manipulations of three separate IPOs and eight publicly traded securities. Using traditional boiler-room and pump-and-dump schemes, microcap stocks were represented to investors as pursuing 'cutting-edge, environmentally friendly breakthroughs' with guaranteed federal funding, prosecutors said."

Milada sucked in her breath. Jane said, "There go Frank's green dreams."

"And there goes the sheer stupidity defense. What about our exposure?"

"I'm thinking that with a hundred-plus defendants, including a bunch of high-profile wise guys, Frank's going to pretty much get lost in the shuffle. And anybody who knows Frank and knows us knows he's not involved with DEI."

"Is Martin up to speed on all this?"

"Already called him. He assures me he has his legal eagles at the ready."

"No deals, no cooperation, no talking until we figure out what exactly is going on."

"Martin knows the drill. Do you still want to talk to Garrick?"

"No. Tomorrow. Some of the dust might have settled by then."

"In time for the hail and brimstone to start falling."

Milada smiled. "Please, Jane. No apocalyptic thoughts yet."

• • •

By Tuesday morning the flame in her cheeks had died down, leaving her with a skier's sunburn. Milada sequestered herself in the conference room at Loveridge & Associates. She even dismissed Karen. She wanted to talk to Jane before bringing in Garrick.

"How raineth the hail and brimstone?" she asked when Jane picked up.

"I don't think we need to worry about collateral damage, other than from the tabloids. Turns out Michael's been cooperating with the Feds all along. That's why we didn't see it coming."

"He's been *cooperating?*"

"They wanted to place undercover agents in some of our subsidiaries. Turns out it was part of the sting operation. Anyway, you know how Michael used to love the cloak-and-dagger scene. Probably the most fun he's had in years. Didn't Howard Hughes do something like this with the CIA and a Soviet sub salvaging operation back in the 1970s or something?"

"Who knows? Has Michael explained why he completely failed to inform us of this little operation?"

"To give us deniability. Whatever that means. This is Michael's version of tough love. Zoë would definitely have warned Frank off."

"How is Zoë taking it?"

"She's stormed in and stormed out half a dozen times already. She claims Frank got set up, framed, had nothing to do with it. Et cetera and et cetera."

"Zoë worries me more than Frank does. Even if she's right. We should get her out of the picture. Out of town, if necessary."

Jane said, "Here's Garrick."

The line clicked. "Morning, girls," said Garrick. "Shall I guess what the topic of conversation is?"

"What do you know that we don't?"

"Martin says he can't get Frank to talk to him. Says Frank's got his own counsel, Bobby Blaylock. At least that's what Frank told Zoë and what Zoë told me."

"Has anyone told him that it is less than a good idea being represented by a mob lawyer in this particular situation? Considering the company he's been keeping?"

"Bobby is pretty good at what he does."

"And there's that whole guilt-by-association thing too."

"Frank claims he's ready to take responsibility for his own actions. Doesn't want to have to rely on the family. Or so says Zoë."

"A little late in the game for that. He could have come to that realization a century or two ago."

"See here," said Garrick. "However it falls out, the Feds aren't going to tag Frank as a major player. And this whole thing is completely unrelated to DEI—in fact, vice versa, if what I'm hearing about Michael's involvement is correct. So we get Michael to dial down the pressure a bit and Frank and Alan to cooperate with the authorities. The two of them ante up to the SEC for a few hundred grand in fines and walk away with a few slaps on the wrist."

"*If* the hole he's digging himself into is not too deep," Milada said. "Oh, and Jane, I care not one whit which lawyer Frank wishes to have represent him. Tell Martin to shadow the case anyway. We'll need him when the reality of the whole thing finally hits Frank. As, *this time,* I am sure it will."

Milada stopped and took a breath. Exhaled slowly. "All right. My thinking right now is, I'll return to New York by week's end. Who do you have ready to take over?"

Garrick said, "Kim Thesman. Should be there by tomorrow. I'll e-mail you an itinerary."

Milada nodded to herself. "Kim is a good choice. My driver will pick her up. Have you had time to read through my memo?"

"I like it. Gets me thinking that there's more room to grow. Link all these research arms together."

"My thoughts exactly. But keep the spotlight on Wylde. Speaking of which, Jane, poke around in accounting and see if you can find someone—a Mormon would be a plus—who knows the area, is familiar with the culture, and would not shrink from spending a fair amount of time in Salt Lake City. I need a liaison between Kammy and me and Mr. Wylde. He strikes me as the type who builds his deals upon personal relationships. We're talking about an overgrown family business here. I expect there to be some serious hand-holding in the near future, and I cannot afford to be the hand holder."

"To begin with, it's hell on your skin," Jane quipped.

"What's that?" Garrick asked.

"Nothing," Milada said. "Please ignore Jane's asides."

"Jane's asides are usually the best part. What, did you get yourself sunburned?"

"Let's not go there, okay?"

Milada knew Garrick was grinning when he said, "Aye, Milly, what won't you do to seal the deal?"

What she wouldn't do indeed.

Chapter 44

She's not long for this world

RACHEL SAW JENNIFER IN HER DREAMS, lying in the isolation room at Deseret Children's Hospital, surrounded by machines and attended to by knights wearing strange suits of white armor. She saw the same thing when she was awake. Except the dragons weren't real. Or perhaps they weren't real only in her dreams.

Jennifer's room was filled with dragons. They unfolded their great golden wings, clawed at the smooth tile with obsidian-sharp talons, ready at once to snatch this child's soul from death's stubborn hold and wing her far away from Hades' gate and across the walls of heaven. These were terrible dragons that feared no fiend or demon. Dragons that slept aside the throne of God until dispatched and returned to his presence when the Valkyrie called.

A rush of wind was all it'd take, and she'd be gone. Rachel pulled Laura to her side tightly, lest she too be drawn away in the fierce vortex of the dragons' wake.

Rachel put on her suit of armor and sat at Jennifer's side in the fragile stillness. She held her daughter's small, white hand in her gloved mitt. *Remember, Jenny? Last summer in Maine with Grandpa and Grandma?* Portland Head Light, the cool summer morning just before dawn. A light mist on the steel-gray bay. The long, low growl of the fog horn filling the air with the sound of distant dragons, calling to them across the infinite chasm. *There, look!* A wyvern gliding down the sound, skimming above the lobster buoys, slipping away behind the shrouded isles. The dragons, they knew even then. They had followed her here, had sought her out in the shadow of these towering battlements of stone. They had come to take her away, to take her home.

Rachel didn't know where her daughter's home was, except that it was not here. And not knowing hurt like death itself.

The end was nigh, and the family flew in like a flock of starlings, paying their last respects outside the glass of the isolation room, as if attending a wake. Rachel wanted to scream, *It's a hospital bed, not the bloody zoo!* But there she was as well, standing guard like a terracotta soldier over this life-size china doll.

"Nothing personal, Rachel," Carl said. "But it kinda creeps me out."

"Carl!" their mother said, giving him a well-practiced cross look.

But Rachel was with Carl on this one. So she was glad when Laura broke the mood and said, "You should see Mom's new outfit. It's so cool."

"A new outfit?"

"Our neighbor gave it to her. She's from Romania, and she's real rich. Andy Millington threw up on her, so she gave it to Mom."

Laura's grandmother looked unsure how to react to this information. Rachel said perfunctorily, "I don't think that's an appropriate subject for this occasion, Laura."

Laura almost stamped her feet. "Jenny's still alive! Quit treating her like she's dead already!"

Instead of answering, Rachel gave her daughter a heartfelt hug. Laura seemed to know that she was speaking for her mother now and didn't wriggle out of her embrace.

Later that night, while they were clearing the table, Rachel's mother brought up the subject Rachel knew had been weighing on her mind and on the mind of David's parents as well. She said, with a cautious nonchalance, "Are you still trying to have children, Rachel? We could help out, you know."

It was a tremendously funny way of putting it. She meant money for the fertility treatments. Rachel shook her head. "It's not like we ever stopped trying, Mom. But we've had other priorities. And there comes a point when you've just got to stop fighting nature."

She smiled gamely. Oh, but what a lie *that* was. Give her half a chance, and she'd beat nature senseless with a stick.

Chapter 45

It's all over but the shouting

THE M&A TEAM CAMPED OUT at Loveridge & Associates knew Kim Thesman. Kim belonged to Garrick's entourage, not DEI's. She represented the new breed of young executives, cross-training their way to the top. She'd played basketball at UConn and followed that up with a Harvard MBA. She could be one of the boys when she had to and dress to kill when she wanted to. She had a healthy tan. She was everything Milada was not, and Milada strongly suspected the team was just as happy that Kim was taking over.

Back at the office, Kim Thesman popped open her attaché and handed Milada a folder. It was the curriculum vitae for one Curtis Matheson. Milada scanned down the sheet. "BYU Graduate School of Accounting. Very good, Jane," she murmured to herself. She said to Kim, "I'll brief him myself before I send him out. He'll mostly be working with Kammy and Mr. Wylde."

"How quickly do you want to move on the WMI proffer?"

"Slowly. Let's get Mr. Matheson on site first. We need to win over the rest of the family before we start exploring the financials. I expect there to be a few skeletons in the closet, and I don't want any big surprises before we get into the particulars of a hands-on audit."

Thursday morning Milada introduced Kim to the WMI board. The rest of the day they spent going over the books with the KMPG crew.

Milada ended her participation at four-thirty. Karen helped her collect her things and followed her down to the lobby. "Is there anything I can do to help?"

"I'm fine."

"Will you be coming back soon?"

Milada smiled. "I'll be back and forth over the next few months, but you should be seeing much more of my sister Kammy."

"Your sister? Oh, yes, with the long hair. You can't miss the family resemblance."

Milada bowed her head before the glass wall of the isolation room and crossed herself. Nothing could induce her to face the sermons to come in a real house of worship. In each of the three synoptic gospels, Jesus had issued the same warning: *Whoso shall offend one of these little ones, it were better for him that a millstone were hanged about his neck, and that he were drowned in the depth of the sea.*

The Elizabethan language rang hauntingly in her ears. She knew these King James verses well and stood condemned by them, having surreptitiously attended the funeral of every child that had fallen into her grasp.

I am the resurrection, and the life, Jesus said to the sisters of Lazarus. *He that believeth in me, though he were dead, yet shall he live: And whosoever liveth and believeth in me shall never die.*

"I don't believe in you," Milada whispered to herself. And when would she ever die? When would incorruption put on the corruptible? When would her life be swallowed up in a victory for the dead? *A time to prepare to meet God,* the child had explained. How long would that take? Longer than even she would live. She crossed herself again, turned to leave, and found herself face to face with Rachel Forsythe.

"Milada—" Rachel said.

"Rachel," Milada replied with a nod of her head, suppressing the same shock of surprise she'd felt the first time they'd met. Why did this woman remind her so much of the Mother Superior? Sister Gertrude, who had been right about Rakoczi, who had fought to keep them at the orphanage. But Rakoczi had money, and the bishop had decided—what with the sale of a profitable indulgence and three fewer mouths to feed—and so that was that.

Milada was glad to leave, glad to leave the insufferable nun behind her forever. Just as she would be glad to put Rachel Forsythe behind her forever. She looked at her again, and Rachel had tears in her eyes. "Thank you, Milada. Thank you for everything."

Milada nodded again, almost a bow of contrition. "I'm sorry," she whispered.

Rachel shook her head.

Milada hesitated and then said, "I should have told you earlier—and I know this will sound self-serving—but that night your daughter spoke to me. She knew who I was, and she knew my name. She told me to tell you that God never walks away from an honest wager. I have no idea what that means." Or anything else the child had said, words Milada would repeat to no one else.

Rachel shook her head again.

At a loss for words, Milada said, "The lasagna was quite good." Rachel almost laughed at the non sequitur. "I'm leaving tomorrow. A small family emergency came up. Uncle Frank has managed to get himself into more trouble than usual this time." She sighed. "Hardly the end of the world. But—"

"You love him anyway."

"Yes," she said with a crooked smile. "He must be saved from himself." With that, Milada nodded again and then went to brush past her. But Rachel reached out and caught her and put her arms around her and held her tightly, the same way Sister Gertrude had that last time, knowing that Milada was leading her sisters into hell. For a moment Milada's composure almost crumbled.

Only for a moment.

When they separated, their eyes did not meet. Milada did not stop. She did not turn around. She did not look back. Some Bible stories she had taken to heart.

Chapter 46
Nothing's so bad but it might be worse

RACHEL READIED HERSELF FOR THE INEVITABLE. She readied herself for the heartfelt sympathy, the trite and meaningless reassurances of faith, and the litany of scriptures surely to come. Her favorite had no deep theological import attached to it other than a simple statement of reality: *Thou shalt live together in love, insomuch that thou shalt weep for the loss of them that die.*

Except that Jennifer refused to die. A perverse air of disappointment haunted this growing realization. Like a fireworks display interrupted by a sudden downpour, the big finale turning into an emotional fizzle. At first, in the words of the hospital staff, Jennifer was "holding on." Then she was "soldiering on." Then she was "out of the woods." Then going from "strength to strength."

"Her FDP is in the basement, and her ANC is through the roof," said Dr. Ingebretsen. In other words, the blood factors of a *healthy* child.

The flock of her extended family finally figured out that the news of Jennifer's death was very much exaggerated and with a collective shrug winged their way back to more comfortable climes.

And then Jennifer was "awake and alert." She opened her eyes and smiled and said, "Hi, Mom. Hi, Dad," as if she'd just gotten off the bus from day camp. She cast her eyes around the room. "Where's Milada?" she wondered.

Rachel and David exchanged curious glances. Rachel said, not questioning the thinking behind such an odd question, "She had to go back to New York."

"Oh," said Jennifer with a small, pouting frown. She quickly brightened. "How about Laura?"

"She's at school. We weren't expecting you to wake up so suddenly."

"When can I go back to school?"

"Not so quick," her father cautioned but with a broad smile that said, *Yes! My child's a trooper!*

Two weeks later Jennifer was declared as healthy as could be expected of a leukemia patient who'd camped out at death's door for the past six months—except for a persistent normocytic anemia revealed in her CBC that responded well to Epogen and blood transfusions. But Dr. Ingebretsen was sure her bone marrow only needed time to recover, and he sent her home.

Lingering concern about opportunistic diseases kept her out of school and wearing a surgical mask whenever she went out, which she treated as a comical disguise. To her mother's great delight, Jennifer was *Jennifer,* in all her resurrected exuberance, everything she treasured about her.

But a shadow grew on Rachel's soul. Nothing she had read—and she'd become a walking encyclopedia on the subject—suggested that a child in Jennifer's condition should recover this fast. When Jennifer's CBC dropped too low, she plainly declared, "Mom, I need blood." Watching the phlebotomist feed the line into her daughter's vein, Rachel restrained herself from blurting out, "Why not let her *drink* it and see what happens?"

Jennifer hated the needle. But after getting a transfusion, she would sit in the passenger's seat in a kind of rapture, completely blissed out for most of the ride home.

Once Jennifer's hair began to grow in, Rachel's fears were confirmed. Dr. Ingebretsen remained unconcerned. The hair of cancer patients, he explained, often grew back in a far different fashion than before. But Jennifer's silver-white hair—her pale skin—her once sky-blue eyes now the color of cut glass—could mean only one thing.

Laura was the first to state the obvious. "She looks like Milada."

Rachel could no longer keep the truth at arm's length. In the end Milada had bowed to her wishes and infected Jennifer. And then she'd left, convinced that she had killed her just as she had killed all those other children. Rachel knew she should contact Milada and explain what had happened. But every day she didn't was another day Jennifer was hers alone.

Worse, Jennifer somehow knew. *Remind my mother that God never walks away from an honest wager.* Rachel had made the offer, and the bookie had accepted the bet. The only question was when she would be forced to give God or the devil their due.

• • •

Jennifer raised the subject again as they were tucking her into bed. "When are we going to go see Milada?" A subtle but demanding tone crept into her voice.

"I don't know," her mother said. "She's very busy with her work. She has her own family to tend to."

Here she was, lying to her own daughter.

David began to wonder as well. "How does she know Milada? I thought Milada left before Jennifer came out of the coma. Why does she keep talking about some deal they made together?"

Rachel thought carefully about which question to answer and how to answer it. She held a pillow under her chin and pulled on the pillowcase. "I, um, promised we'd go see her when she got better."

"Oh," David said, following suit on his side of the bed.

"Remember I told you Milada came to the hospital to see Jenny? I think she developed quite an attachment to her."

"To be honest, she didn't strike me as the type."

"No," Rachel agreed. "But we should go see her. It's important to Jenny." Except that the moment Milada saw her, she would realize what had happened. Rachel set the pillow against the headboard and got into bed. "David, do you remember the story of Samuel and Eli?"

"You mean, when Samuel thinks Eli is calling him and gets up and goes to his bedside, and the third time Eli tells him that it is the voice of the Lord calling him?"

"Yes, but do you remember what happens before that?"

He thought it over for a minute. "What did happen before that?"

"Hannah, Samuel's mother, promised that if she had a son she would give him to the Lord for all the days of his life. That's why she took him to Eli in the first place."

"Ah yes. I believe Laura calls it the Rumpelstiltskin story. Or was it Rapunzel?"

"Rapunzel."

"Maybe it's just me, but the humans in these fairy tales often behave as badly as the witches and goblins."

"It's not just you," Rachel said quietly.

"So at least Hannah followed through."

Rachel sighed to herself. If only David were more suspicious, more inclined to read between the lines. He would grab her and shake the truth out of her the way frustrated men did with their wives in television dramas. She knew he was puzzled, curious, and confused about his daughter's remarkable recovery. But confronted with something beyond his expertise, like most men he resorted with a helpless shrug to Occam's razor: the simplest, most logical, most obvious explanation—especially when it came to truths with emotional baggage attached—was presumed correct until proved otherwise.

Maybe metaphysical truth or existential truth or scientific truth would make her free. But it was better to live with some lies than drive people crazy with the cold, hard facts. The best lie told in all the scriptures is the lie God tells Abraham. Sarah laughs when told she will bear a child, but when God brings the proposal to Abraham, he tells him that his wife was concerned that she was too old to bear children. *Exactly* what a guy would tell another guy.

Except that's not what Sarah said. She said that menopause aside, she just didn't think the old codger could get it up anymore.

Funnier yet, Abraham was pretty sure that's what she *was* laughing about, but Sarah denied it. Two lies in a row.

So Rachel was in good company. Small comfort.

Chapter 47
A guilty conscience needs no accuser

MILADA SAT BEHIND HER DESK in her Midtown Manhattan office and stared out the window at the wet, gray day. Fog rolled in off the river. The same as the day Garrick and his men had come for Rakoczi. She and her sisters were sent to Cheapside. Their previous lives were summarily thrown away.

Why should the memory of such a fortuitous day wear so heavily on her soul?

The cold rain weighed down her spirits, yet her body burned with a low, pleasant fever. She'd come to the office directly from the hotel. She kept a change of clothes on hand just for these occasions. She couldn't even remember the man's name. He'd volunteered no more information than she had. He'd claimed he was single.

Perhaps he was. She never looked for that telling white shadow on the ring finger. But if not, did taking away a memory also take away the guilt? For that matter, did taking away the guilt take away the memory? Was that what she was afraid of losing? Some small, perverse part of herself that missed what they'd had together, just the three—the four—of them, once upon a time in London?

Jane poked her head into the office, breaking her out of her reverie. "Garrick says to turn on your cell phone."

When she answered her phone, that was Garrick's first question. "When did you start turning off your phone?"

"Sorry. A bad habit I acquired in Utah."

"About the proffer—do you want your first offer to appear tough but generous or just tough?"

"Generous enough to make them bite, but not so generous that they'll settle on the first offer. Give Wylde some push-back room. It'll strengthen his bargaining position and improve his standing among the shareholders. He's still got to deliver the unregistered shares."

"Right now Kim's looking at fourteen and change."
"Sounds good to me."
"*Ciao.*"
"See you, Garrick." After hanging up, she checked to see if she had missed any other calls. A voice message from Garrick: "Milly, turn on your phone!" Before that, a text message from Kammy received at 11:55 the night before, which meant 9:55 Mountain Daylight Time: *7 yr old fem. CCR5D32x2!! DCH invoice. WTF???*

Milada decoded the message: *Seven-year-old girl with two CCR5 Delta 32 alleles. Test invoiced to Deseret Children's Hospital.*

A cold chill ran down her spine. She felt the actual shiver. The message must have been sent from Wylde. How could Kammy have found the record so quickly? Why would she be asking her about it? Milada set the phone down on her desk and stared at the display, her forehead resting against her hands.

"Stupid," she said to herself. "*Stupid.*" All she'd ordered was the CCR5 test. No normal person did that. It would stand out like a sore thumb. But with nobody to trace it back to—

Milada leaned back and closed her eyes and concocted her excuse: she was putting Wylde's B2B operations to a real-world test. There wasn't anybody to trace it back to. The child was dead. One more notch in her belt.

There *wasn't* anybody to trace it back to. The child *had* died. She was certain. But she'd never checked. She was certain. But she didn't want to know. She straightened her chair and picked up the phone and scrolled through the address book.

The nurse's station on the DCH bone marrow transplant unit. For some reason she'd saved the number.

Her thumb rested against the button. She hesitated. Perhaps her instincts had been right all along. Except that if she was right then it would be a relief to know. And if she was wrong—let some sleeping dogs lie, and they'd bite her leg off.

She pressed the button. Two thousand miles away, the phone rang at the nurse's station on the third floor of Deseret Children's Hospital. "DCH BMT," a woman's voice said.

Milada softened her accent to sound more like her sister. "Hello, this is Dr. Daranyi. I was wondering if I could get the current status on Jennifer Forsythe."

A pause, and the nurse's voice raised half an octave. She said, positive *cheer* in her voice, "She's on outpatient status. She was discharged last week. I could transfer you to Dr. Ingebretsen—"

"No, that's fine." Milada forced calm into her voice. "I'll be seeing him later. Thank you anyway."

She set down the phone. Her hand was shaking. She pushed the chair back and walked to the window. She folded her arms across her chest, pressed her forehead against the tinted glass. *Deep breaths.* She felt something strange on her cheek and brushed her fingers against the skin. A tear like a small bead of glass. She stared at it with a sense of wonder that only brought the foreign emotions closer to the surface.

Milada hurried to her private bathroom and washed her face. "Jesus, God, what have you done?" she asked her reflection. The white-faced woman in the mirror had no answer.

She collected her wits, returned to the office, and dialed Jane's extension. "Something just came up. How early can you get me into Salt Lake?"

"Today?"

"Today."

Jane called back five minutes later. "The earliest seat available is on the 3:15 from JFK. Gets into Salt Lake City at 6:35."

Milada pressed her fist hard against her temple and clenched her teeth. Almost twelve bloody hours, and she had no idea what Kammy would be doing. "Yes. That's fine. Have the limo pick me up at my place. Oh, and reserve a rental. It'll be late enough by the time I arrive."

"Will do." A touch of concern crept into Jane's voice. "Anything wrong?"

"Oh, no," Milada said, with all the nonchalance she could muster. "Odds and ends." She added, "But as far as anybody else is concerned, I'm out of the office for the rest of the day. Incommunicado or whatever."

"Got it." Jane didn't sound convinced but let the matter drop.

Milada packed only a carry-on and her laptop. Her mind couldn't focus on work. She ignored the solicitations of the flight attendants and closed her eyes and tried to figure out what she had done wrong. This was so unlike her. Running the numbers. Playing out the scenarios. Looking at the big picture. Taking the long view. That's what she did for a living. Why not in her personal life?

She'd acted like a shortsighted, impulsive child. Like Zoë. She'd acted the same way she had acted four hundred years ago. She hadn't learned a thing in all the time since.

No. Her instincts hadn't been proven wrong. She didn't *actually* know what had happened to the child. She didn't *actually* know what Kammy had figured out. Perhaps Kammy was simply curious. Perhaps the hospital had released Jennifer so she could die at home.

Wishing another child dead.

And if she was alive? Milada wracked her brains. For as often as Kammy had accused her of living in the past, she'd forgotten too much. *What happens next?* Jennifer would lose her incisors. She'd shed her palate. Her fangs and new incisors would erupt. Her hair and skin would change. *How long did each step take? In what order?*

Kammy would know.

Milada pressed her hands against her face. This was the same mistake she'd made as a child. She'd let her fears take hold and her imagination run loose.

Facts, facts, *facts*. Profit and loss. Earning per share. Return on investment. She didn't wonder and worry while calculating worst-case scenarios. She acted on objective knowledge.

She reached for the phone on the seatback in front of her, rehearsing the script she would follow: *Don't react. Feign ignorance. It was only a test.*

The phone rang three times. Then her sister's voice.

"Who is she, Milada?"

So loudly that Milada cast a nervous glance at the forty-something businessman in the aisle seat. She switched the phone to her other ear and scrunched over next to the window.

"Kammy—"

"Who is she?"

"How did—"

Entirely the wrong question. She had indicted herself.

"Whenever I get my hands on a database like this, I always check the CCR5 data for additional markers."

"Checking on me?" Guilty as charged, but still she felt offended.

"No, you idiot. Checking to see if there are any more of *us* out there. That time you weren't asking hypotheticals. It was a real case! Dammit, Milly!"

"It was only a test." Like that excuse was going to work now.

"Give me a break. It's not your genome. What's going on?"

Milada felt her own temper rising. "It's not important, Kammy. I can handle it."

"It's not important? The invoice says the report was sent directly to Loveridge! So *not* important that you had a courier deliver it? Yeah, don't worry, I deleted the record. Damned lucky it wasn't archived."

Milada closed her eyes. *What a mistake.* "Kammy, leave it alone." The tension gathered in her voice. "Leave it alone."

"You're always pulling crap like this, Milly. Same as in London."

The line went dead. An arrow went through her heart. Milada had to exercise every ounce of self-control to keep from slamming the phone against the seatback in front of her. When she'd calmed down sufficiently, she snapped it back into its cradle.

The businessman glanced at her. "Family, huh?"

Inexplicably, Milada felt a small smile come to her face. "Yes. Worse, it's my fault." She somehow felt better confessing the truth.

The man shook his head in a gesture of empathy. "Don't I know it. Been there, done that."

She tried calling again. Kammy had turned off her phone, which meant she wasn't talking to her or she was at the hospital. Or both. Milada cracked open the window shade and glanced down at the flat expanse of the northern Great Plains crawling by seven miles below.

For the next two hours, the entirety of the world was out of her control. That awful feeling swept through her again. *Helplessness.* She was helpless to do anything for those who depended on her without making their lives so much worse in the process.

Chapter 48
Fools and children tell the truth

MONDAY NIGHT RACHEL SAT AT THE COMPUTER composing the family newsletter. Laura and Jennifer were camped out in front of the television with their father exploring the ins and outs of the latest Nintendo game machine. David had easily been persuaded to make the purchase as a coming-home present for Jenny.

Rachel was brimming with good news to share with their friends and relatives. But she had long since stopped typing and instead sat and watched her husband and children. It was better than any movie. Laura and Jenny finally figured out the controllers and shouted and danced around playing a game of electronic tennis.

The doorbell rang.

"I'll get it," Rachel said. Nobody else noticed.

Sunlight streamed through the glass panels on either side of the front door, painting bright rectangles on the hardwood floor.

"Yes?" Rachel said as she opened the door.

The sun was almost even with the horizon, clipping the roofs and slanting through the side yards, making her squint. A girl in her late teens stood on the porch. The western sky at her back set her brilliant white hair afire. Clear eyes shone out of her shadowed face.

"Milada, come in—" Rachel said. In that same moment, she knew the girl was *not* Milada. But that was the only logical connection her brain could make.

The girl looked back at Rachel with an equally startled expression. She was perhaps an inch shorter than Milada. Her hair was pulled back from her face in a ponytail. She was wearing green hospital scrubs. She could have passed for any of the medical students Rachel saw all the time at DCH—if not for her extraordinary complexion and strange outfit.

The mention of Milada's name told the girl what she needed to know. "Excuse me," she said. She pushed past Rachel and strode into the foyer and down the hallway, hesitating briefly at the stairway and then becoming aware of the commotion radiating from the family room.

"W-wait!" Rachel said, coming to her senses and hurrying after her.

David glanced over his shoulder, expecting to see his wife. He leapt to his feet. "Who—?" he started to say.

The girl's eyes focused on him briefly and then fell on Jennifer, as the gaze of a circling hawk falls on its prey. She stepped forward. David held out his arms, shielding his children from this stranger.

Rachel's frantic mind finally connected a name with the face. The picture she'd seen on Milada's kitchen counter. "Kam—" she started to say.

Kamilla whirled on her, teeth clenched, her eyes bright with shock. "What did she do? WHAT DID MILADA DO?"

Rachel stared at her dumbly. "It—it was my idea," she felt compelled to say.

"*Your* idea? How could it be *your* idea?" Kamilla's eyes narrowed. She seized Rachel's chin and turned her head to one side and the other. Though there was nothing to see, Rachel's hand reflexively went to the invisible scars on her throat.

"I didn't sleep—" Rachel said defensively. She choked off the rest of the sentence.

David stepped forward to defend his wife from this incomprehensible hostility. "Look here—"

Kamilla stretched out her right hand toward him, a gesture made with such resolute authority that David yielded to its force. She focused her eyes on Rachel. "I have the test results. So don't tell me—"

"The test results?"

"The genetic test Milada ran through Wylde. *Damn* it! What were you *thinking?*" Rachel sensed that the question was directed as much at Milada as herself.

"Hey!" said David. "You don't use that kind of language—"

"Stay out of this!" she snapped.

"Stay out of what? What are you talking about? What's Milada got to do with this?"

"But—but she refused," Rachel said. "I asked her. But she refused."

"Refused to do *what?*" the girl growled.

Another horror seized Rachel. The girl's body eclipsed her husband's presence, creating a small pocket of privacy between them. "*Please.*" Rachel's voice fell into a harsh whisper, the air barely escaping her lips. "*He doesn't know.*" Truth stood before her, ready to destroy her utterly, and all she cared about in that moment was the lie. Rachel would have knelt before the girl if she believed it would further her cause.

The few seconds of tense quietude was all David needed to gird up his loins. "I don't know who you are or what you're doing here, but you're going to have to leave." He stepped forward and grabbed the girl by the wrist, placing his left hand against her shoulder to leverage her away from his wife. Rachel could not remember the last time he had laid hands on another person in anger.

She didn't budge. Rachel blanched. "*Don't touch her—*" she gasped so desperately that he dropped his hold as if touching a hot iron.

Kamilla shot her an icy glare. "Give me some credit. Please."

David had not exhausted all his courage. "What is going on? What was she looking at Jennifer like that for? What does she have to do with Milada?"

"She's her sister," Laura and Jennifer piped up together.

The three adults turned as one. Laura and Jennifer were backed up against the far wall of the family room, looking alternatively aghast and enraptured by the drama unfolding in front of them.

"Well, it's obvious, isn't it?" Laura shrugged a nonchalant teenage shrug. "Or maybe she's another vampire."

David gaped at his older daughter. Rachel clenched her fists and closed her eyes and prayed.

"Laura, be serious," her father said.

"Yes, Laura, be serious," echoed Kamilla.

The abrupt, absurd turn of the argument drained the energy from the room. The air fell still. Kamilla again stepped toward Jennifer, and again David blocked her way.

"I have to see Jennifer."

"Why?"

Rachel found her voice again. "Kamilla's the doctor I told you about."

David stared at her, this girl who looked only a few years older than Laura. "You mentioned a genetic test. Is this is an experimental drug your company is working on?"

Kamilla seized upon the assumption. "Something like that."

"Then why didn't you say so earlier?" David asked. Rachel felt a cold hand tighten around her heart as he turned his eyes on her. Her house of cards came tumbling down. "You made this decision on your own? Shouldn't we have discussed it together?"

"Probably. Probably." Her desperate sense of conviction returned. "Yes! Okay? *Yes!* But it made no sense. And you never would have agreed. Nobody in their right mind would." The same argument Milada had once used against her. Tears spilled from her eyes. "This was the only chance Jenny had. And I—I didn't think Milada would. She was furious when I brought up the possibility. She said she wouldn't. I thought—"

David turned his attention back to Kamilla. "And you didn't know it was given to Jenny until just now." Give him time and the proper motivation, and David could put the pieces of any puzzle together. Even if what he came up with didn't look exactly like the picture on the box.

"This is not a tenable—*protocol*," Kamilla said. "It works only if the patient possesses a specific pair of mutations."

"You're talking about gene therapy?"

Rachel heard wonder and horror mingling in his voice.

"RNA interference using an in-vivo retrovirus as the vector." The terminology rolled smoothly off Kamilla's tongue, one truth eclipsing the broader lie.

"Would *you* have approved this treatment for my daughter?"

"No," Kamilla answered flatly.

"Because of the side effects."

"Among other things. This—*protocol*—is not according to FDA procedures."

Kamilla was reacting just as Milada said she would. "But it *worked*," Rachel insisted.

"What side effects?" David pressed.

"Besides the hypomelanism? Persistent anemia, to start with," Kamilla answered carefully. "Hypersensitivity to sunlight. Functional changes to the periodontium and surrounding tissues. Retardation of the aging process."

"But it *worked*," Rachel insisted again. "I was with Jenny every day. *Every day*. There weren't any alternatives left. Like you said, David. Like Dr. Ingebretsen said. There wasn't any hope left. *But it worked.*"

"That doesn't make it right!" Kamilla's voice rang out in frustration, the flush of righteous anger darkening her white countenance.

"Then what good is it?" Rachel answered with equal vehemence. In this one instance, Milada had gone ahead and hacked through the Gordian knot. In this one instance, Rachel had no desire to see the frayed threads tied back up in a nice bow. "Sometimes the ends do justify the means!"

"What good is it?" Kamilla's voice rose in barely contained rage. "Do you know the mortality rate under this so-called *protocol* for those who *don't* have the mutation? *One hundred percent!* The nurses and doctors treating Jennifer had *no* idea what they were dealing with. And you felt justified exposing them to that risk? To get what *you* wanted?"

Rachel felt the blood drain from her face. The thought had never occurred to her. "I'm sorry," she said in a tiny voice. "I'm sorry. I'm sorry." She bowed her head in contrition. "But what—what do we do now?"

Hearing no response, Rachel looked up. A slight tremor passed across Kamilla's face. Rachel saw in her countenance an eighteen-year-old girl who, out of the clear blue, found herself bearing a weight of responsibility beyond her wildest dreams.

"I—I don't know."

Kamilla's arms flopped to her sides. Her head slumped. As if finally realizing she was an unwelcome stranger in these unfamiliar surroundings, she wandered in a daze to the sliding glass door and leaned her head against the dark glass.

Cautiously, Laura and Jennifer emerged from their father's shadow.

"Milada's sister?" Jennifer asked.

"Yeah," said Laura.

"Look!" said Jennifer. "It's Milada!"

They turned as one. Rachel remembered that she'd left the front door open. Milada must have simply walked in. She stood at the foot of the short flight of stairs. Her eyes wide. Her mouth half-open. Out of breath.

Rachel glanced at Kamilla. Kamilla stared at her sister. Rachel watched as the anger slowly suffused her face, years of frustration distilling into human language. She shouted, "You want to know why I don't work in pediatrics? *This* is why I don't work in pediatrics!"

Milada's eyes, showing only guilt and fear, flicked to Jennifer and then back to Kamilla.

Kamilla stepped forward. "Do you have any idea what you've done?" Already a more plaintive tone of bewilderment was creeping into her voice.

The question hung there in the air. Raw desperation contorted Milada's face. "One child." A plea. "One child." An entreaty. A prayer. "One child to live after all the children I—"

Kamilla's head snapped around, terror on her face, her mouth opening in a roar of pain. A primal scream. Rachel felt her heart lurch. Jennifer and Laura jumped, holding their hands up to their ears. Even David took a step back.

A sharp retort in a Slavic tongue. Milada nodded, abashed, *ashamed*. Kamilla strode forward. Milada backed away until the wall stopped her. She did not raise her arms to defend herself. Kamilla seized her by the shoulders.

"He killed them. *He* killed them." Kammy shook her sister's shoulders with sufficient force that Milada's head knocked against the wall with an audible thud. "He *deserved* to die. You made the right decision. Milly, please. *We aren't what our pasts made us.*"

Milada nodded again. She looked so numb and fragile and weak. She slumped against the wall, hiding her face in her hands and drawing ragged breaths. Kamilla looked at her until she could apparently stand it no longer and turned away, biting her lip. She sat down on the arm of the couch, ragged exhaustion clouding her face. The family room grew still except for the quiet sound of Milada's weeping.

Rachel was so focused on Milada that she didn't notice Jennifer until her daughter stood at Milada's feet. Jennifer waited until first Kamilla and then Milada noticed her. Wonder showing on her face at this creature she had wrought, Milada crouched down so their eyes could meet. Cautiously, wondrously, she ran her hand across the soft white down of the child's head.

"Jennifer. I'm sorry. I truly am."

Jennifer shook her head. "It's okay. We're going to be okay."

Milada reached out, the child rushed forward, and Milada took her into her arms. As she stood, lifting her up, Jennifer's small arms clinging to her neck, Rachel instinctively reached for her daughter as well. But she was too far away and by now out of her grasp.

Chapter 49

The heart knows what the mind denies

THREE MONTHS PASSED.

Milada found an empty seat in the baggage claim area of the Salt Lake airport. Through the plate-glass windows, she watched the snow swirling through the headlight beams of the cabs and shuttle buses in front of the terminal.

The skies had been dark and the air freezing cold and filled with ice that late afternoon in London as well. The Little Ice Age had begun, she imagined, the day she was born and plumbed its depths the day Rakoczi died.

White snow fell on her shoulders. Her heart was black as coal. Fear weighed heavily upon her as the guards escorted her through the catacombs of Newgate Prison to the Master's cell. Rakoczi's desiccated body lay on a dirty straw mattress. The fetid air smelled of rotting flesh. He had the cell to himself. No one would approach him or even touch him. The way his skin sloughed off in white flakes, the way the air itself ate away at his tissues until there was hardly anything left of him but powder on bones—the guards imagined he must be dying of leprosy or plague or some even more terrible disease.

Yet somehow still alive. His eyes focused on her. "I have missed you, Milada."

"I betrayed you."

"You had the right."

She turned away and wept. Her last moment of true human sorrow in four hundred years, and for this man of all men. "You must not die, not like this."

His voice rose in a disjointed monotone, quoting the seventeenth chapter of Leviticus: "*Whatsoever man there be of the house of Israel, or of the strangers that sojourn among you, that eateth any manner of blood, I will cut him off from among his people.*" He said, "It is so lonely."

His voice spent, he expelled his last breath. His chest collapsed in a cloud of gritty ash.

Ashes to ashes.

The guards—no, the prisoners, commanded and threatened and forced by the guards—burned the mattress, scorched the stone with oil of vitriol, and washed the remains into the dank sewers, into the mud, into the sea.

We all fall down.

For Kammy, the moving finger, having written, moved on. She couldn't stand to hear Milada say it, but children *did* become their parents. The image of the man who sired them was imprinted on Milada's mind and soul. For all her exasperation, Kammy never really denied Milada's culpability. Deep down in her subconscious, she knew it was true: Milada wanted a family, companions to share the long night of eternity with. Yet it was their time with *him* that she clung to as the ideal.

And like her sire, not all of her desires lent her their abilities. She was in no way prepared to be a parent, a job that would fit Kamilla like a glove.

You met the wrong sister, Milada had told Rachel Forsythe, and she was right.

The squawk of the warning bell shook Milada out of her reverie. The luggage carrel began to revolve. A minute later, the suitcases and backpacks and skiing paraphernalia started arriving, spilling off the end of the conveyor belt and tumbling down into the stainless-steel carousel.

Jennifer planted herself in front of the conveyer. Her pink knapsack was strapped to her back, the bright green tail of the Dilbert dragon poking incongruously out of the top. Kamilla hovered over her, hands resting lightly on her shoulders, as they took turns guessing which of the suitcases crawling up the ramp would be theirs.

"There's mine!" Jennifer shouted. And then, "We missed!"

Kammy laughed. "C'mon," she said, taking Jennifer's hand and skipping around the carousel in the opposite direction. "We'll sneak up on it."

Milada had thought that giving Kammy a company in which she could invest her intellectual passions would make her happy. But nothing like this. *Nothing like this.* Kammy needed only to be reminded about what she was capable of, and she could do it. She'd always been that way, and her older sister was the person to provide the motivation.

This was not a responsibility Milada could shoulder. *The iniquity of Eli's house shall not be purged with sacrifice nor offering.* Rachel had promised her forgiveness. But Milada had left off the last word of that verse: *forever*. She had eaten from the tree of life and would live forever in her sins.

The taste of that bitter fruit had grown almost palatable. It might grow sweet in time. She harbored no expectations. This was simply the way the world was. Some truths about herself were not difficult to accept. In any event, she made a good aunt.

"Miss Daranyi."

"Oh, Steven." Milada glanced up with a tired smile. "Your service wasn't sure you'd be available."

"School doesn't start until the middle of January," he explained. He picked up her garment bag and looped the strap over his shoulder.

"You're still on holiday, then?"

"We didn't go anywhere this Christmas. Cynthia's parents invited us to their place, but I guess there comes a point when your family is who you go home to every night. I'm sorry, did you have any other luggage?"

"Milly!" Kammy called out on cue. Jennifer chimed in, "Come and get your stuff!"

"Yes," Milada said. "And speaking of which, you've got a few more passengers this time around."

Chapter 50

Blood is thicker than water

JENNIFER FORSYTHE REAPPEARED in Cottonwood Estates as unexpectedly as she had vanished. Over the Christmas holidays she attended church with her parents and sister, accompanied by a striking young woman with fair skin and clear eyes, her long white hair drawn back in a ponytail.

"I swear they look like sisters."

"Just like that other woman who was here—what was her name?"

The story went around that Kamilla was Jennifer's au pair. An amended version said that she was her nurse. Kamilla sat in the foyer during services reading *The New England Journal of Medicine*, and Jennifer ran to her with a bright smile when Sunday school let out.

The bishop didn't have to tell Troy Ellis to leave Kamilla alone.

And then she and Jennifer were gone again, without a word of public explanation. Some said they'd seen them around downtown Salt Lake. Some said they'd moved back to New York. Sister Millington said that Rachel told her Jennifer had been enrolled in a long-term cancer study sponsored by Deseret Children's Hospital and Wylde Medical Informatics, thanks to a grant provided by the DEI Foundation.

Rachel deflected all further inquiries with a sad smile. A few short months before, she had steeled herself to listen again to the final stanza of the poem by Milton:

> *Then thou the mother of so sweet a child*
> *Her false imagined loss cease to lament,*
> *And wisely learn to curb thy sorrows wild;*
> *Think what a present thou to God hast sent.*

Attending the Bromleys' funeral, the verse had struck her as hollow comfort. There was nothing falsely imagined about such a loss, these *thoughts that do often lie too deep for tears*. The separation felt to her as must the phantom pain from a severed limb.

And yet — what an unexpected gift her daughter had brought back with her from across the river, a grace so vast it reached into the Underworld to redeem the living dead.

Now, instead, other words echoed though Rachel's mind: *The Lord killeth, and maketh alive. He bringeth down to the grave, and bringeth up.* The hymn Hannah sang as she handed Samuel over to Eli's eternal care.

About the Author

Eugene Woodbury was born and raised in the upstate New York community of Scotia-Glenville. After serving for two years in the Tokyo South Mission, he graduated from Brigham Young University with degrees in Japanese and TESOL.

His stories have appeared in the *New Era, Sunstone, Cricket, American Gardener*, and *Clubhouse*. He has twice been a Utah Original Writing Competition finalist and is a recipient of the Sunstone Foundation Moonstone Award for short fiction.

He lives in Orem, Utah, where he works as a freelance writer and translator. He can be reached via his website at www.eugenewoodbury.com.

Additional Titles Published by Zarahemla Books

Brother Brigham—In this novel by D. Michael Martindale, C.H. Young has sacrificed his dreams to earn a living for his family—until one day he receives an amazing supernatural visitation. As Brother Brigham's appearances and instructions grow increasingly bold, C.H. struggles to hold together his faith, his marriage, and his sanity.

Hooligan: A Mormon Boyhood—Detailing the author's years growing up in Provo, Utah, during the Depression and World War Two, Douglas Thayer's memoir shares literary DNA in common with Frank McCourt's *Angela's Ashes*, Mark Twain's *The Adventures of Huckleberry Finn*, and William Golding's *Lord of the Flies*.

Hunting Gideon—Jessica Draper's Mormon-flavored cyber-crime novel tracks two crack employees of the FBI's National Infrastructure Protection Center. Through her feline avatar, Sue Anne Jones stalks the V-Net along with her partner, ex-cracker Loren Hunter. Embarking on a wild chase through both virtual and actual reality, they scramble to avert the ultimate online disaster.

Kindred Spirits—In this novel by Christopher Kimball Bigelow, Utah-bred Eliza Spainhower has carved out an independent life for herself in Boston. After she makes a love connection with a local native on the subway, she's forced to reckon in new ways with her Mormon identity and her sometimes-overactive religious imagination.

Long After Dark—In these award-winning stories and a new novella, Todd Robert Petersen takes the reader on expeditions to Utah, Arizona, Brazil, Rwanda, and into the souls of twenty-first-century Mormons caught between their humanity, faith, and church.

On the Road to Heaven—This exuberant and groundbreaking autobiographical novel reveals Coke Newell's hard-won path to meaning, faith, and forgiveness. *On the Road to Heaven* is a love story about a girl and a guy and their search for heaven—a lotta love, a little heaven, and one heck of a ride in between.

Available at ZarahemlaBooks.com

Also available at Amazon.com and other booksellers

www.ingramcontent.com/pod-product-compliance
Ingram Content Group UK Ltd.
Pitfield, Milton Keynes, MK11 3LW, UK
UKHW041951230426
12048UKWH00008B/263